SKELMERSDALE

11. DEC 07

COX, G.   A F SF

TITLE   Loose ends

No, Liz thought. *Not him. It can't be.*

The voice, deep and raspy, jolted Liz's memory like an electric shock. Shivering for reasons that had nothing to do with the temperature, she shoved her way through the throngs of shoppers to get a look at the voice's owner, ignoring complaints and protests of the people she elbowed past. "Wait just one minute, young lady!" a woman in a Hawaiian shirt called out, but Liz wasn't listening. She *had* to see whom the irate voice belonged to, right now, this very minute. Standing on her tiptoes, peering frantically over the shoulders of a bunch of frustratingly immovable tourists, she spied the upset customer: a burly Caucasian man wearing a red vinyl jacket and a bright orange hunter's cap. Reddish-brown stubble covered his chin and jowls, while his broad, belligerent face was flushed with irritation.

Liz recognized him right away. *Oh my God*, she thought. An icy chill suffused her entire body, and, without thinking, she clutched her stomach protectively. *It's him. It's really him.*

The man who nearly killed her...

ROSWELL™

#1 LOOSE ENDS

Be sure to look for new titles in this suspense series

Available from POCKET BOOKS

Don't miss any books in the original series:

ROSWELL HIGH

#1 THE OUTSIDER
#2 THE WILD ONE
#3 THE SEEKER
#4 THE WATCHER
#5 THE INTRUDER
#6 THE STOWAWAY
#7 THE VANISHED
#8 THE REBEL
#9 THE DARK ONE
#10 THE SALVATION

Available from POCKET PULSE

ROSWELL™
LOOSE ENDS

Greg Cox
**From the television series
developed by Jason Katims**

POCKET BOOKS
New York   London   Toronto   Sydney   Singapore

08434775

This book is a work of fiction. Names, characters, places and incidents are products of the author's imagination or are used fictitiously. Any resemblance to actual events or locales or persons, living or dead, is entirely coincidental.

An *Original* Publication of POCKET BOOKS

POCKET BOOKS, a division of Simon & Schuster, Inc.
1230 Avenue of the Americas, New York, NY 10020

™ & Copyright © 2001 Twentieth Century Fox Film Corporation, Regency Entertainment (USA) Inc. and Monachy Enterprises B. V.

All rights reserved, including the right to reproduce this book or portions thereof in any form whatsoever. For information address Pocket Books, 1230 Avenue of the Americas, New York, NY 10020

ISBN: 0-7434-1834-4

First Pocket Books printing May 2001

10 9 8 7 6 5 4 3 2 1

POCKET and colophon are registered trademarks of Simon & Schuster, Inc.

Cover photograph ™ & © 2001 Twentieth Century Fox Film Corporation.
Front cover illustration by John Vairo, Jr.

Printed in the U.S.A.

For Laura and Katie,
honorary alumni of West Roswell High

Acknowledgments

Thanks to John Ordover, for recommending me for this assignment, to Ingrid van der Leeden and Samantha Schutz for providing plenty of editorial support, and assistance, and to my agents, Russ Galen and Anna Ghosh, for working out the legal details.

Also, thanks to the talented cast, crew, and creators of *Roswell* for supplying both inspiration and enjoyment, and to the helpful folks at alt.tv.roswell and CrashDown.com for much invaluable information on *Roswell* lore and trivia.

Finally, thanks as ever to Karen and Alex, for help on the home front while I was writing this book.

"As far as I know, an alien spacecraft did not crash at Roswell, N.M., in 1947. . . . If the United States Air Force did recover alien bodies, they didn't tell me about it, and I want to know."

—President William Jefferson Clinton, December 1995

PROLOGUE

"What are you doing? I told you never to call me here. It's too dangerous!"

"Shut up. This line is secure, believe me. Have you got it?"

"Not yet, but I will. I know where it is, and I know how to get to it."

"You'd better. There's a lot at stake here, for both of us. Don't screw it up."

"I won't! I promise! Everything's on schedule, just like we planned."

"Good. You know where to meet me. Be there on time, and don't even think about double-crossing me. You know what happened to the last guy who tried that...."

1

"So, you really think Hilary might be a Skin?"

"I'm not saying it's for sure. I'm just saying that it's a possibility."

Max Evans and Michael Guerin huddled over a copy of *USA Today*, intently examining the day's news in search of hints of hostile alien activity. Max didn't need a highlighter to mark the article in question; he just ran his finger over the black-and-white newsprint and the selected headline acquired a bright yellow background. "What about Kathie Lee?" he asked, turning to the next page of the paper. "I always thought there was something kind of unnatural about her."

Says my favorite human-alien hybrid, Liz Parker thought silently. But that wasn't really fair, the petite brunette admitted to herself; in many ways, and despite his extraterrestrial origins, Max was the most human person she knew. As she knew better than anyone else, there was nothing alien at all about his heart.

It was a quiet Thursday afternoon at the Crashdown

Cafe, Roswell, New Mexico's finest alien-themed diner, and the gang's usual after school hangout. Watercolor paintings of strange alien creatures decorated the walls while a mannequin in a silver spacesuit greeted customers by the front door. Liz sat at one of the restaurant's rear booths, opposite Max and Michael, while Max's sister Isabel, and their friend Alex Whitman, occupied the adjacent booth, close enough to take part in the proceedings if they felt like it. Liz knew that Alex would have preferred to have had Isabel all to himself, but guessed that he'd settle for just sharing the same booth with her. *Hope things are going okay between them,* Liz thought. *Isabel can be pretty moody sometimes.*

"Kathie Lee?" Maria DeLuca asked, rolling her large olive-green eyes. Her silver waitress's apron mimicked the unearthly countenance of your standard-model alien abductor as she stood beside the two rear booths. Shiny tinfoil antennae bobbed above her long, strawberry-blond hair. The dinner rush hadn't started yet, so Maria was free to kill time with her friends. "Don't you think maybe you guys are getting a wee bit paranoid?"

Michael bristled indignantly, not unlike his unruly brown hair. "This is serious business. Maybe you can joke about it, but some of us can't afford to overlook any possibilities." Empty bottles of Tabasco sauce littered the tabletop, evidence of his and Max's strenuous strategy session. "You can never tell where the Skins might strike next."

"Hey, you don't need to bite my head off, alien-boy," Maria retorted. Scanning quickly to make sure that no new customers had arrived, she slid into the booth beside Liz. "I know all about the evil alien invasion, remember? I was just trying to give you guys a much-needed reality check."

"Oh, is that what that was?" Michael asked sarcastically. A scowl made him look even more ticked off and discontented than usual. "I thought you were busting my chops about things you obviously don't understand or appreciate." He eyed the pad of green order slips tucked into the belt of Maria's E.T. apron. "Maybe you should stick to the customers' checks from now on."

Maria immediately shifted into combat mode. "Yeah, right, and maybe you never want to see the inside of the eraser room again?" she replied, referring to their usual make out spot at West Roswell High. "Heck, summer vacation's coming up soon, and you could be looking at a long, lonely summer, Michael Guerin."

Liz winced at the heated words exchanged between the on-again, off-again couple. Granted, Maria and Michael bickering was nothing new, but there seemed to be more of an edge to it than usual. She glanced across the table at Max, who appeared oblivious to the escalating spitting match going on right next to him. Beneath his neatly-trimmed black bangs, lines of worry and concentration creased his brow as he vigilantly perused the newspaper, occasionally highlighting a suspicious headline or photo caption. A chocolate Dark Side of the Force milkshake sat more or less ignored next to his uneaten Grilled Lunar Cheese Sandwich. Liz's heart ached in sympathy. He looked like he was bearing the weight of the world on his shoulders. Maybe more than one world…

"Cool it, you guys," she told Michael and Maria. If she couldn't relieve Max of most of his unfair burden, at least she could play peacemaker between his squabbling friends and allies. "We're all kind of stressed-out, I think." *And who wouldn't be,* she thought, *after all we've been through lately?* "Let's cut each other some slack, okay?"

"Yeah, I guess so," Michael agreed, looking a little chastened. He shrugged, which was about as close as he ever came to an apology, and cast a conciliatory look at Maria, who relaxed her own combative body language a notch or two. "I just want to be ready, you know? For the FBI. For the Skins. Everything."

"Are you sure we should be talking about this here?" Isabel asked anxiously from the next booth, looking over the back of her own seat at Liz and the others. Like her brother, she looked tense and worried, while her voice, if anything, sounded even more nervous and apprehensive. Her immaculate, cover-girl appearance belied her chronic uneasiness. "What if somebody heard you?"

"Like who?" Maria snorted. A devout advocate of aromatherapy, she fetched a tiny glass vial from her pocket, and uncapped it beneath her nose. Sniffing the fragrant oil seemed to ease her frustration with Michael. "Look around," she said, "this place is deader than Senator Whitaker."

Sitting across from Isabel, nibbling on a stack of golden Unidentified Frying Objects, Alex tried to reassure her. "Besides, don't forget, this is Roswell, the unofficial capital of Close Encounters land," he said, a grin upon his boyish face. The tourists *expect* to hear us discussing crashed alien spaceships and top secret government conspiracies. Heck, we should probably be talking louder, just to do our part for the local economy."

His glib attempt to lift Isabel's spirits failed miserably. "That's not funny, Alex," she said curtly before turning her attention back to the four teens in the other booth. Liz pretended not to notice the crushed look on Alex's face, which he attempted to hide as quickly as it appeared. "We never know who might be listening," Isabel continued. "We've been spied on before, with hidden cameras and listening devices and who knows what else."

True enough, Liz thought. *But you could go crazy thinking about that 24–7.* She picked absently at her Little Green Mint sundae while a new song by Dido played over the diner's music system. *Where did you draw the line,* she wondered, *between being careful and being paranoid?* And was it fair of her to judge Isabel for being so high-strung and fearful? Liz had only lived with the Big Secret for two years now; Max, Michael, and Isabel had been hiding their alien heritage for their entire lives.

"Liz is right," Maria announced decisively. She swept the faces around her with a knowing gaze. "We're all a bunch of nervous wrecks. We need some serious R&R and I mean soon. Just for this weekend, we should forget all about hidden secrets, fiendish enemies, etcetera, and do something fun for a change." She plucked the spread-out newspaper out from under Max's nose. "And that means you, too, glorious leader. All work and no play makes Max a dull spaceman."

Max looked more startled than annoyed by Maria's impulsive action. Michael scowled, though, and tried to snatch back the crumpled papers, which Maria stubbornly held up over her head, out of his reach. "Look, babe," he pleaded, making an obvious effort not to lose his temper, "I don't want to get into this with you again, but there's an interplanetary war going on. We haven't got time for fun and games."

"Oh yeah," Maria challenged him. "You think I don't

ever watch The History Channel? Even back during World War One or Two or whichever war it was, the soldiers took time out occasionally, for shore leave and USO shows and all that Andrews Sisters boogie-woogie bugle boy stuff. They had to, or they'd just wig out. It was important to their—whatchamacallit—morals?"

"Morale," Liz corrected her gently. She was surprised and relieved to see that Max seemed to be giving Maria his full attention, listening to her whole spiel with a thoughtful expression. "You know, she may have a point, Max," Liz added, seeing a chance to lighten his load a little, if only for one weekend. "We could all use a break."

"Right, exactly! That's what I'm saying," Maria declared, vindicated by Liz's vote of support. She settled back into her seat, the decision a done deal as far as she was concerned, and stroked her chin as she considered their options. "I'm thinking: Road Trip. But to where? That's the question."

An idea suddenly occurred to Liz. "I know!" she blurted out. "We could go to Carlsbad Caverns. It's only a couple of hours away, and Ms. Hultquist in earth sciences said she'd give extra credit to any student who went to the caves and wrote a report on their trip."

"Spoken like the science nerd you are," Maria teased her best friend. "I'm thinking wild teenage hijinks and you want to go on a field trip!"

"No, no, it will be fun, really," Liz insisted. "My parents used to take me to the Caverns when I was little, and it was always really cool." A surge of nostalgia hit her with unexpected force, bringing back bittersweet memories of childhood pleasures and simpler times, before her life grew so very complicated. A lump formed in her throat and she felt her eyes watering. *Guess I need a vacation as much as anybody else,* she realized. *A vacation back to a more carefree me.*

As if he could sense her longing for a little harmless childhood regression, Max nodded solemnly. "Carlsbad Caverns works for me," he stated with quiet authority. His dark, serious eyes surveyed the faces around him. "What do the rest of you think?"

No surprise, Michael was unconvinced. "What do I care about earth sciences," he said sourly, making another unsuccessful grab at the stolen newspaper. "I'm not even from Earth."

Maria gave him a warning glare. "Don't be such a Czechoslovakian party pooper," she said, using her preferred euphemism for *extraterrestrial*, "or I might forget that you're the love of my life."

Michael sank back sullenly against the back of the booth, clearly resentful, but apparently unwilling to push his luck much further, at least for now. "Okay, make that three votes for the Caverns," Maria said smugly. She craned her head to peer into the next booth over. "What about you, Alex? You up for a journey to the center of Earth?"

"Er, I think so," he answered, awkwardly searching Isabel's exquisitely made-up face for some clue to her preferences. "Umm, what do you think, Iz?" He smiled broadly, trying too hard to sound cheerful and upbeat. "Sounds like it could be fun."

Isabel, in turn, turned to her brother for guidance. "Are you sure this is a good idea, Max?" she asked, her uncertain tone making it sound like they were discussing a root canal rather than a joy ride. Liz wondered, somewhat uncharitably, if Prozac worked on aliens.

"It couldn't hurt, Iz," Max said softly. Liz couldn't help noticing how tenderly he handled his sister's frayed and fragile nerves. How could he doubt that he was born to be his people's leader? Isabel's hand gripped the wooden divider between the two booths, and Max gently placed his own hand atop hers. "Plus, it might be exactly what we all need."

"Okay," Isabel assented. She managed a wan smile, making an effort to get into the spirit of things. "A change of scenery might be nice at that."

"That settles it, then!" Maria said triumphantly. "You're outvoted, Michael, five-to-one." A burst of organizational energy animated her entire body, setting her antennae bobbing vigorously. "I'll borrow the Jetta from my mom, Max and Isabel can get their Jeep; Liz and Michael, you stock up on munchies, sodas, and Tabasco sauce, and we'll be all set. Saturday morning, we're hitting the road for Carlsbad Caverns!"

Maria's enthusiasm was infectious. Liz grinned at Max, who smiled back at her. Beneath the table, she playfully rubbed her foot against his ankle. *It's great to see him looking relaxed again,* she thought, starting to get genuinely excited about the weekend ahead. She couldn't remember the last time the two of them had just been able to have a good time together, enjoying each other's company, instead of running and hiding and agonizing about various earthly and unearthly threats.

The more she thought about it, the better it sounded. *A fun-filled weekend outing is just what the doctor ordered,* she decided. *For all of us.*

She couldn't wait to get going.

2

"Believe it or not," the park ranger explained, "this entire region was once at the bottom of a huge inland sea. Two hundred and fifty million years ago, these caves began as a series of underwater reefs. Eventually, however, the sea dried up and the reef was buried beneath tons of sediment. Over the centuries, geological pressures gradually pushed the reef system back toward the surface where rainwater, seeping through cracks in the limestone, began carving out the caverns all around us."

Liz tried to imagine the arid Chihuahuan Desert, now about seven hundred feet above them, covered in seawater, but it was hard to visualize, especially after driving all the way down from Roswell through almost a hundred miles of sun-baked, reddish-brown New Mexican landscape. Fortunately, they had gotten off to an early start this morning, before the June heat hit its peak.

"Isn't this amazing, Max?" she said, taking in the spectacular subterranean scenery all around them. Jagged stalactites hung like gigantic stone icicles high above their heads, while fanglike stalagmites reached toward the ceiling. Massive calcite columns, formed when the stalactites met their inverted counterparts, rose dramatically like the pillars of some ancient pagan temple. In places, the limestone walls of the spacious cavern resembled frozen waterfalls, or overlapping sheets of petrified drapery. Colored lights, positioned strategically throughout the caves, displayed its natural wonders to their best advantage, providing an eye-catching array of shadows, hues, and textures. Time had polished many of the formations, giving them a pearly, opalescent sheen. *It's like an alien world,* Liz thought, *right here on Earth.*

"It is impressive," Max agreed, his arm around her waist as they strolled along with a large herd of tourists, making an effort to stay within earshot of the friendly ranger giving the group a guided tour of the King's Palace section of the caverns. Max ducked his head to whisper into her ear, "This place makes the Pod Chamber"—where he and the other alien children had been buried after the Crash— "look like a gopher hole."

"And this is just a small fraction of what's down here," Liz commented, flipping through the guidebook she had bought on the surface. "It says here that there are over eighty-five caverns in the Park, of which only ten or so are open to the public."

"You hear that, folks?" Maria chimed in. She and Michael were right behind them, followed closely by Alex and Isabel. "Nobody get lost, 'cause I don't want to go poking around in spooky, bat-filled caves looking for you."

"Maria was traumatized by *The Adventures of Tom Sawyer* at an early age," Liz teased, recalling the sequence where

Becky Thatcher and Tom were stalked through an underground labyrinth by the murderous Injun Joe. "She used to hide behind the couch whenever we got to that part on the video."

"Funny, I don't remember being alone behind that couch," Maria stated. She gave Liz a playful punch from behind. "Admit it, Parker, you were just as creeped-out as I was."

"Well, we were only ten at the time," Liz said. "I like to think I'd be a bit braver now."

"After the Skins and the Special Unit," Max said, "I'm sure of it." He tightened his hold on her waist, giving her an affectionate squeeze.

"Just the same, everybody stick to the lighted trails," Maria insisted, clearly getting in touch with her inner Den Mother. "And, remember, if we get separated, everybody meet back at the elevator."

Michael snorted. "Like I'm really going to be tempted to go exploring on my own." He regarded the surrounding stalagmites and such with a distinctly unimpressed air. "I mean, it's just a humongous hole in the ground. What's the big deal?"

Maria pulled away from Michael, glaring at him balefully. "You know, you could at least *try* to have a good time, for my sake. Or would that spoil your whole image as a Rebel Without a Planet?"

"Hey, so I don't feel like oohing and aahing over a bunch of pretty lights and rock formations. Is that such a crime?" he groused. Slouched shoulders advertised his lack of enthusiasm for the entire expedition. "Give me a break. Lighten up."

By now, Maria was fuming visibly. She turned on him angrily, green eyes flashing. "No, *you* lighten up, Michael Guerin, and another thing...!"

"Sssh!" a middle-aged tourist, wearing a souvenir Carlsbad Caverns baseball cap, shushed the teenagers, an annoyed look on her face. Liz blushed, embarrassed even though it wasn't really her fault, and even Maria and Michael looked a little abashed. They all lowered their voices as they hurried to catch up with their tour guide, who was now explaining why one particular formation was known as the Frustrated Lovers. *Well, that's appropriate,* Liz thought wryly, particularly where Maria and Michael were concerned.

Flashbulbs flared as a mob of tourists elbowed and jostled their way forward, trying to get a better view of the petrified Lovers. The one problem with hitting the caverns on a sunny summer weekend, Liz realized, was coping with the inevitable crowds. There seemed to be hundreds of people exploring the various caverns today, which made sightseeing a bit of a hassle. The crush of would-be spelunkers squeezed the small band of high school students together, making it easier to converse without raising their voices.

"You know," Alex remarked, now that he and Isabel were right next to Liz, "this whole thing is cool and all, but I can't help thinking that the public parts of the caverns have been domesticated too much. You've got paved trails, electricity, lights, guardrails, even waste baskets every fifty yards or so." To prove his point, he slam-dunked a wadded-up candy bar wrapper into the nearest convenient trash receptacle. "Don't you think it would be spookier and more atmospheric if these caves actually looked more like caves and less like an underground mall?"

"I see your point, Alex," Max said amiably, sounding more at ease than he had for weeks, maybe months. "Although I think there are some more caverns nearby that have been left in something closer to their natural state, for more serious cavers, and other caves that have barely been explored at all." He leafed through the guidebook in Liz's hands. "Yeah, it says here there's Slaughter Canyon Cave, Spider Cave, and some that don't even have names yet."

"Now there's an idea!" Alex enthused. "What do you think, Isabel?" He grinned goofily at Max's sister. The wiry would-be musician and the pristine prom queen made an odd-looking couple, but Liz had more or less given up trying to figure out their relationship. "Later on, you want to go looking for a cave of our own?" He wiggled his eyebrows, Groucho-style, trying to coax a laugh or smile from his glamorous (but emotionally elusive) dream girl. "Just you, me, and a couple thousand bats."

"I don't think that would be safe," Isabel responded, more or less missing the point. Although she dutifully held onto Alex's hand, her manner remained distant and preoccupied. "Why don't we just listen to the ranger's lecture, okay?"

"Yeah, sure, that's fine, I guess," Alex muttered, disappointed once again in his never-ending struggle to get past Isabel's considerable defenses. Liz had to admire his persistence, even if she sometimes thought he was fighting a losing battle.

She sighed sympathetically, taking stock of the fracture lines dividing her friends. At the moment, it seemed as though only she and Max were making the most of today's excursion. *That's too bad,* she thought, squeezing Max's waist even tighter, *but I'm not going to let Michael and Maria's problems, or Alex and Isabel's, spoil my own day with Max.* After risking her own life and happiness to save the entire world from alien invaders, she figured she was entitled to be a little bit selfish, if only for just one weekend.

The park ranger, who obviously knew every nook and cranny of the King's Palace caverns by heart, led them deeper and deeper into the vaulted, subterranean chambers of Carlsbad Caverns. Despite the wool sweater she had prudently remembered to bring along, Liz found herself shivering slightly as the temperature within the caves dropped along with their elevation. Glancing at her wristwatch, which read 10:45 A.M., she guessed that it was probably over ninety degrees back on the surface; eight hundred-plus feet below, however, it was noticeably chilly. *Brrr!* Liz thought, wishing she had brought a jacket as well. (Then again, the unseasonably cool air *did* give her an excuse to huddle closer to Max.)

After leading them in and out of the King's Palace, pausing periodically to take in such colorfully-named attractions as the Bashful Elephant and the Queen's Chamber, their guide dropped them off at the underground rest area near the elevator to the surface. "Well, I hope you enjoyed the tour," the ranger said. "If you want, you can now take the elevator back to the Visitors Center uptop, or you can take a self-guided tour of the Big Room." He pointed at a subterranean archway directly behind them. "If you haven't seen the Big Room yet, then you really don't want to miss it. We're talking one of the largest underground spaces in the world, spacious enough to hold over a dozen full-size football fields."

"Ooh, boy, an even bigger hole," Michael said sarcastically, eliciting a venomous look from Maria.

"Not as big as the one you're digging for yourself," she

warned him. *Ouch*, Liz thought. She wouldn't want to be in Michael's shoes when Maria finally got him alone.

According to the guidebook, it took about an hour and a half to explore the Big Room completely, so they decided to take a combined snack and bathroom break first. Fortunately, a genuine cafeteria, complete with rest rooms and gift shop, had been constructed near the elevator, a mere 750 feet belowground. Liz waved good-bye to Max as the group temporarily split apart, each going in search of munchies or whatever. She wasn't feeling hungry just yet, so, after a quick trip to the ladies' room, she decided to browse a bit in the gift shop. *Maybe I can find a nice gift for Max or my folks,* she thought.

After growing up in Roswell, it felt odd to be in a souvenir store that wasn't packed to the ceiling with tacky UFO and alien knickknacks. Where were the inflatable E.T.s and cheesy "Take Me to Your Leader" postcards? Instead the underground gift shop traded heavily in rubber bats, cheap imitation kachina dolls, and a wide variety of overpriced, cave-related merchandise: mugs, ashtrays, pennants, souvenir spoons, snow globes, etc. Weaving her way through a pack of bargain-hunting tourists, Liz rifled through a rack of postcards near the front of the shop. One card in particular caught her eye: a color photo of some ancient Native American line carvings found just beyond the entrance of the cave. *Interesting,* she thought; a couple of the timeworn carvings vaguely resembled some of the alien symbols she and the others had discovered in caves around Roswell. Could there be a connection?

She grabbed a copy of the card, to show to Max, and started to make her way toward the cash register. As she neared the checkout counter, an angry voice, coming from right up ahead, froze her in her tracks.

"Five ninety-five? For this piece of crap? What do you think I am, a moron?"

No, Liz thought. *Not him. It can't be.*

The voice, deep and raspy, jolted Liz's memory like an electric shock. Shivering for reasons that had nothing to do with the temperature, she shoved her way through the throngs of shoppers to get a look at the voice's owner, ignoring the complaints and protests of the people she elbowed past. "Wait just one minute, young lady!" a woman in a Hawaiian shirt called out, but Liz wasn't listening. She *had* to see whom the irate voice belonged to, right now, this very minute. Standing on her tiptoes, peering frantically over the shoulders of a bunch of frustratingly immovable tourists, she spied the upset customer: a burly Caucasian man wearing a red vinyl jacket and a bright orange hunter's cap. Reddish-brown stubble covered his chin and jowls, while his broad, belligerent face was flushed with irritation.

Liz recognized him right away. *Oh my God,* she thought. An icy chill suffused her entire body and, without thinking, she clutched her stomach protectively. *It's him. It's really him.*

The man who nearly killed her...

The Crashdown Cafe, almost two years ago:

It had all happened very quickly. One minute she was waiting tables with Maria, trading quips and gossip, when suddenly a loud argument broke out at one of the side booths. Two rough-looking men, whom Liz had never seen before, started fighting over money. Before anyone else in the diner had a chance to react or call the police, the heavier of the two men drew a gun on his companion, who grabbed onto the gunman's arm in self-defense. The two men wrestled for control of the pistol and then, without warning, the gun went off.

Standing a few yards away, near the kitchen door, Liz heard a tremendous bang and felt a sudden pain in her stomach, below her ribs. Before she knew it, without really understanding how she'd got there, she was lying on her back upon the cool tile floor, staring up at the fluorescent lights in the ceiling. The pain in her belly burned like fire, but the rest of her felt very, very cold. People shouted and Maria screamed, but the confused cries seemed to be coming from somewhere very far away. The icy numbness spread through her body, and somehow Liz knew that she was dying. *Oh my God,* she thought in a daze. *I've been shot.*

The fluorescent lights seemed to dim, and a murky darkness began encroaching on the periphery of her vision, blocking out the light. Something wet, warm, and sticky pooled atop her stomach, soaking through her uniform. Liz wanted to sit up, inspect her injury, but she couldn't even lift her head. Her arms and hands lay uselessly upon the floor, lacking the strength to move. All her strength and vitality was slipping away, consumed by the blazing fire below her ribs. *It's not fair,* she thought, barely managing to keep her eyes open. *I can't be dying. It's too soon.* The darkness crept in on her from all sides, making it harder and harder to think. Her heartbeat grew slower and fainter every second. A sense of profound regret came over her, driving out the fear and pain. *I'm only seventeen! I haven't even—*

And, all of sudden, Max was there, calling her back from

the abyss, his soulful face and caring brown eyes staring down at her, filling her vision. He tore open her uniform and laid his hand upon her stomach, quenching the fire there with the cool depths of his spirit.

Her life was never the same again....

The two men, Maria had told her later, had fled the Crashdown as soon as the gun went off. They were long gone before Sheriff Valenti and his deputies showed up to investigate. Everyone figured they'd skipped town, and Liz had never expected to see the man who shot her again.

Until now.

Without thinking, Liz gasped out loud. The memory was so strong she felt like she had been shot all over again. She could practically smell the gunpowder in the air, hear the sharp report of the gunshots echoing within her ears. She glanced down at her stomach, half-expecting to see the blood leaking through her fingers. *Help me!* she thought irrationally. *Somebody help me! I've been shot!*

She staggered backward, accidentally knocking over a display of official Carlsbad Caverns snow globes. The fragile souvenirs, containing molded plastic replicas of the cave's stalactites and stalagmites, crashed to the floor, shattering loudly and spilling their liquid contents all over the tiles beneath Liz's feet. The noisy crash attracted the attention of everyone in the shop, including the beefy, loudmouthed man at the cashier's counter. Looking up in shock and confusion, Liz found herself staring directly into the surly, bloodshot eyes of the man who shot her that day at the Crashdown.

He peered at Liz with a smug, sadistic expression,

clearly enjoying someone else's embarrassment, then re-acted with surprise once he got a good look at her face. He squinted quizzically, a scowl forming amid his stubble, as he examined Liz more closely from across the room.

Panic gripped Liz's heart. *Did he recognize me?* she thought, suddenly terrified. *Does he know who I am?* An over-powering need to get away came over her, and she turned and ran frantically out of the gift shop, leaving behind a mess of broken glass and water. She barreled through the crowds, both in and out of the cafeteria, and didn't stop run-ning until she was all the way to the opening of the Big Room. Her heart was pounding in her chest and she felt like she could hardly breathe. A scream of utter terror and dis-may formed at the back of her throat and she had to bite down on her lower lip to keep from shrieking hysterically. She was afraid to look behind, afraid that she'd see the gun-wielding man chasing after her. She flinched in anticipation of another ear-shattering gunshot tearing her world apart....

"Liz!" Suddenly, Max was there, right in front of her, and she gratefully ran into his arms, grabbing onto him like he was a life preserver in the middle of a stormy sea. She buried her face against his chest and began sobbing uncon-trollably. "You're white as a ghost! What is it?" he asked, alarmed by her obvious distress. "What's the matter, Liz? What happened?"

Racing footsteps pounded upon the paved concrete trail, and soon they were surrounded by Maria, Alex, Michael, and Isabel, all looking confused and concerned. "Are you okay, girlfriend?" Maria asked, offering Liz a cup of lemon-ade from the snack bar. "Here, have a sip of this."

It took a few seconds, but Liz eventually lifted her face

away from Max's chest. She wiped her cheeks with the back of her hand while she tried to get her sobbing under control. The lemonade helped, a little, but her eyes kept searching anxiously for the man from the shop.

"Everything's fine. Nothing to see here," Michael called out to a bunch of passing sightseers, who had paused to see what the matter was. "Just a bout of claustrophobia, that's all," Michael assured the strangers.

"Please, Liz," Max urged her softly. She felt his warm arms holding onto her tightly, and she remembered how, on that terrible day at the Crashdown, he had healed her with his special powers. "Tell me what happened," he pleaded.

She nodded weakly, anxious to share her fears with him and the others. But first she needed to put still more distance between her and the site of her terrifying encounter, just in case the man in the red jacket was looking for her. "Not here," she whispered plaintively. She tilted her head toward the entrance to the Big Room. "Let's just go a little further, please?"

"Okay," Max said, looking puzzled but willing to do whatever it took to make her safe again. He draped her arm over his shoulders, lending her support as he guided her toward the cavern opening. "In there," he instructed the others, taking the lead while exchanging worried looks with both Michael and Isabel. No doubt he had to be wondering, Liz realized, whether one of their human or inhuman enemies had caught up with them again.

Not this time, she thought ruefully, leaning against Max as they walked along the underground trail, gladly letting him prop her up. For once, this wasn't an alien thing; it was Liz's own past that had come back to haunt them.

The Big Room was just as awe-inspiring as she remembered it. Hundreds of stalactites hung from the ceiling, over twenty-five feet above their heads, while the vast underground chamber stretched out before them like some enormous subterranean cathedral. "Wow!" Alex exclaimed, impressed despite the crisis with Liz. "It looks like you could fit most of downtown Roswell in here and still have room to spare."

But Liz was in no shape to appreciate the stupendous natural wonders surrounding her. Max led her gently into one of the Big Room's many vaulted grottoes. A towering stalagmite, the size and width of some ancient Egyptian obelisk, loomed over them as he slipped out from beneath her arm in order to look her directly in the face. "Is this far enough, Liz?" he asked solicitously. "Can you tell us what happened now?"

"I-I think so," she stammered, swallowing hard and sniffling. Although still badly shaken, she was starting to feel a little calmer now; the initial panic was fading, giving way to a feeling of slightly greater security now that she had Max and her friends to comfort and protect her. They were all clustered around her now, watching her with concerned and caring eyes as they waited nervously to find out what had frightened her so badly. "It's him, Max," she whispered finally. "The man who shot me at the Crashdown. He's here."

"What!" Max reacted explosively. "Where?"

Quickly, she told them about her chance encounter with the man at the gift shop, and how she had fled the scene in terror. Saying the words somehow made the entire awful experience even more real, and she had to pause for a second before continuing. Isabel thoughtfully handed her a napkin to wipe her eyes and nose with, and she dabbed at her face with the paper towel while she struggled to regain her composure. *Now what do we do?* she wondered, scared and uncertain. *Is there anything we can do, or should do?*

Max, on the other hand, had apparently heard enough. "That son of a bitch!" he exclaimed with uncharacteristic rage. His expression darkened and he clenched his fists before stepping back and glaring furiously at the way they had come. Without warning, he stalked away from the group, heading straight for the exit.

"Hey, Max!" Michael called out, taking off after him. "Where do you think you're going?"

"The rest of you take care of Liz," Max shouted, not even looking back. He was halfway out of the grotto by now. "I'm going to get the slimeball who shot her!"

"Whoa there, man!" Catching up with Max, Michael laid a restraining hand on his friend's shoulder. "Hold on! We've got to think about this."

Max spun around angrily. For a second, Liz thought he was going to punch Michael in the face; she couldn't remember the last time she had seen Max look so enraged. "What's to talk about?" he snapped, brusquely knocking his best friend's hand aside. "That bastard nearly killed Liz!"

Michael looked around furtively. Max had deliberately selected a natural alcove off the beaten track, but he and Michael's tense confrontation was still starting to draw stares from the handful of other tourists present. "Chill out, man," he whispered intently, indicating with a gesture that they should lower their voices. "We don't want to attract any unnecessary attention, right?"

A lifetime of cautious anonymity seemed to supersede Max's seething fury, at least in part, and he weighed Michael's words carefully. His blazing eyes swung back and forth between Michael and the route back to the gift shop, as if torn between conflicting impulses. "I don't know," he said through gritted teeth, his fists remaining clenched at his sides. "He might get away."

"Let's just talk this over for a few minutes," Michael insisted. Despite the upsetting circumstances, Liz couldn't help noting how bizarre it was to hear Michael acting as the voice of reason; usually, Michael was the impetuous one, while Max advocated common sense and caution. She didn't know whether to be flattered or alarmed by Max's violent reaction to her unplanned reunion with the shooter. *I never realized he hated that guy so much.*

With open reluctance, Max returned with Michael to where Liz and the others were standing, in the shadow of the colossal stalagmite. "Make it fast," he said impatiently. "I don't want that trigger-happy scumbag to get away." He looked back at the exit, then glanced at his watch. "For all we know, he's already heading for Mexico."

"Hey, how about if I keep an eye on him," Alex volunteered, "while the rest of you plot strategy or whatever." He shrugged his lanky shoulders, as if it were no big deal. "I wasn't there that day at the Crashdown so he doesn't know me from Adam."

Max frowned, clearly wanting to go after the shooter himself, but not seeing any obvious flaws in Alex's proposal. "You sure you can identify him?" he asked skeptically.

"Big guy, red jacket, orange cap, bad attitude?" Alex recited, quoting the description Liz had given them. "No problem."

"Sounds like a plan, then," Michael agreed. Liz knew what he had to be thinking: If nothing else, Alex seemed to be in lot calmer state of mind than Max, and thus less likely to cause a scene that might attract undue attention. "Go for it."

"Be careful, Alex," Isabel said as Alex took off back toward the gift shop. He grinned back at her, visibly delighted by her concern. Liz hoped that Alex wouldn't take any unnecessary chances just to impress Isabel.

The remaining teens huddled beneath the giant calcite peak. "Okay," Michael said, looking around warily to make sure no strangers were listening. "How do we want to handle this?"

"Are you kidding?" Maria asked incredulously. She had draped her own arm protectively over Liz, who was still trembling like a rabbit caught in a trap. "We've got to tell the police right away!" She scratched her head with her free hand, puzzled by a new thought. "Er, do park rangers count as police?"

"Not so fast," Michael said. "The last thing we want to do is call the authorities' attention back to that incident at the Crashdown. Officially, remember, there was *no* shooting. Max healed Liz before the cops showed up."

But I was shot, Liz recalled. Her hands strayed once more to the spot where the bullet had entered her body. There wasn't even a scar there now, she knew, thanks to Max's miraculous powers, but that didn't mean she couldn't still recall the sudden burning pain in her belly, and the horrible way she felt her life slipping away through the hole in her stomach. *Darkness closing in on me. Blood soaking through my uniform...*

"Michael is right," Isabel declared. She lingered at the back of the grotto, a strained expression on her immaculate face. "It's too dangerous. We can't take the chance."

Maria stared at Michael and Isabel in disbelief. "But we have to do something!" she objected, sounding totally appalled at the notion of doing nothing. "We can't just let this guy walk out of here scot-free. He shot Liz, for pete's sake!"

Liz appreciated Maria's loyalty, but realized that Michael and Isabel had a point. They had all spent two stressful years covering up what had really happened at the Crashdown the day she was shot; did they really want to drag all that up into the light again? There was only so far Sheriff Valenti could protect them from outside scrutiny. "I don't know," she said hesitantly. "Maybe it's too complicated."

"Right!" Michael asserted. "What do we care about some lowlife, **trigger-ha**ppy hood? We've got enough problems with **alien inva**ders, rogue FBI agents, shapechangers, etcetera. **I s**ay we forget about him."

Easier said than done, Liz thought. She'd always known, intellectually, that the shooter was still out there somewhere, but now, having discovered firsthand that he could reappear in her life at any time, she wasn't sure she would ever feel safe again.

Max seemed to feel the same way. "You're all forgetting one thing," he reminded the others. Liz could hear the brooding intensity in his voice, sense the pent-up fury contained in his coiled muscles and posture. "This guy saw Liz, too. If he recognized her, he knows she can identify him. That puts Liz in danger."

I hadn't thought of that, Liz thought, feeling the panic flare up again. She shuddered violently, and received a comforting hug from Maria, who also offered her a sniff from one of her ubiquitous vials of soothing scents. "I'm not sure I can face him again," Liz confessed, dreading the very idea of running into the volatile gunman one more time. "I'm afraid to budge from this spot." Apprehension tied a knot in her stomach, and her legs felt like soggy french fries. "What if next time he recognizes me for sure?"

"Well, we can take care of that easily enough," Isabel declared. At least a foot taller than Liz, she reached out and ran her open palm over Liz's long brown hair. Molecules rearranged at the alien teenager's delicate prodding and Liz's cocoa-colored tresses turned a bright shade of scarlet. "There," Isabel stated, "instant redhead." With another pass of her hand, she shifted the hue of Liz's wool sweater from dark green to lemon-yellow, then stepped back to inspect her work. "Not bad," she pronounced. "I doubt that anyone will recognize you now, let alone some jerk who only saw you once before, two years ago."

Maria whistled appreciatively. "Boy, you must save a fortune on cosmetics and clothes," she remarked enviously to Isabel.

"I could change her eye color and hairstyle, too," Isabel said with a shrug. She produced a compact from her purse and offered the tiny mirror to Liz. "But that might be overkill."

Probably, Liz thought, marveling at the startling transformation revealed in the mirror. *So that's what I look like as a redhead.* She had to admit that Isabel had done a good job of changing her appearance, which made Liz feel somewhat safer and more secure. *A good disguise works wonders, I guess.*

"Thank you, Isabel," Max said to his sister. "That was a smart idea." He eyed Liz curiously, no doubt trying to get used to her striking new look. "It's still just a temporary solution, though. As long as this guy is loose, he's a potential threat to Liz." Liz recognized the look of determination in his eyes; he had made his decision. "I don't know about the rest of you, but I'm going to track this guy down and make sure he never hurts anybody again—even if I have to do it alone."

3

I think I'm starting to get the hang of this sneaky stuff, Alex Whitman thought. *Who would have guessed?*

Except in his wilder daydreams, Alex had never imagined himself the James Bond type. Yet here he was, trailing a dangerous, possibly lethal, suspect through the exotic setting of a gigantic cavern, eight hundred feet below the ground. *It's amazing,* he thought, *what hanging around with aliens can do to perk up an otherwise dull lifestyle.*

Locating Liz's mysterious assailant had been no problem; Alex had found the scruffy, heavyset stranger milling about outside the gift shop, looking impatient and irritable. The tricky part was going to be keeping an eye on the nameless shooter without blowing his cover. Alex hung out by the entrance to the underground cafeteria, pretending to be fascinated by a rock formation in the shape of an ice cream cone. *Too bad there's no newsstand down here,* he lamented; in the movies, private eyes and secret agents always hid behind their newspapers when shadowing suspicious characters.

Watching the alleged gunman out of the corner of his

eye, Alex couldn't blame Liz for being spooked by this joker. Even if he hadn't already shot one of Alex's best friends, the big, imposing bruiser just looked like trouble. A trucker, maybe, or a convict, or both. The kind of brutal, bullying thug that ate mild-mannered high school kids for breakfast. *Did he have to be quite so big and mean-looking?* Alex asked silently, registering a complaint with whatever higher power was plotting his fate. After all, unlike Max or Michael, he wasn't equipped with his own personal force field and death ray. *What do I do if he catches me following him? Run like heck, I guess.*

Alex suddenly remembered the disposable Kodak camera he'd purchased at the Visitors Center uptop. He had intended to use the small plastic camera to snap some candid shots of his friends as they explored the caverns, but now a more devious application occurred to him.

Fishing the camera from the pocket of his jacket, he took a few random shots of the spacious cavern, just to establish his cover, then waited until Mr. Bad Attitude's sullen pacing brought him in front of a suitably photogenic stalagmite. Alex's index finger hovered over the shutter-release button of the compact camera, stalling until the elusive gunman was framed in the center of the viewfinder, then clicked the button.

The resulting flash was brighter than he would have preferred. Gulping, Alex felt his blood rushing toward his feet as the flashbulb's momentary discharge caused Bad Attitude to glance in Alex's direction. He hurriedly shot several more photos, in every direction *except* the mystery man's, before furtively risking a glimpse back at his unwilling (and highly intimidating) photographic subject. To his relief, the surly gunman was no longer paying any attention to Alex, having shrugged off the presence of the lanky teenage shutterbug. *Thank goodness!* Alex thought, feeling his racing pulse slow to something closer to a normal human rate. Now the only question was, having already pressed his luck this far, did he really have the nerve to keep on trailing the dangerous suspect?

His resolve was tested only ten minutes later when the looming target of his surveillance checked his watch and grunted in approval. Carelessly tossing an empty candy wrapper onto the concrete floor of the rest area, Bad Attitude stomped toward the passage to the Big Room. *What was he waiting for?* Alex wondered, giving the guy a few seconds' head start before sticking his camera back in his pocket and taking off in pursuit.

Once he realized the shooter was definitely heading for the Big Room, Alex grew worried that Bad Attitude was going to run right into Liz and the others. He considered running ahead to warn them, but quickly decided that would be jumping the gun, no pun intended. The Big Room was *big*, after all; chances were, the burly gunman would completely miss Liz and Co. in the vast, crowded recesses of the enormous cavern.

Certainly, Bad Attitude wasn't interested in sight-seeing. He hiked right across the paved, level surface of the Big Room, ignoring such popular attractions as the Painted Grotto and the Rock of Ages. Instead he marched straight to the far end of the gargantuan cavern, where he paused in front of a gaping chasm that a nearby sign identified as THE BOTTOMLESS PIT.

Alex gulped, finding it all too easy to visualize the bad-tempered hoodlum throwing him bodily into the Pit, where he would probably fall for several long minutes before ending up impaled on some razor-sharp stalagmite. *Knock it off,* he told his overeager imagination. *No more of that now.* Taking a deep breath to steady his nerves, he ambled casually over to the end of the cave, faking an interest in one odd-shaped calcite deposit after another. *Boy, could I use that newspaper!* he thought yearningly.

Meanwhile, Bad Attitude waited with growing impatience by the Pit, tapping his foot restlessly while searching the faces of the tourists parading past the chasm. He was looking for someone, Alex deduced, but was it Liz? At one point, the man's bellicose gaze passed directly over Alex without any flicker of recognition or interest, and Alex had to resist an urge to sigh loudly in relief. Despite the chill atmosphere, he was sweating heavily beneath his sweater, the perspiration causing the fabric of his T-shirt to cling to his back. "Keep cool," he whispered to himself, avoiding eye contact with the menacing lone gunman. "We can do this, for Liz's sake."

The hefty suspect, who had been known to fire off guns in public places, had grumpily checked his watch at least three times before another man finally approached him. "About time," Bad Attitude snarled, his raspy voice not sounding any friendlier or less intimidating than the rest of him. "You're late."

The newcomer murmured something in reply, but Alex couldn't quite make it out. He took a second to scope out the Johnny-come-lately, risking a quick stare at the stranger, before concentrating, or so it seemed, on a rounded rock formation that bore a surprising resemblance to a Teletubby. *Don't mind me,* he thought, wishing he possessed some small fraction of Isabel's telepathic gifts. *I'm just checking out Tinky-Winky here. Nothing for you to worry about...*

Bad Attitude's tardy visitor could not have been more different than the disreputable-looking gunman. Clean-cut and neatly groomed, the second man wore an unscuffed leather flight jacket, aviator-style sunglasses, and newly-pressed blue slacks. Alex had relatives in the military, so he recognized the type right away. *Some sort of cop or soldier,* he guessed, a theory confirmed only seconds later when he heard Bad Attitude address the other man as "Lieutenant."

Probably from Fort Bliss or White Sands, he surmised; both military bases were only a few hours' drive from Carlsbad—and strictly off-limits to civilians. *What sort of business could this lieutenant possibly have with a gun-wielding thug like Bad Attitude?* He considered trying to snap a photo of the nameless officer, but was afraid that would give him away for sure. The region around the Pit was murkily lit, the better to show off the colored spotlights illuminating the chasm; there was no way either the gunman or the lieutenant could miss the flash when it went off, and Bad Attitude had already let Alex take one "accidental" snapshot of him. Trying for a second surveillance photo would definitely be pushing his luck, maybe all the way into the waiting Pit.

"Over here," the shooter said gruffly, nodding toward a vacant corner of the cave, where they could better converse in privacy. As the two men relocated, Alex stealthily circled around the nearest gnarled stone column, keeping the immense pillar between him and the unlikely pair. He still couldn't hear everything being said—the cavern's irregular contours made for strange acoustics—but he could make out snatches of the conversation.

"Look, Morton, I got (*inaudible*) as soon as I could," the Lieutenant complained. From his tone, Alex could tell this was no friendly rendezvous. "You don't understand the pressure I'm under.... (*something, something*) watching me all the time."

The shooter, whose name was apparently Morton, was less than sympathetic. "Yeah, yeah. Have you (*mutter, mumble*) the merchandise?"

The lieutenant lowered his voice, making it harder for Alex to eavesdrop. "(*Something*) hidden... (*mumble*) not here... (*whisper*) too public... (*mutter*) the money?"

"You'll get the money when (*something*)," Morton said firmly, if not entirely audibly. Alex wished he could somehow turn up the volume on the two co-conspirators. Whatever they were up to, it was obviously something fishy. "Tonight. Midnight. (*Mumble, mumble*) Slaughter Canyon."

Alex recognized the name as the site of one of the less touristy caverns Max had mentioned earlier, a short drive away. Slaughter Canyon sounded like something out of a Scooby-Doo cartoon, but it was a real enough place to serve, so it seemed, as the locale for some sort of illicit transaction between Morton and the lieutenant. *Is this about drugs?* he wondered. *Military secrets? Illegal aliens, of the non-extraterrestrial variety?* This close to the Mexican border, it was easy to imagine all kinds of nefarious smuggling operations. *We never did find out,* he recalled, *what that gunfight in the Crashdown was all about.*

Having dispensed with the meat of their discussion, the two men wandered back toward the Pit, forcing Alex to shift position in order to keep out of their line of sight. "You stay here for a while," he ordered the lieutenant, making it pretty clear who was calling the shots in this partnership. "Don't leave too quickly." He spit rudely onto the floor of the cavern. "Let me get out of here first."

"Sure," the lieutenant said nervously. "Of course." Alex guessed that the unnamed military man was acutely afraid of being caught at whatever shady business he was up to; why else would he be wearing shades eight hundred feet below ground?

Thoughts of international espionage raced through Alex's hyperactive mind. *What in the world have we gotten into this time,* he wondered, his heart pounding, *and when did my life turn into a never-ending episode of* The X-Files?

Assuming that Morton would be heading for the elevator next, Alex decided he needed to report back to Max and the others before Morton left the caverns entirely. Making a break for it, he darted out from behind the tapered column and made tracks for the secluded grotto where he had left his friends, zigzagging through and around clusters of strolling tourists. *Damn it,* he thought impatiently, in a hurry to get where he was going, *did the Big Room have to be so darn* big?

By the time he reached the grotto, maybe ten minutes later, he was out of breath and panting. At first he didn't recognize the redhead in the yellow sweater, tucked between Max and Maria, then he did a double take when he realized it was Liz. *Whoa,* he thought. *That's just too weird.*

Bent over gasping, his hands resting on his knees, he hastily told the others what he had seen and overheard. "Morton's probably on his way to the elevator now," he concluded, "although I got a pretty good start on him."

"Good work, Alex," Max said succinctly. His stony expression belied the volcanic intensity of his eyes. Max was your classic still-waters-run-deep kind of guy, Alex knew, but it was obvious that those waters were pretty stirred up at the moment. Max's fist collided with his open palm and he stared past Alex with a keen, determined gaze.

"Now it's my turn," he said.

4

"**W**hat are you talking about?" Michael challenged Max. Water dripped somewhere nearby, each steady drop echoing through the subterranean grotto. "Haven't you heard a word we've said? It's too dangerous, Max!"

The dark-haired alien teen was undaunted by his friend's fervent outburst. "I told you all before," Max said. The once and future king of a distant alien world, he had seldom sounded more resolute. "I'm not going to let him get away."

Isabel approached her brother, laying a concerned hand upon his shoulder. "But you don't have to follow him now," she pointed out. "You heard what Alex said. We know where he's going to be tonight. At that place, Slaughter Canyon."

Slaughter...The name sent a chill through Liz, rattling her already jangled nerves. She knew she ought to have some opinion about Max's reckless plan, but she was still too stressed-out to think straight. Every time she tried to concentrate, she kept flashing back to that day at the Crashdown. *Angry voices exploding. A noisy scuffle at the booth. Watch out! He's got a gun!*

"I don't care," Max said. "What if he gets spooked and doesn't show up at midnight?" He paced restlessly across the floor of the grotto. "I'm not going to take that chance."

"Okay, okay," Maria conceded, knowing as well as any of them how stubborn Max could be when he felt strongly about something. *Like when he tried to get me back,* Liz thought, *after that whole scene with Tess.* "But don't you at least want to know what Morton's up to before you do something stupid?"

It felt strange, Liz thought, to actually have a name for the man who had once nearly killed her, and even stranger that she had gone all this time without knowing it. *Morton.* It was a surprisingly mundane label for such a malignant presence in her life. *Is that his first name or his last name,* she wondered, *and did that really matter?*

Meanwhile, Maria was still reading the riot act to Max. "Use your super-powered, Czechoslovakian brain, Max!" She threw up her hands in sheer exasperation. "Right now you have no idea what you'd be getting yourself mixed up with."

Her cautionary words must have gotten through to Max, because he paused and mulled them over before replying. "All right," he said, sounding slightly less combative. "I won't do anything rash until we know more. But I *am* going to follow him and find out where he's going now."

"Okay," Michael grudgingly agreed. "But I'm going with you, just to make sure you don't get carried away on this whole avenging boyfriend kick."

Was that what was driving Max? Liz asked silently. Even in her own distracted state, she was aware that Max was acting more recklessly than usual. *Does he feel he has to pay Morton back for hurting me? Or does he blame Morton for making him reveal his powers, putting them all in danger from the Special Unit and the Skins?*

"Fine," Max told Michael. "Let's go." He marched briskly toward the grotto's exit, then paused right underneath the natural limestone archway. "The rest of you, look after Liz. Make sure she gets out of here okay." He slowed long enough to look back at Liz with concern. "We'll hook up with you again later."

A sudden fear that Max was going to get himself hurt, or worse, over some misguided chivalric impulse flashed through Liz's brain. She saw the murderous gunman firing his weapon again, this time at her boyfriend and soulmate. "Please, Max," she urged him. "Be careful!"

"Yeah," Maria seconded that anguished emotion. "Both of you, play it safe, will you?" Worry radiated from her naked, openly emotional face. "Remember, we *know* this guy is armed and dangerous."

"So are we," Max reminded them before disappearing into the tunnel outside the grotto. Liz listened as his and Michael's footsteps swiftly receded into the distance.

"Boy," Alex commented, shaking his head in disbelief. "When did Max turn into such a hard-ass? He was starting to sound like Dirty Harry there."

"He's just worried about Liz...I think," Maria said doubtfully. "The scary part is, we're expecting *Michael* to be the sensible one?" She gave Liz another encouraging hug, perhaps to reassure herself as much as her shell-shocked best friend. "Well, what do you say, girlfriend? Are you up to blowing this underground popsicle stand? I don't know about you, but I'm ready to see the sun again." She toyed with the silver pendant around her neck. "If cool chicks like us were meant to live underground, then we wouldn't look so great with a tan."

"Okay, I guess," Liz said. Her legs still felt a little rubbery, but she supposed she could manage to make her way back to the surface again. *Maybe I'll feel less trapped, less frightened, once I get out of these endless caves.* A pang of regret stabbed her heart as she wondered whether her upsetting run-in with Morton had ruined the caves for her forever. Only this morning, Carlsbad had represented carefree childhood memories to her; now she just wanted to get as far away from these gloomy caverns as possible.

Her arm around Liz's shoulders, Maria guided Liz out of the grotto, into the press of foot traffic surging through the Big Room. Alex stuck close to Liz as well, so that she was bracketed protectively between her friends as they slowly made their way back toward the rest area. "Isabel?" he called out after a moment or two. "You coming with us?"

The glamorous alien teenager shook her head. "Not right away. There's something else I have to do first."

"Huh?" Alex said, mystified. He lingered upon the trail, blocking traffic somewhat, torn between keeping up with Liz and Maria and finding out what his frequently enigmatic dream girl was planning. "Why? What—?"

"No questions, Alex," she instructed him decisively. Like her brother, Isabel could seldom be dissuaded once she'd made up her mind. They were royalty, after all, Liz remembered, albeit not from this planet. "Help Maria get Liz to the surface. I'll join you there later."

"But—?" Alex began, completely disoriented by this baffling turn of events. Liz had to admit that she didn't understand either.

"Just do it, Alex," Isabel insisted, turning her back and heading the other way. Alex strained his neck to keep her in view, but, within moments, she had disappeared into the milling mob of amateur spelunkers.

"Come on, Alex," Maria said, calling him back to the task at hand; namely, ferrying Liz back to the world above. "I'm sure our friend, the space princess, will find us once she's finished her mysterious alien business." Lowering her voice, she whispered clandestinely into Liz's ear. "What on earth is *that* all about?"

I have no idea, Liz thought.

Lieutenant David Ramirez, currently assigned to White Sands Missile Range, was wishing he'd never heard of Joe Morton. *How the hell did I get mixed up in this mess?* he asked himself gloomily, but he already knew the answer. Morton had plenty of dirt on him—the drugs, the gambling, the whole thing—plus connections with enough cash to let Ramirez pay off his debts and start a new life somewhere else if he had to. Blackmail and bribery were a potent combination, one that he had been unable to resist. *I should have never opened my mouth about that damn UFO!*

He leaned against the metal guardrail, staring morosely into the unplumbed depths of the Bottomless Pit, which seemed about as black and abysmal as his current prospects. He had no illusions what would happen to him if his superiors found out about his dealings with Morton. At best, he'd be talking court-martial; at worst, he'd just quietly "disappear" without any fuss, as though he had never existed at all. This was high treason, after all, involving some of the government's most closely-guarded secrets.

Maybe it won't turn out that way, he thought desperately. *Maybe the entire operation will go off as planned.* He had to think so, otherwise he might just as well hurl himself into the Pit right now. *Think of the money,* he told himself, trying hard to look on the bright side. *If I don't get caught, if Morton comes through with his side of the bargain, I'll be set for life.* He could just serve out his term of duty, exit the air force with an honorable discharge, then settle down to live a life of luxury someplace very far from here, where no one has ever heard of Roswell or the Crash. . . .

"Yeah," he murmured wistfully. That was the ticket. Someplace nice and warm, on a beach, maybe, with a big house, big cars, and a sexy babe or two, with long blond hair and built like—

"Excuse me, do you have the time?"

Startled, he looked up from the Pit to find his fantasy standing right next to him, only inches away. He blinked behind his sunglasses, taken aback by the breathtaking vision that seemed to have stepped right out of his steamier daydreams.

She was young—eighteen, nineteen, probably—and quite simply gorgeous. Lustrous, sandy-blond hair falling down over her shoulders. Glossy, pouting lips. Smooth, flawless skin. Even bundled up against the coolness of the caverns, wearing a partly opened tan suede jacket over a blue cashmere sweater, she obviously possessed the enticing curves of a good, old-fashioned pinup girl. Seductive brown eyes locked onto his, and Ramirez felt his heart skip a beat.

"The time?" she asked again. She had a throaty, sultry voice that pushed his buttons in all the right ways. He was over six feet tall, but she was tall enough to look him directly in the eyes. *Talk about hot!* he thought eagerly.

"Oh, yeah, right. No problem," he burbled. Somehow he managed to tear his eyes away from hers long enough to peek at his wristwatch. "It's about 12:45," he told her helpfully.

"Thanks," she said with a smile. Encouragingly, she didn't seem to be in any hurry to move on now that he'd answered her query. "Sorry to bother you, but there's just no way to tell what time it is down here, away from the sky and all." She unzipped her jacket the rest of the way, revealing more of the amply-filled blue sweater underneath. "It's like we've stepped outside of time, you know? Into a whole new world, with completely different rules."

I'd like to break a few rules with you, he thought lewdly. Part of him knew he had more important things to worry about than trying to make time with some chick, no matter how sensational she was. Another part of him, however, welcomed the distraction. God knows this babe was easy on the eyes, and a hell of a lot more appealing than Joe Morton. "Yeah," he agreed readily. "This place is pretty impressive, isn't it."

"I'll say!" she breathed huskily. She leaned over the guardrail, gazing down into the Pit. "Wow, that's a long way down," she exclaimed, then stumbled backward, tottering unsteadily upon her shapely, denim-clad legs while placing a hand over her forehead. "Ooh, I feel dizzy...," she whispered, swooning so dramatically that he had to rush forward to keep her from collapsing onto the floor of the cavern. His arms slid deftly beneath hers as her weight sagged against his chest.

"Hey, there!" he said, feeling her taut body press against

his. The heady scent of her hair filled his nostrils, while his hands gently stroked her back through, in his opinion, far too many layers of clothing. "Are you okay?" he asked, marveling inwardly at his luck. *This keeps getting better and better!*

"I'm fine, I think," she murmured, her head rested on his shoulder. She clung to him for support, perhaps waiting for the dizziness to pass. He was perfectly happy to hold onto her for as long as necessary, and then some. "Just a touch of vertigo." She shivered delectably. "You must think I'm terribly weak."

"No, not at all," he assured her. As far as he was concerned, her sudden vulnerability just made her sexier. "That's a pretty steep drop-off." He laughed in what he hoped was an irresistibly debonair fashion. "They don't call it the Bottomless Pit for nothing."

She lifted her head to look up at him with grateful brown eyes. A devastating smile melted away the worries of the day, at least for the moment. "That's sweet of you to say so," she declared, "but I'll bet you're never afraid of heights."

How could he resist a cue like that? "Actually, I'm a test pilot," he volunteered, "for the air force."

"Really!" Her awestruck tone was a tonic to his ego, which had been seriously battered by recent events. *Never fails,* he thought smugly. *Chicks love the whole* Top Gun *thing.*

Blushing, she seemed to realize that she was still snugly clasped in his arms. He repressed a frustrated sigh as she (reluctantly?) extricated herself from his grasp and took a few steps backward. She was still close enough, though, that he could smell her hair and savor the contours of her voluptuous figure. "My name's Isabel," she said. "Isabel…DeLuca." She looked him over flirtatiously. "What's yours?"

He hesitated, uncertain whether to divulge his real name. There was a lot at stake here, and he didn't want to make a fatal mistake just because this girl was a knockout. *Then again,* he thought, scoping her out from top to bottom, *where's the harm?* He wasn't violating any regulations by spending the weekend at Carlsbad; as far as anyone knew, he was just checking out the local tourist attractions—and talent. Behind his shades, his eyes greedily devoured Isabel as, fanning herself with one hand, she slowly slipped out of her jacket, which she folded over the metal guardrail. She leaned back languidly against the rail, coyly watching him watching her. *In fact,* he rationalized, mouth watering, *he might get himself into more trouble if he started fabricating things unnecessarily. What was that old saying about lies and tangled webs?*

"Lieutenant David Ramirez at your service," he said confidently. Throwing caution to the winds, he removed his sunglasses and tucked them into one of the inner pockets of his flight jacket. "Currently stationed at White Sands Missile Range."

Her eyes widened just like he hoped they would. "Isn't that where they're testing the 'Star Wars' missile defense system?" she asked, displaying rather more knowledge of current events than he expected. "Are you involved with all that?"

Conveniently, he had a perfectly legitimate excuse for being evasive. "I'm afraid I'm not at liberty to discuss my specific duties," he said ominously. A little intrigue and mystery could only enhance his image, he figured. "Matters of national security, you understand. Strictly classified, on a need-to-know basis."

"Oh, right. Of course," she said, nodding. "I should have realized." Her baby-doll pout deepened, and she peered up at him through thick, curling lashes. "Can't you give me just a hint, though?"

"Sure," he said lightly, "but then I'd have to kill you." He laughed again, to make it clear he was joking, sort of, while hastily pondering his next move. Should he try to lure her back to his motel room in Whites City, or just try to get her phone number? A red-hot afternoon fling would sure take his mind off his midnight meeting with Morton, and everything that could go wrong there, but what if she accidentally stumbled onto the merchandise? Then he might have to kill her for real.

"So, are you from around here?" he asked curiously. If she was a tourist, visiting from God knows where, then he'd have to move quickly if he wanted to score with her. Even with the whole Morton mess hanging over his head, it would be a crying shame to let an opportunity—and a hottie—like this go to waste.

"Oh, sure," Isabel replied. "I was born and raised in...Artesia."

"That's south of Roswell, right?" Until today, he hadn't gotten off the base much.

"By about fifty miles or so," she confirmed. "Midway between Carlsbad and Roswell, actually." Sultry, brown eyes probed his. "You ever been to Roswell?" she asked innocently.

He mentally kicked himself for even mentioning the R-word, just when he was finally succeeding in getting his mind off classified government secrets and their sale. "Say, you got any plans for this afternoon?" he inquired impulsively, changing the subject. "Maybe we could go for drinks, or something?"

This isn't too smart, he realized, even as he stepped closer to the alluring young woman, flashing his most ingratiating smile. Now that he knew she was local, he should just play it cool and look her up after his business with Morton was wrapped up. *I can't help it, though,* he thought, unable to resist the almost magnetic attraction drawing him onward. *I mean, look at her!*

Unfortunately, her immediate response to his invitation was an embarrassed wince. "Gee, that sounds great, but I promised my friends I'd hook up with them uptop." She glanced at the paved walkway leading away from the Bottomless Pit. "In fact, I'm probably running late already."

Damn! He knew a brush-off when he heard one. *So much for a world outside of time,* he thought irritably. His restored spirits, and mounting excitement, went into a nosedive. *Time-wasting little tease! Don't tell me she wasn't flirting with me shamelessly this whole time.*

Then, after he had already written her off, Isabel smiled slyly and said, "You know, Mr. Lieutenant, I'd love to see you in uniform sometime. I'll bet you look just like Tom Cruise." She reached over and adjusted the lapel of his flight jacket. "Maybe you can give me your phone number?"

Maybe his lurid fantasies weren't quite dead after all. "Sure," he said, "if you'll give me yours."

Another sheepish wince, followed by an inviting gaze. "I'd rather give you a call, if that's all right." She shrugged her shoulders, tossing her flowing blond hair at the same time. "It's complicated," she explained vaguely.

A jealous boyfriend? he speculated. *Overprotective parents?* Frankly, he didn't need those kinds of hassles, either. Seeing nothing to lose, and plenty to gain, he scribbled down his cell phone number on a scrap of paper he found in his wallet. "Here," he said cheerfully, handing her the improvised note. "You can reach me there most of the time, except when I'm on duty, of course."

"Naturally," she replied. She folded the slip of paper carefully and placed it in her back pocket. "I've got to run," she said, retrieving her jacket and slipping it back on. "But I'll be in touch, I promise!"

I sure hope so, Ramirez thought, eyeing her hungrily as she hurried onto the trail back to the rest area and the elevator. Chances were, he might never hear from her again, but even still, his accidental meeting with this hot little number was the luckiest break he'd had in a long, long time.

Now he just had to get through this weekend without ending up behind bars.

Or worse.

Men! Isabel Evans thought with disdain. Human or alien, they were all the same; flirt with them a little, bat your big brown eyes adoringly, and you could get them to do almost anything. Lieutenant Ramirez hadn't even put up a fight. Whatever his full story was, he'd been just as easy to manipulate as the high school boys she was used to wrapping around her little finger.

As she rushed back toward the elevator, she worried briefly about whether she had maybe laid the vamp act on a little too thick. Had that whole dizzy spell routine been too much? What if she'd tipped her hand when she fell into his arms, raising his suspicions instead of lowering his defenses?

Naah, she decided promptly. He'd fallen for it hook, line, and sinker, she could tell. Another woman would have seen through that transparent ploy right away, but, as she'd learned repeatedly since sixth grade at the latest, subtlety was lost on most members of the male gender. Sometimes you couldn't be too obvious, especially where men were concerned.

Besides, she reflected, *I could have been even more blatant, given the setting.* Stalagmites, caverns, unexplored nether regions...the possibilities for smutty double entendres had been almost too readily available. *Not that I needed them,* she thought with a smirk.

Her confidence in her own time-tested techniques and tactics gave way to unsettling fears and suspicions as she considered the information she had managed to extract from the lecherous lieutenant. *Classified military experiments at White Sands?* Isabel chewed nervously on her lower lip, disturbed by the possible implications of Ramirez's background. Visions of top secret alien autopsies and extraterrestrial artifacts paraded behind her fretful brown eyes, awakening deep-rooted fears and anxieties that were never very far from her thoughts.

What was an air force test pilot doing with the man who shot Liz two years ago? Could these shady goings-on have anything to do with Roswell's hidden alien secrets? The last few years had taught Isabel to be distrustful of almost everything and everyone, including herself. A high school counselor, a congresswoman, a deputy, a waitress, new friends and admirers...all had proven to pose hidden dangers. She couldn't help worrying that her unearthly heritage was about to catch up with her again.

Won't it ever end? she asked bitterly, waiting in line for the elevator back to the surface. *Won't we ever be safe, anywhere on this planet?*

5

"So," Alex said, flagrantly trying to take Liz's mind off her nerve-racking brush with Joe Morton, "there's just one thing about this whole alien royalty bit I don't understand. If Max is Luke Skywalker, Michael is Han Solo, and Isabel is Princess Leia, what does that make the rest of us?"

"Hmm, I can't speak for myself," Maria said, "but I always thought there was something very C-3PO about you."

"Thanks a lot!" Alex replied in mock indignation. He balanced on the back of a wooden bench outside the Visitors Center, his tennis shoes resting on the timbered seat of the bench next to Liz and Maria.

"Hey, don't complain," Maria warned. "I could've said Chewbacca. Or Jar Jar Binks." She glanced at Liz, playfully punching her preoccupied best friend in the shoulder. "What do you think, Liz? Is Alex more of a 'droid or a Wookiee?"

Liz mustered a feeble smile at her friends' lighthearted banter. She knew they were both working overtime to raise her spirits, and she didn't want to disappoint them, but she couldn't help it; she still felt like an emotional basket case.

Her nerves were shot, and she jumped at every unexpected noise or movement. Her eyes restlessly scanned the surrounding scenery, half-expecting to see Joe Morton, gun in hand, reappear without warning. *I've never felt this scared before,* she thought, *not even when the FBI or the Skins were chasing us.*

Granted, there was nothing overtly threatening about their present location. The three teenagers, all one hundred percent human, sat outside the Caverns's bustling Visitors Center. The blazing sun, burning brightly overhead, baked the packed parking lots and arid desert terrain around them, keeping the temperature in the upper nineties, even in the shade. Spiny cacti and flowering red agave and ocotillo bushes sprouted stubbornly from the dusty brown soil surrounding the low, one-story Visitors Center. A nearby wooden kiosk displayed a variety of posted notices regarding park safety and regulations. None of the notices, Liz guessed, said anything about how to cope with fearsome, trigger-happy monsters from your past.

She watched a vulture circle slowly in the cloudless blue sky stretching over the desert, the grim harbinger of death doing little to dispel the disturbing memory of her own excruciating brush with mortality, lying wounded and bleeding on the scuffed tile floor of the Crashdown. Nor did the scorching sun drive away the numbing chill that seemed to have settled into her flesh and bones for good. The rocky Guadalupe Mountains loomed on the horizon, harsh and forbidding, like her life now seemed to be.

"How're you holding up, kid?" Maria asked sympathetically, abandoning her and Alex's happy act.

"I don't know," Liz confessed, grateful for a shoulder to

cry on. "I can't stop thinking about it. The shooting at the Crashdown, I mean." Her yellow, formerly green, sweater was crumpled into a ball on the seat of the bench, but she was still overdressed for the torrid heat of the New Mexican summer. The Visitors Center, only a few yards away, was air-conditioned, but she just wasn't ready to deal with a building full of strangers right now. Despite the raging sun cooking the three teens to a crisp, Liz craved privacy and quiet more than she needed relief from the heat. "I know, I should be over it, after all this time. Max healed me right away, so I was really only hurt for a couple of minutes, but, ever since I saw Morton again, it's like it's happening all over again!"

Perched atop the back of the bench, Alex kept looking over at the front door of the Center. Liz knew he had to be wondering what was keeping Isabel. "That's perfectly understandable," he assured Liz. "I got beaten up on the way home from school once, and for weeks afterward, I couldn't walk that route without looking over my shoulder the whole time." He squinted into the glaring sunlight, keeping an eye out for Isabel and/or Morton. "I got over it, eventually," he told Liz. "So will you."

I hope so, she thought despairingly. She hated feeling so weak and fragile. *I've been captured by alien shapeshifters, for heaven's sake, and lived to tell of it, so why has this left me such a wreck?* She choked back a sob as she buried her face against Maria's shoulder. Tears streamed from her eyes.

Sighing in sympathy, Maria held onto Liz's shaking frame. "Oh, gee," she murmured, sounding choked up herself. Maria took a restorative sniff from a vial of rosemary oil, then waved the tiny glass bottle under her distraught friend's nose as well. "Look, Liz, if you want, I can drive you home in the Jetta right now. Alex can wait for our alien buddies, and hitch a ride home in the Jeep."

"Sure," he volunteered readily. "No problem. You can take off whenever you want." His gawky frame, seated above Liz and Maria, provided a bit of welcome shade for his friends. "Don't worry about me."

Liz shook her head vehemently. The rosemary oil had done little to soothe her anguished spirit. "No, I can't. Not yet." She was in no shape to face her parents, not in the frazzled and fragile state she was in. They had no idea what had almost happened to her in the Crashdown that day, let alone everything she'd been through since. *There's no way I could hide what I'm feeling from Mom and Dad,* she realized.

"Okay," Maria said soothingly. "No rush. Just wanted you to know you've got the option, whenever you feel up to it."

"Thanks," Liz managed with difficulty. She knew she couldn't stay here, sitting on this bench forever, but the mere thought of doing anything else, taking any kind of decisive action, was just too daunting. *Where are Max and Michael?* she fretted in an agony of suspense, terrified that something horrible would happen to them while they were trailing Morton to who knew where. *Shouldn't they be back by now?* She needed to know that Max was safe and coming back to her soon. *Who will heal him,* she tormented herself, *if both he and Michael are shot?* In her mind's eye, she could see Morton taking aim at the only boy she had ever really loved....

BANG! A sudden loud explosion caused Liz to leap to her feet and let out a gasp of sheer terror. Her heart pounded like a jackhammer, and she was suddenly back at the Crashdown again, feeling the bullet slam into her belly, knocking her to the floor. The smell of smoke and burned gunpowder filled her throat, and she clutched her stomach in alarm. *Help me! Max! Maria! I've been shot!*

"No, Liz! It's okay!" Maria grabbed onto Liz's arm to keep her from running away in fear. She thrust her face in front of Liz's, trying urgently to penetrate the instant panic stampeding through her friend. "It was just a car, Liz! Backfiring in the parking lot." Behind her, Alex jumped awkwardly from the bench onto the sidewalk, coming to their assistance, a dismayed look upon his face. "Only a car, that's all!"

A car? Liz didn't understand. Adrenaline flooded her body, spurring an uncontrollable urge to run for safety. She tugged on her arm, trying to break away from Maria's steady grip. Her frantic eyes searched wildly for Joe Morton and his smoking gun. *A car?* she dimly registered, blinking in fright and confusion. *But I was shot, wasn't I?* Pain, or the memory of pain, throbbed below her ribs. She looked down apprehensively, expecting to see blood gushing from her abdomen, seeping through her lightweight cotton T-shirt, but saw nothing of the kind, not even a single, charred bullet hole in her shirt. "A car?" she asked uncertainly.

Her friends flanked her on both sides, offering her reassurance and support. "That's right," Maria insisted once more. She took Liz's hand and gave it a comforting squeeze. "It was just a car, Liz."

Alex seconded Maria's emphatic assertions. "It's okay, Liz," he said, taking hold of her other hand. "There's nothing to be afraid of. Everything's fine."

Really? Liz wondered hopefully. The unreasoning panic began to subside as her friends' calming words sank in. She felt her pulse slowing to something closer to normal. Her breathing grew softer and more regular as she shakily contemplated the adjacent parking lot, which was crammed with dusty station wagons, SUVs, and vehicles from all over the country. *It* could *have been a car,* her fear-stricken mind gradually conceded. *That ear-shattering, nerve-jangling bang* might *have been just a routine backfire, brought on by a faulty muffler or carburetor.* But what about the pain, the agonizing impact of the bullet striking her flesh? She could've sworn that she'd been shot once more.

Liberating her hand from Maria's consoling clasp, she gripped the bottom of her T-shirt and tugged the fabric upward, needing to see for herself that she was indeed unharmed. Her worst, most dire fears and expectations were not at all allayed when both Alex and Maria gasped out loud at the sight of her exposed belly. Filled with fear and trepidation, she looked down and let out a startled cry herself. "Oh, my God," she whispered.

There was no wound, no blood, but something else caused her eyes to widen and her jaw to drop. There, emblazoned on the quivering flesh of her bare stomach, was a phosphorescent silver handprint, glowing brighter than the noonday sun.

6

Good thing we don't have heat vision, Michael Guerin thought. Otherwise Max's ferocious glare would have burned a hole in the back of Joe Morton's skull.

The alien youths lurked at the back of the elevator, accompanying the mysterious gunman on his way back to the surface. Fortunately, Morton's size and girth made it fairly easy to keep track of him, even in the crowded elevator. Michael figured the odds that the scruffy stranger, who reminded him unpleasantly of his vanished foster father Hank, would recognize him and Max from the Crashdown were incredibly remote. Morton and his sleazy confederate had fled the scene of the shooting well before Max called attention to himself with his miraculous (and highly imprudent) laying of hands upon Liz. He never knew that his single bullet had changed all of their lives forever.

The baleful intensity with which Max's eyes shot daggers at Morton made Michael uncomfortable. It wasn't like Max to lose control like this. Usually he was more cautious, more thoughtful—except, of course, for that day at the

Crashdown. *Maybe I've got good reason to be worried,* Michael thought; the last time Morton threatened Liz, Max had risked everything by using his powers in public. Who knew what rash action Max might take now that, after all these months, the deadly gunman had reentered their lives?

Seven hundred and fifty feet later, the elevator disgorged its occupants into the Visitors Center atop the caverns. Morton ignored the various educational displays on the history of the park, featuring large mounted photos of such earthly luminaries as Calvin Coolidge and Herbert Hoover visiting the caves, and headed straight for the nearest exit. Max and Michael chased after him, trying hard not to be too conspicuous about it.

At the last minute, right before stepping through the swinging glass doors to the outside, Morton turned and looked behind him. Michael's heart jumped, and he hurriedly feigned interest in a map of the surrounding parklands, but Morton paid no attention to either Max or him, glowering instead at the sealed doors of the elevator. *Right,* Michael guessed, with a strong sense of relief, *he's not looking at us. He's checking to make sure the lieutenant is still underground and not leaving the caves at the same time.*

Having assured himself that his nameless co-conspirator was nowhere to be seen, Morton left the Center. Michael counted to five, then took off after him, disturbed to see that Max was already several steps ahead of him. "Slow down, man!" he whispered forcefully to Max, catching up with his longtime friend. "Cool your jets, okay? You're going to blow our cover!"

After spending the last few hours in the cool, artificially-lit recesses of the caverns, stepping out of the Center into the heat and glare of summer came as quite a jolt. Michael squinted, raising a hand to shield his eyes. Days like this, he wished he had a protective inner eyelid, like Mr. Spock on *Star Trek. Guess we're a different sort of alien,* he thought wryly, searching for the designated target of their amateur manhunt. At first he couldn't locate Morton amid all the other tourists coming and going outside the Center. Then, despite the blinding sunlight, he spotted a familiar bright orange cap rising above the stationary vehicles crowding the large, spacious parking lot. "Over there," he alerted Max, pointing toward the departing figure. Morton was obviously planning to say adios to the park.

Max nodded grimly, no doubt reaching the same conclusion. "Get the car," he instructed Michael tersely, tossing him the keys to the olive-green, army-surplus Jeep he and Isabel shared to get around. "I'll stick with Morton."

"Are you sure?" Michael asked, a dubious expression on his face. The way Max was acting, he was reluctant to leave him alone with Morton, even for only five minutes or so. "How about the other way around?"

"Just do it," Max ordered, his intent gaze never leaving their unsuspecting quarry. He proceeded briskly along the edge of the parking lot, continuing the pursuit without a single glance backward.

Fuming in frustration, Michael kicked a discarded Pepsi can at Max's retreating back. *Tell a guy he's the rightful heir to a distant alien civilization, and suddenly he thinks he can call all the shots.* Realizing there was no arguing with Max in his present mood, Michael hustled to carry out his friend's instructions. He raced across the overpopulated parking lot, sliding between the tightly-packed vehicles until, only moments later, he reached the Jeep, right where they'd left it. Hopping into the driver's seat, he fired the ignition and backed out of their parking space, taking care not to run over any strolling tourists or (worse yet) bang into Maria's precious red Jetta, parked right next door.

Figuring that Morton, once he got into his own car, would be headed for the exit at the northeast end of the lot, Michael drove that way as well. Sure enough, he found Max waiting alongside the exit, looking impatient enough to spontaneously combust. Michael pulled up next to him, and Max bounded into the front passenger seat, not even bothering with the Jeep's door. "That's him," he snapped, pointing at the access road leading out of the park. "The blue Chevy convertible with the Texas plates." He vibrated with frustrated antagonism. "Don't let him get away!"

The Jeep accelerated out of the parking lot, onto N. Mex 7. Michael spotted the navy-blue Chevy Max was talking about, two or three vehicles ahead, and got into the same lane. He wondered how long Max was willing to follow Morton. All the way to Texas, or to hell and back?

I'm betting on that last one, he thought sourly. He still wasn't convinced that this was a good idea. *We don't have enough troubles and enemies on our hands, we have to go looking for more?*

Keeping one hand on the wheel, he snatched a half-empty bottle of Tabasco sauce off the dashboard and took a deep gulp of the bottle's fiery red contents. The refreshing liquid heat coursed down his throat, tantalizing his alien tongue and taste buds. *Ahh*, he thought appreciatively, *that really hits the spot*. He offered the rest of the bottle to Max, but Max brushed it aside with a curt gesture, obsessively focused on the blue Chevy and its occupant.

Without stopping, Morton passed through the tiny tourist trap of Whites City, heading northeast on National Parks Highway, better known as El Paso Road, toward Carlsbad itself, about half an hour away. Sun-baked desert plains, spotted with occasional stands of mesquite or yucca plants, stretched out monotonously on both sides of the park highway. Pushing the speed limit, the Jeep's forward motion generated a cooling breeze that helped to make the sweltering heat slightly bearable.

Michael cautiously kept a couple of vehicles between the Jeep and the Chevy, much to the frustration of Max, who kept urging him to close the gap. "You're too far away," he complained, restlessly drumming his fingers upon the dashboard. "We're going to lose him."

"No, we're not," Michael assured him for what felt like the fifteenth time. *Talk about your role reversals,* he thought. *I'm supposed to be the reckless, impulsive one.* "Do you want him to figure out we're tailing him?" he asked Max in exasperation. "This snazzy Jeep of yours is pretty conspicuous."

Max did not respond, instead falling silent as he continued to stare darkly at the speeding Chevy. His icy expression and smoldering eyes spooked Michael, who tried to figure out just where his friend's head was at. *I haven't seen Max so angry,* he thought, *since that final confrontation with Agent Pierce.* "So what's the master plan?" he asked worriedly. "What exactly are you planning to do once we find out what this creep is up to?"

"Whatever I have to," Max said, looking straight ahead, his seething gaze glued to Morton's convertible.

"What the hell does that mean, Max?" Michael didn't like the tone of his friend's voice. His hands gripped the wheel tightly as he let Max know exactly what he thought. "Are we talking murder here, Max? Is that the plan? Are you planning to kill Morton yourself, to avenge Liz Parker's sacred honor?" Squeezing the wheel so hard his knuckles whitened, he cast an accusatory look at the obsessed alien teenager sitting next to him. "Just how far are you planning to go, Max?"

"I don't know," Max answered, after too long a pause. His expression darkened as he considered his options where Joe Morton was concerned. His jaw twitched and an angry vein pulsed along his brow. "Far enough, I guess."

"Oh yeah?" Michael challenged him, dividing his attention between the road, the Chevy, and Max Evans. "Let me clue you in on something, glorious leader. Killing another person, human or otherwise, isn't like skipping class or lying to the cops. It's something you have to live with, every day for the rest of your life."

He spoke from painful experience. It had taken him months to come to terms with having killed Agent Pierce, and that had been in self-defense. Sometimes he still had nightmares about it, vivid flashbacks that woke him up in the middle of the night. He could just imagine the torments Max's anguished conscience would put his best friend through if Max actually killed Morton in cold blood. "You don't want to do that, man."

Max looked unconvinced, but at least he appeared to be considering what Michael had said. His fingers stopped drumming violently on the dashboard and his stormy gaze turned inward for a time. *Let's hope I got through to him,* Michael prayed, *before he does something we all regret.*

They drove in heavy silence for maybe fifteen, twenty minutes or so, before Michael saw the Chevy's right turn signal flash on. A stretch of cheap motels lined both sides of the highway, and Michael watched intently as Morton turned his car into the parking lot of a Motel 6. He exchanged a wordless look with Max, acknowledging that they'd both noted the detour the Chevy had just taken. *Guess we're not driving to Texas after all,* Michael concluded somberly. *Which makes sense, I suppose, if Morton really is planning to meet the lieutenant at Slaughter Canyon tonight. He wouldn't want to get too far from the Park for the time being.*

To avoid tipping off Morton, Michael drove past the Motel 6. Max squirmed impatiently as he did so, but recognized the necessity of maintaining their cover. He waited stiffly, tapping his foot against the floor of the Jeep, as the army-surplus vehicle circled back, eventually coming to rest in front of the Days Inn directly across the street from Motel 6. The minute Michael hit the brakes, Max hopped out of the Jeep and ran to the edge of the road, peering across the highway at the motel parking lot where they had last seen Morton's convertible. Michael didn't know whether to be relieved or disappointed that the blue Chevy was still parked prominently in front of Motel 6.

"Let's go," Max said as soon as Michael joined him at the roadside. Apparently, locating Morton's temporary lodgings was not good enough for Max; he was determined to take this foolhardy expedition another step further.

"Wait," Michael cautioned him. "We ought to do something else first." Max grudgingly let Michael drag him back into the parking lot, where they hid from sight between two oversize sports utility vehicles. Michael looked up and down the narrow space between the two humongous gas guzzlers, making sure no one was watching them. "Isabel had the right idea," he explained, "just so Morton doesn't recognize us from the elevator."

Concentrating, the way Nasedo had taught him, Michael ran his hand through his hair. A mop of disorderly brown hair lightened dramatically, all the way to bleached white. "Let's find out if blonds really do have more fun," he cracked. With a few more passes of his hand, he changed the cut and color of his clothing, replacing his black T-shirt and jeans with a bright blue football jersey and khaki slacks. A pair of dark sunglasses added a final layer of anonymity. "Your turn," he told Max when he was finished.

Nodding, Max disguised himself as well. Perhaps in solidarity with Liz, he gave himself sandy red hair, then changed his flannel shirt and jeans into a white tank top and a pair of cutoffs. "Good job," Michael commented, barely recognizing Max with his new look. "The sweat stains are a nice touch."

"Those are authentic," Max said dryly, glancing up at the sun. He put on his own shades and stepped out from between the parked SUVs, into the full heat of afternoon. "C'mon, we haven't got all day."

Actually, we have until midnight, Michael recalled, but didn't bother to correct Max. He wanted to get this over with, too, and return to Maria and the others. *Wonder how they're doing back at the caverns?* He hoped Maria was doing a better job of calming down Liz than he was doing with Max. *Which one of us got the tougher assignment, I wonder.*

Crossing the busy highway was not easy. They had to

hike about a half mile up the road, breathing in lungfuls of gritty dust and exhaust, before finding a lighted crosswalk. Heat waves rippled over the hot asphalt, giving their time-consuming trek a feverish, hallucinatory quality. More than once, Max had been tempted to make a dash for it, but Michael successfully convinced him that turning themselves both into road pizza was not going to do Liz any good—or put Joe Morton safely behind bars.

Once across the highway, they had to backtrack the same half mile to reach Motel 6 at last. The whole time, Max had worried that Morton would pull up stakes and move on before they got back to the blue Chevy, which they ultimately found parked right outside room #19, facing the highway. Treading softly upon the cement walkway running past the wing of cheap motel rooms, Max placed his ear up against the door of #19. A few feet away, standing guard in case anyone came along, Michael thought he could hear voices coming from the other side of the door. "Is it him?" he whispered to Max.

Max held up a finger to silence Michael and listened some more at the door, his face screwed up in concentration. "I think so," he said finally, stepping back from the door. "But there's somebody else in there with him. Another man."

Michael scowled, not liking what he was hearing. Another stranger, besides Morton and the lieutenant? This whole thing was getting too damn complicated. How many people were in this stupid conspiracy anyway, assuming that there was, in fact, some kind of criminal conspiracy going on?

"What now, fearless leader?" he asked Max sarcastically. He certainly hoped Max wasn't seriously thinking about barging into Morton's room right this very minute. They had their special powers to fight with, of course, but Morton and his unknown associate almost certainly had guns, and the willingness to use them. *C'mon, Max,* he urged silently. His mouth was dry and he would have killed, figuratively speaking, for another spicy sip of Tabasco sauce. *Let's not get crazy here.*

Fortunately, Max wasn't that far gone yet, no matter how out of character he had been acting. "I have a plan," he announced after a moment's thought. Indicating that Michael should follow him, he walked to the far end of the outdoor walkway, then stationed himself in front of the ice machine roughly ten yards away from Morton's door. "This should be far enough," he stated cryptically. "Get ready."

"For what?" Michael asked, having no idea what Max had in mind. "What's the big plan?"

"Watch," Max instructed. He closed his eyes and took a deep breath, marshalling his preternatural mental energies. Then he opened his eyes and extended his arm, pointing his index finger at the dusty blue hood of Morton's convertible, several yards away.

Abruptly, the Chevy came alive, as though struck by lightning. Its horn honked and its car alarm blared. The windshield wipers whipped back and forth across the curved glass, while the sprinklers squirted cleaning solution over and over. Even the car's engine surged to life, roaring beneath the hood of the Chevy like a prehistoric monster. "Hey, pretty cool, man!" Michael enthused, impressed despite himself. *I've got to remember that trick,* he thought.

No surprise, the earsplitting automotive commotion drew Joe Morton from his room in a hurry. The door slammed open and he came charging out, a Smith & Wesson semi-automatic pistol clutched in his hand. Gulping, Michael wondered if Max had figured on the gun when devising this ingenious plan. Morton ran to his car and hastily shut off the alarm, wipers, sprinklers, etc., all the while looking for the parties responsible for the disturbance. His bloodthirsty eyes fixed on Max and Michael, over by the ice machine, and Michael could practically see him calculating the distance between the Chevy and the two teenagers. "Hey, you kids!" he hollered, sounding perplexed as well as irate. "Did you see anybody messing with my car?"

"No, sir," Michael shouted back quickly, not trusting Max to respond without giving away his true feelings. Fortunately, he'd had a lot of practice at playing dumb. "We just got here."

Morton must have ruled them out as suspects, since, without even thanking Michael for his eyewitness report, he paid no more attention to the pair of disguised teens. "What the hell—?" he muttered irascibly, giving his front tires a savage kick just for the hell of it. He removed his orange cap, revealing a sizable bald spot atop his cranium, and scratched his head in confusion. "I don't get it. How the devil—?"

"What is it?" a new voice asked nervously from the threshold of Morton's motel room. "What's the matter?"

A second individual emerged from #19: a nerdy-looking Asian guy, at least a foot shorter than Morton and a lot less menacing in appearance, wearing a pair of black-rimmed glasses and a *Buffy the Vampire Slayer* T-shirt. He furtively looked up and down the row of motel rooms, as if fearful of being seen in Morton's company. The new guy had "guilty" written all over his skinny fan-boy face, prompting

Michael to wonder again what sort of crooked deal was in the works. *A thug, a lieutenant, and a geek,* he thought, mentally running down their ever-growing list of suspects. *Talk about your strange bedfellows.*

Max reacted even more strongly to their first glimpse of the newcomer. "What?" he murmured under his breath, too low for Morton or his roommate to hear. "I know that guy. I've seen him before."

Huh? Michael thought. He was positive that the little Asian dude had not been the second man at the Crashdown on the day Liz was shot, so where else could Max know him from? The UFO Museum in Roswell, maybe? That was the only thing Michael could think of right away. "What do you mean, man?" he whispered fervently. "How do you know him?"

It took Max a couple seconds to place the guy. "Las Cruces University," he said eventually. Surprise and puzzlement temporarily drove the simmering animosity from his face. "I saw him at the university that one time, when I snuck into the particle physics lab to sabotage that experiment. He was one of the lab technicians performing those tests on Agent Pierce's bones!"

"What?" Michael asked, stunned by this latest revelation. He could hardly forget the incident in question; *if not for Max,* he recalled pointedly, *I'd probably be serving time for Pierce's murder right now.* He watched numbly as the alleged science guy frantically convinced Morton to put his handgun away and step back inside the motel room. The painted turquoise door slammed shut, leaving Max and Michael alone outside the motel, with far too many questions to keep them company. "Are you sure?" Michael asked in disbelief. *This can't be right. It doesn't make any sense!*

"Positive," Max insisted. His intense gaze remained fixed on the door to #19. Michael didn't hear a trace of doubt in his voice. "He was there, with Congresswoman Whitaker and the others."

That Whitaker had ultimately turned out to be a Skin did not make Michael any happier. *Okay,* he thought, *now I'm really feeling paranoid.* It was one thing when he thought Morton was just another lowlife hood, and the shooting in Crashdown nothing more than a routine drug deal gone wrong, but now the surly gunman appeared mixed-up with something far more complicated and unnerving, something that conceivably tied in with the life-or-death dangers and deceptions that had become part of their daily existences, ever since Max first stopped Liz Parker from bleeding to death on the diner floor. *What was Joe Morton doing in Roswell that day?* he fretted anxiously. *And what is he plotting now?*

"All right, you win," he told Max sourly. "We need to find out more about this guy. A lot more."

7

"Post-traumatic stress disorder," Alex diagnosed. "That's what you're experiencing, Liz. I'm sure of it."

And here I thought I was just going crazy, Liz thought ruefully, sitting in a booth next to Maria, across from Alex and Isabel. The oppressive heat had finally driven them indoors, not long after Max's sister had rejoined them on the surface, to the family-style restaurant attached to the Visitors Center. Liz picked unenthusiastically at a cooling plate of cheese-coated nachos while ignoring the milkshake and tamales her friends had treated her to. At the next booth over, a temperamental infant threw a tantrum, banging a metal spoon against the tray of its highchair while shrieking its lungs out simultaneously. Liz flinched involuntarily every time the spoon noisily struck the tray. The baby's high-pitched screams scraped away at her already raw and hypersensitive nerves. "Post-traumatic?" she repeated, not entirely sure what Alex was getting at.

"Exactly," he said with utter confidence. "I should have realized it earlier." He dipped a nacho into a gooey pool of melted cheese. "I wrote a term paper on the subject for psychology last semester, and you're practically a textbook case, Liz. Well, except for the glowing handprint, that is."

Hard to overlook that, Liz thought. Even though the luminous sigil was once again concealed beneath her T-shirt, she was half-convinced she could feel the silver handprint shimmering upon her belly. Her skin tingled where the handprint marked her, exactly where Max had healed her two years ago. He'd left an identical brand upon her on that unforgettable occasion, but the splayed silver fingers had eventually faded after a day or two. Why had the handprint returned after all this time? Max had not needed to heal her down in the murky caverns. He hadn't even touched her stomach.

"Explain," Maria prompted Alex. Tiny vials of therapeutic scents were arrayed like toy soldiers next to her plate. Beneath the molded Formica tabletop, she placed a sympathetic hand on Liz's knee. "Isn't post-traumatic whatchamacallit something Vietnam vets suffer from?"

Alex nodded in agreement. "Soldiers, disaster victims, and anyone who goes through some kind of severe trauma and doesn't get the right kind of psychological counseling afterward. Liz's symptoms fit the profile perfectly: flashbacks, nervousness, heightened sensitivity to sudden noises and surprises, inability to concentrate or make decisions." From the look on his face, he must have suddenly realized what a discouraging litany he had just recited, and he hastened to add, "It's nothing personal, Liz. Nothing you need to be ashamed of. It's a perfectly normal psychological response to getting shot."

"But that was almost two years ago," Maria objected.

Carefully selecting one of her vials, she inhaled deeply of its supposedly calming aroma. "Why would she be having this reaction now?"

Alex stood by his original diagnosis. "Like I said, it's textbook. Sometimes the symptoms of post-traumatic stress disorder can pop up years after the traumatic incident. My guess is that seeing Morton again stirred up Liz's repressed memories of the shooting itself." He scratched his bushy black hair, and Liz remembered that his vocational testing exams, administered by the late Agent Topolsky, had actually deemed best-suited to a career in psychiatry. "Actually, when you think about it, Liz was a prime candidate for P.T.S.D. because she never really had a chance to emotionally deal with, or seek counseling for, the experience of being shot, since she had to pretend, for Max's sake, that it never happened." He gave Liz a playful smile. "Heck, kiddo, I'm amazed you haven't cracked up on us before now."

"Well, I've been kind of busy, you know." Liz had to admit there might be something to what Alex was saying; she sure felt like all those old memories from the shooting had snuck up and walloped her from behind. "Saving the world and all."

"No one's saying you haven't been through a lot," Isabel assured her. The aloof young alien princess had already filled them in on what she'd managed to glean from her conversation with Lieutenant Ramirez, even if, for the sake of Alex's feelings, she'd been a bit vague about the nature of that discussion. "We all have."

"Okay, okay," Maria said, still not entirely satisfied with Alex's explanation, "I'll give you that Liz almost certainly has issues regarding her shooting, but what about that freaky silver handprint?" She squeezed Liz's knee to express her concern for Liz's emotional and physical well-being. "How do you explain that, Dr. Freud?"

Alex grimaced and munched on a nacho to buy an extra moment or two. "Well, yeah, that's the tricky part," he admitted eventually. The three women stared at him expectantly, waiting for a more informative response. He sighed and threw up his hands. "Fine. Here's a crazy idea, and I realize I'm going out on a limb here: What if the handprint is simply a psychosomatic manifestation of her post-traumatic stress disorder?"

"Huh?" Maria laughed. "You're joking? That's the best you can do?"

Sitting next to Alex, Isabel looked skeptical as well, although she refrained from contradicting her constant admirer directly. Liz appreciated her restraint. After all, Alex was just trying to help.

"No, no, think about it!" he insisted, caught up in his theories. "Isabel, didn't Nasedo tell Michael that all your alien powers are actually *human* powers, that you're really just tapping into parts of the human brain that the rest of us haven't figured out how to use yet?"

Isabel nodded soberly. "That's right," she said, regarding him with uncertain eyes. "So?"

Alex's face lit up as his latest theory came together in his mind. "Don't you see? There's no reason why Liz's unconscious mind couldn't mimic what Max did to her way back when, especially if her cells retained some sort of genetic memory of the original handprint." He gulped down a mouthful of Mountain Dew, fueling his cascading imagination with yet more caffeine. "Or maybe all of Liz's mind-melds with Max have stimulated Liz's own brain enough to fake the shiny handprint on her own."

"Like with *stigmata*?" Liz suggested, the budding scientist in her intrigued despite the topic's unsettling personal implications. "All those people who spontaneously develop wounds and marks on their bodies?"

"The same sort of thing, I'll bet," Alex theorized. "The unconscious mind is capable of all kinds of weird stuff, and Lord knows you've given it plenty of bizarre material to work with lately." He chewed thoughtfully on a soggy nacho. "Yeah, the more I think about it, the more plausible this sounds. I'm pretty sure, Liz, that it's your own brain creating that handprint." He turned to Isabel for confirmation of his genius. "Not a bad job of figuring things out, eh?"

Much to his obvious disappointment, however, Isabel still looked dubious. "That could work, I suppose," she said in a less than ringing validation of Alex's hypothesis.

"Says the woman who can listen to CDs without a CD player," Alex pointed out indignantly, "or go traipsing through other people's dreams. After all the wacko garbage we've been through, from skin-shedding alien bodysnatchers to time travel, is one little stress-induced handprint too much to accept?"

Even through her own agitated emotions, Liz thought she heard an extra touch of irritation in Alex's voice, more than Isabel's admittedly lukewarm endorsement of his theory really warranted. *He's probably a little ticked-off and jealous,* she speculated, *because he knows, just like we all do,*

*exactly how Isabel wormed all that information out of the lieu-
tenant.* You didn't have to be Mata Hari to imagine how that
scene went down; Isabel could vamp members of the opposite sex like nobody's business.

Liz felt sorry for Alex's bruised feelings, but she was too
freaked-out herself to do much more than try to bring the
discussion back to where they started. "But even if you're
right, Alex, if I'm really suffering from this post-traumatic
stress disorder, what am I supposed to do about it? I feel
like I'm having a nervous breakdown." One booth and a
highchair away, the unhappy baby yowled again, causing
Liz to grip the edge of the table with white knuckles. The
spoon banged against the tray, and she had to clench her
teeth to keep from jumping out of her skin. "How," she
asked, after the torturous moment passed, "am I supposed
to get over this?"

"I don't know," Alex confessed quietly, his concern for
Liz taking priority over his problems with Isabel. "Ideally,
according to the psych textbooks I read, you ought to get
special counseling from an expert trained in treating
P.T.S.D., but I guess that's not really an option in this case,
unless you want to spill the beans about you-know-what
to some shrink." He nervously cast a sideways glance at
Isabel, acutely aware that she wasn't going to like that
idea.

"No," she said immediately, rejecting that notion once
and for all. She had already placed Max's secret in danger
too many times; no matter how messed-up she was, she
wasn't going to let her problems jeopardize anyone else's
safety again. "Talking to a psychiatrist is out."

Alex nodded. "I figured as much. In that case, all I can

recommend, based on what I've read, is that you shouldn't try to repress the traumatic memories again, because you've got to acknowledge the stress before you can work through it." His angular face was full of sympathy and regret. "Somehow or another, you need to confront your repressed fears and anxieties regarding the shooting, and come to terms with them." He shrugged glumly. "Easier said than done, I know."

Tell me about it, Liz thought bitterly. *I can't even confront a backfiring car—or a crying baby—without falling to pieces.*

"You know we're here for you," Maria reminded her gently. She slid one of her tiny translucent vials across the table toward Liz. "We all are."

"I know," Liz said gratefully, offering a weak smile in return. She dutifully sniffed from the miniature vial, more to please Maria than in any serious expectation of deriving comfort or peace of mind from the bottled scent. Despite the pungent odor, she couldn't help worrying about Max, however, and wondering what had become of him and Michael. They had been gone for a couple of hours now, without checking in. Liz knew that part of her would never be able to relax until she knew that Max was okay. What if Morton had surprised them somehow? What if he was pointing his gun at Max right this very moment?

Crash! The irate baby pounded upon his tray like it was a cymbal, the constant *rat-a-tat-tat* causing Liz to flinch visibly with every beat. The infant's high-pitched squeals climbed into the upper decibels, drowning out the restaurant's overhead Muzak system and pushing Liz close to the breaking point. How was she supposed to think, let alone confront her fears, with that hellish caterwauling going on? She pressed her hands against her ears, desperately trying to hide from the noise. She squeezed her eyes shut, only to see Joe Morton rise up from her tormented imagination, waving his handgun wildly in the middle of the Crashdown. In her mind, the baby's shrill cries merged with Maria's screams of terror as the pistol went off, *rat-a-tat-tat*, unleashing a hail of bullets that turned a row of stacked water glasses into a rain of broken shards before striking Liz right below her ribs, again and again and again. "Stop it," she whimpered hoarsely, tears leaking from the corners of her eyes. "I can't stand it anymore!" It was unclear, even to her, if she was talking about the baby or the flashbacks. "Please, make it stop."

"Hang on," Isabel said decisively. Without another word, she deftly slipped out of the booth and strolled casually toward the salad bar, passing the screaming baby's highchair on the way. Only those who knew her well, and were privy to her special talents, would have noticed the way her slender fingers brushed the back of the highchair as she sauntered by.

A second later, the baby slammed the rounded bowl of his spoon against the tray again. Instead of producing a sharp knock, however, this time the impact yielded only a soft, gooey splat. Confused and startled, the puzzled infant stopped crying long enough to examine his former noisemaker, an intrigued expression upon its chubby little face. Experimentally, it stuck the spoon in its mouth, and immediately started gurgling happily, almost as if the stainless steel utensil had miraculously changed into some kind of chewy chocolate treat. By then, of course, Isabel was already on her way back from the salad bar with a couple of fresh breadsticks.

"Thank you," Liz said sincerely, drying her eyes on a napkin. It was a small mercy, but one she appreciated immensely. *If only all our problems could be solved so easily,* she thought, *and with so little danger.*

Where were Max and Michael?

8

"Over three hundred thousand bats currently reside in the bat cave below," the park ranger announced. "Mexican free-tailed bats, to be exact. At the moment, they're sleeping upside down inside the cavern, about a half-mile past the main entrance, but soon all three hundred thousand will come spiraling out of the cave in search of dinner: mostly moths, mosquitoes, and other flying insects. Trust me, it's a pretty impressive sight when all those bats come flapping out of the cave all at once!"

Dozens of tourists packed the outdoor amphitheater, waiting for one of Carlsbad Caverns's biggest attractions: the nightly Bat Flight. Constructed of solid stone and concrete, the amphitheater looked down onto the natural entrance of the main cavern, a dark oval gap at the bottom of a rocky cliff. To the west, the sun was already sinking toward the horizon, so the expectant throng knew that the bats would be making their promised appearance soon. Restless children, bored by the ranger's educational lecture, climbed up and down the wide stone steps of the amphitheater, squirmed impatiently between their parents, or attempted to frighten their younger siblings with black rubber bats purchased earlier at a souvenir shop. Near the back of the open-air theater, some joker played the theme music from *Batman* on his portable boombox.

"Why are we here again?" Max asked, as impatient as any of the unruly toddlers. Along with Liz and the others, he sat on one of the tiered stone benches overlooking the cave entrance. Only Michael was missing; according to Max, he had volunteered to stay behind at the Days Inn to keep watch over Morton's motel room, freeing Max to return to the park to find the rest of his friends and relatives. Liz had originally been startled by Max's newly-blond appearance, but he'd quickly restored his hair to its usual raven-black hue once he realized that the disguise bothered her. Her own tresses, however, remained brilliant red, for safety's sake, as well as for her own peace of mind.

"Because the Visitors Center is closed, and this is what people do at the Caverns at sunset," Maria said testily; Liz guessed that she wasn't happy about Michael being left behind to baby-sit an armed criminal of uncertain intentions. "You're the one who's always telling us to blend in and not attract attention." She was two seats down from Max, with Liz nestled between them. It was still warm out, but the summer heat was cooling to more bearable levels. "Besides, the bats are cool."

"I guess," Max sighed, peeking at his watch. Liz knew he was counting the hours and minutes before he could go spy on Morton's midnight rendezvous with the lieutenant. *How far is Slaughter Canyon from here,* she wondered, *and do I really want Max out tailing Morton through the desert?*

They had already spent several minutes comparing notes after Max got back from his earlier surveillance mission. He had told them about the science guy inexplicably sharing a room with Morton, while Isabel had filled her brother in on what she had learned from Lieutenant Ramirez. Liz wasn't sure what any of this meant, and doubted that any of the others did. All this mystery was the last thing she needed right now, rattled as she still was by her resurrected psychological baggage from the shooting, but she had to admit that the entire situation was looking increasingly suspicious and alarming. A particle physicist with Morton? Conspiring with an air force pilot from White Sands? What could this possibly be about—except maybe more alien-inspired intrigue left over from the Crash?

She shivered, hugging herself and wishing that she could just curl up into a fetal ball somewhere far from Roswell, New Mexico and its secrets. This was supposed to be a vacation from all that, she recalled with bitter irony, but so far it wasn't working out that way.

"How are you doing, Liz?" Max asked softly, searching her face with those soulful dark eyes. She guessed that someone, maybe Alex or Isabel, had also brought Max up to speed on her precarious emotional state. "I know you've been having a rough time." She detected a trace of guilt in his voice. "I'm sorry I haven't been around more."

"That's all right," she consoled him. In a crisis, she had learned from painful experience, there often wasn't time for togetherness. "You were doing what you had to do—for my sake." She turned toward him, looking up at the troubled face she knew so well. "Morton's my problem, not yours."

"I just wish I could do more," he said passionately. "The idea that he's still out there, up to no good, after hurting you!" His expression hardened and he clenched his fists, as if newly enraged by the very thought of Morton. A baseball-size chunk of concrete, resting by his foot, abruptly exploded in a shower of dust and gravel. Embarrassed and flustered, he guiltily peeked at the strangers around them; fortunately, no one besides his friends appeared to have noticed the brick's unnatural disintegration. "It just makes me crazy," he offered by way of explanation. "You can't imagine."

Out of the corner of her eye, Liz saw Maria observing Max warily, eyeing him as she would a ticking time bomb. Isabel and Alex were discreetly monitoring Max as well. Liz felt her friends' shared discomfort, even as she appreciated their reluctance to intrude on her private moment with Max.

"I know," she said to him. Watching him simmer in anger and frustration, she wondered who had been most disturbed by Morton's return, she or Max? Once again, she was tormented by the possibility that Max might get hurt trying to avenge her shooting. *I'd never forgive myself*, she thought, *if something happened to him because of me.* "You don't have to do this, Max," she urged him. Her moist brown eyes pleaded with his for an end to this disastrous expedition. "We could just turn around and go home, pretend we never saw him."

He shook his head. "It's too late for that, Liz. Things have gone too far. We need to know what Morton is doing with that scientist and the air force guy, for all of our sakes." A rueful smile lifted the corners of his lips. "Anyway, Michael and I have already rented a couple of rooms at the Days Inn for us."

The better to keep Joe Morton under twenty-four hour watch, Liz realized. The idea of staying that close to where the murderous gunman was hiding out made her sick to her stomach. *I'd rather camp out in the bat cave, with three hundred thousand–plus flying mammals.* She knew that Max was probably right; Morton needed watching. She wished she could do more to help Max get to the bottom of the mystery, but, in her present state, she was no good to anyone. *When will I feel like myself again?* she asked hopelessly. *How long can constant terror last?*

Down at the foot of the amphitheater, the loquacious ranger wrapped up his lecture, glancing toward the setting sun and checking his wristwatch. "It should be any time now, folks," he announced, although predicting exactly the bats' big moment was something less than an exact science. "Please remember, no flash photography."

An eager hush fell over the gathered tourists, quieting all but the most obstreperous youngsters. Danny Elfman's pounding *Batman* score echoed beneath the dimming desert sky as several dozen eyes turned toward the cavernous opening at the base of the cliff. "Have you ever seen this before?" Liz asked Max, trying to enjoy the moment as best she could.

"Once," he admitted, "when we were just kids." A gentler smile temporarily lightened his brooding demeanor. "Isabel was terrified the bats would get caught in her hair."

"Too bad Michael's missing this," Maria sighed. "Guys like bats and snakes and things, right?"

Before either Max or Liz could respond to her query, a loud rustling sound came from the mouth of the cavern, like the fluttery susurrus of millions of shuffling papers. The audience held its breath en masse, leaning forward on their stone benches to get a better look, when suddenly a swirling cloud of black leathery wings burst from the cave, ascending toward the sky like, well, a bat out of hell. Wave after wave of hungry bats, several thousand at a time, poured out of the cavern, spiraling upward like some sort of vampiric tornado before dispersing into the night. Their high-pitched cries bounced off the rocky foundations of the outdoor theater, competing with the shrieks of excited spectators and the thunderous flapping of countless nocturnal predators. "Holy Bat-Surplus!" Alex exclaimed, leaping to his feet while, beside him, Isabel scrunched down as far as she could, protectively placing her hands over her hair. "This is just like Hitchcock's *The Birds*—but with fewer feathers!"

Liz's own reaction caught them all by surprise. Even though she knew what to expect, having witnessed the twilight exodus numerous times as a child, the sudden roar of the bat explosion, the turbulent storm of furry black bodies blotting out the sky, overloaded her senses and sent her heart and soul winging back to the Crashdown and the day she was shot. *Help me!* she thought frantically, her hysterical screams lost in the tumult. Darkness, black as death, closed in on her. Pain flared below her ribs. *Max! Where are you, Max? I'm dying!*

The blackness was still enveloping her as her friends took hold of her and hastily hustled her away from the bat show.

9

A coyote howled mournfully in the night as Max and Michael crouched behind some outcropping rocks atop a ridge overlooking the hillside entrance to the gruesomely-named Slaughter Canyon Cave. They had arrived at the canyon well before midnight, so that they could take up a concealed position before either Morton or Lieutenant Ramirez showed up to conduct their mysterious business. Although the cave itself had closed at sunset, all-night camping was permitted on the park's thirty-something miles of back-country trails, allowing the two teenagers to reach this location without having to sneak past any guards or barriers, like they often had to do on covert missions like this. *So far, so good,* Max thought.

He hated having to leave Liz's side again, especially after her total meltdown at the Bat Flight, but there was no way around it; he couldn't trust this job to anyone else, not even Michael. *If anyone's going to uncover Morton's dirty dealings, it's going to be me,* he vowed silently. *I owe it to Liz—and myself.*

Fortunately, Liz had calmed down some after they'd gotten her away from the burgeoning bats and crowds. In theory, she was resting now in a room at the Days Inn, where Maria, Alex, and Isabel could take care of her. It had torn his heart out to see Liz so scared and miserable, which only increased his resolve to take care of Joe Morton, one way or another. With luck, Liz would feel better, and more like her old self again, once she knew that the loathsome gunman could no longer threaten her.

A cold fury possessed him, spreading from his gut out to his fingertips, which tingled with pent-up psychic energy. He clenched his fist, feeling the red-hot power building within him, waiting to burst free. The alien energies at his command were fully capable of killing a man, Max knew, but was he? He tried to imagine what it would be like, setting Morton's heart on fire with the power of his mind, melting the man's rib cage until it resembled one of the shapeless calcite formations found in the caverns below. The image both horrified and intrigued him.

Could I actually kill Morton in cold blood? he asked himself, uncertain of the answer. A vivid mental picture, of Liz dying on the floor of the Crashdown, blood seeping from her wounded belly, her beautiful brown eyes dimming, sprang into his mind, as real as life. He had never felt so scared, so desperate. *Maria screaming in the background. Michael trying to hold him back. Liz's smooth, soft skin growing cold and still... "No, please, no! You can't die, Liz. You can't!"*

Max shook his head violently, trying to dislodge the awful memories from his thoughts. He shuddered, his body responding irrationally to events that had taken place nearly two years ago. The remote canyon, lit by a thin crescent moon, could not have been more different than the

Crashdown with its kitschy decor, yet he suddenly felt as though part of him, the most important part, was still kneeling on the diner floor, next to Liz's bleeding body. How could anyone do this to her, to Liz of all people? One very special person like Liz, so beautiful, so bright, and so caring, was worth more than a hundred worthless scumbags like Joe Morton. How dare he come so close to extinguishing Liz's life forever? Max's alien blood boiled in his veins and he knew that, at that moment at least, he was more than capable of obliterating Joe Morton for good.

"You okay, *kemo sabe?*" Michael asked. Like his friend, the alien youth squatted in the dirt behind the craggy ridge, and had discarded his blond disguise in favor of his usual mop of messy brown hair. High-powered binoculars, purchased at one of the shops in Whites City, rested on his lap, next to a medium-size bottle of Tabasco sauce.

"I'm fine," Max asserted. "I just want to get this over with, and get back to Liz." He peeked at the Indiglo display on his watch; it was already 11:35 P.M. "Not much longer," he promised Michael.

"So why do you think this place is called Slaughter Canyon anyway?" Michael asked casually. He took a sip of the bright red Tabasco sauce. "Are we talking some sort of ghastly Indian massacre here or what?"

"I have no idea," Max stated, grimacing slightly. His legs were growing numb from holding the same position, so he shifted his weight slightly. "And I don't particularly care." He glanced over at his friend to see how he was holding up.

What he saw sent a chill through his blood. "Michael!" he whispered urgently. "Don't move!" Max froze as well, taking care not to make any sudden movements. "Whatever you do, don't move."

There in the moonlight, coiled in the shadow of a flowering cactus plant, its burnished copper scales glittering, a full-grown rattlesnake lifted its serpentine head, only inches away from Michael's ankle. Diamond-shaped markings along its coils advertised its deadly nature and species, while a forked tongue flicked between its predatory jaws.

At first, Michael looked mystified by Max's whispered warning. "What?" he mouthed silently, taking pains to obey Max's instructions even though he didn't yet comprehend the why of them. Then the rattler shook its tail like a maraca, filling the still night air with a dry, staccato warning. Understanding—and fear—dawned in Michael's eyes. "Oh crap," he whispered.

Would rattlesnake venom affect Michael's alien biology? Max didn't want to find out. Holding his breath, he watched the snake with vigilant eyes, hoping that the poisonous reptile would slither away harmlessly. *Just go about your business, snake,* he pleaded silently, regretting that, unlike some movie aliens, talking to animals was not among his inhuman abilities. *Don't mind us. We won't give you any trouble.*

If the diamondback could read his mind, which was highly unlikely, then it definitely wasn't listening to him. The dry rattle increased in volume and tempo as the serpent appeared to grow more and more agitated by the humanoid intruders trespassing on its domain. The snake hissed again, more vehemently, and Max caught a glimpse of curved yellow fangs, dripping with venom. Its coils rustled atop the dirt and gravel, and the rattler's head reared up, poised to strike at Michael's ankle.

"No," Max declared, unleashing the destructive energy he had been saving for Morton. His outstretched fingers glowed with an unearthly radiance and a bolt of incandescent heat and fury flashed between Max and the attacking serpent. The hiss of burning meat replaced the diamondback's own sibilant vocalizations, and the angry rattling ceased abruptly.

Startled by the strobelike flash, Michael yelped and scrambled away from the zapped rattler on his hands and knees, not looking back until he had put many yards between himself and his former location. "Whew!" he exclaimed, forcefully expelling all the air from his lungs. His chest rose and fell irregularly as he looked back in surprise at what was left of the snake.

Thin white tendrils of smoke rose from a blackened lump of charred bones and skin. The volcanic heat of Max's psychic blast had even scorched the earth around the smoking snake skeleton, leaving a crust of gray-black ash atop the soil. Climbing onto his feet, Michael nudged the cremated remains with the toe of his sneaker. Nothing rattled, since the fiery mental thunderbolt had fused the rattler's natural noisemaker into a single, inert mass of smoldering cartilage. Michael pushed the barbecued snake parts farther aside, revealing a patch of once-gritty sand that had been transformed by the extreme heat into a thin sheet of cracked and discolored glass, like the epicenter of a miniature atomic explosion. The glazed sand reflected silvery fragments of the moonlit sky overhead.

"Yo, Max," Michael said, shaking his head in disbelief, "you have really got to work on your control." Rescuing his bottle of Tabasco sauce from the ground where it had fallen, he took a deep gulp from the bottle, then wiped his mouth with the back of his hand. "Not that I'm not grateful for the timely save, mind you, but, if you don't watch out, you really are going to kill somebody one day."

Max contemplated the smoking debris with a sense of grim satisfaction. It occurred to him, belatedly, that he hadn't needed to incinerate the rattler, that he could have just projected a force field instead, but he had few regrets at the way the scene had played out. *One snake down,* he thought. *One more to go.*

"Boy, what is it about us and creatures that like to shed their skin?" Michael asked rhetorically, continuing to inspect leftover pieces of rattlesnake. Wired by his near brush with terminal snakebite, he stretched his limbs and gazed past Max's brooding form, out over the canyon. His eyes widened suddenly, and he dropped to the ground, throwing up a cloud of dust and sand. Max started to sneeze, but Michael hastily placed a finger beneath his friend's nose, then raised another finger over his own lips, signaling him to silence. "Sssh!" he hushed Max, tilting his head toward the canyon below. "Look."

Crouching lower, onto his hands and knees, Max cautiously lifted his head until he could just peer over the tops of the jutting rocks. He sucked air through his clenched teeth as he spotted what Michael had seen only seconds before.

While they'd both been distracted, understandably, by the overly territorial rattler, Joe Morton had come trudging up the steep desert trail to the entrance of Slaughter Canyon Cave. Brandishing a flashlight in one hand, a pistol in the other, and carrying a canvas backpack upon his beefy shoulders, Morton was breathing heavily by the time he reached the top of the trail, just outside the shadowy gap in the hillside. Posted signs warned hikers not to explore the hazardous cavern except in the company of an experienced guide, but the burly gunman did not look like he was planning any unauthorized spelunking; arriving at the end of the trail, he slipped the backpack off his shoulders, planted his hefty butt on a conveniently flat-topped boulder, and settled down to wait for Lieutenant Ramirez. The night was quiet enough that Max could hear him muttering grumpily about the steepness of the climb, the lieutenant's lack of punctuality, and the general crappiness of life in general. He spit a mouthful of chewing tobacco at the base of a sign listing general park regulations. "Lousy, stinkin' nature," he groused. "Who needs all this nothing anyway? Ought to build a casino here or something."

Squatting behind the craggy ridge, Michael stared at Morton in disgust. "A real class act, this guy," he whispered softly to Max, his voice filled with contempt. "Reminds me of my absent-and-unlamented foster dad, Hank."

Given that Michael's former legal guardian, now happily missing for many months, had been an abusive, bad-tempered drunk, Max knew just what Michael meant. He could readily imagine an irate Hank shooting up the Crashdown the way Morton had, the way Morton had nearly taken Liz away from him forever. *Blood soaking through her goofy, adorable space-waitress uniform, her brown eyes glazing over, staring blankly into the void...*

The very sight of Morton brought Max's simmering rage to a frothing boil once more, throwing him back mentally to all the anger and fear of that terrible day at the diner. Adrenaline flooded his system and every muscle in his body felt primed to explode into action. Veins throbbed at his temples, the rapid, arrhythmic pulse making him slightly queasy. He felt an overpowering compulsion to smash Morton's piglike face in, to wipe him off the face of the Earth and any other planet he could think of. Without thinking, he started to rise up from behind the ridge, his clenched fist emitting an eerie silver glow.

"Max! What are you doing?" Michael frantically grabbed onto Max's arm, tugging him back down behind the rough concealment of the rocky ridge. "Have you lost your mind?"

Michael's blurted words hit Max like a splash of cold water. What *was* he doing? Morton hadn't even met up with the lieutenant yet, let alone revealed the secret of his nefarious scheming, yet he had almost given away his and Michael's position in a moment of unthinking hatred. Max blinked in confusion, staring in shock and disbelief at his own glowing fingers. Resting his back against the stone outcropping, he struggled to regain command of his temper and higher faculties. He panted raggedly, hyperventilating, and Michael worriedly clasped a hand over Max's mouth, forcing him to breath through his nose. Max felt light-headed, out of control, and, for the first time since Liz spotted Morton in the caverns, he wondered if Michael had been right all along, if there really was something wrong with him.

Gradually, though sheer willpower, Max forced himself to come to his senses. His breathing slowed, and the pounding in his veins and temples diminished to a dull throb. He held his hand up before his eyes and watched as the silver glow slowly dimmed until it disappeared entirely. Michael sighed in relief as the eldritch light faded, and he looked quizzically into Max's eyes. Reassured by the restored sanity he found there, he withdrew the hand covering Max's mouth. "Sorry about that, pal," he apologized, "but you looked like you were losing it."

"I was," Max confessed. "Thanks."

Michael smirked and shrugged his shoulders. "No problem, you crazy kid. I dimly recall you've done the same for me."

"Many, many times," Max reminded his impetuous podbrother. Michael had been a loose cannon for as long as he could remember.

"Hey, who's counting?" Michael said with a grin. Confident that Max wasn't going to go berserk in the next few minutes, he raised his head to check on events over by the cave entrance. "Heads up," he alerted Max in a low voice. "Looks like it's show time."

Although anxious to see what was happening in the canyon, Max took a couple of deep breaths first. His temporary mania appalled and disturbed him, and he didn't want to risk losing control again at the sight of Morton. *Keep cool*, he counseled himself, trying to remain focused on tonight's primary objective. *This is a fact-finding mission, not a rumble or assassination attempt. I need to stay cool, keep quiet, and find out what Morton's up to.* He could always stage a showdown with Morton later, after they all had a better idea of what was at stake.

Stealthily turning around behind the ridge, he crouched down and peered over the piled rocks. His eyes widened as he saw that Morton was no longer alone; another man was coming up the trail to Slaughter Canyon Cave, carrying a black attaché case in one hand. Although the newcomer was clad in strictly civilian garb, a leather flight jacket and jeans, Max guessed from Alex's and Isabel's descriptions that this was the mysterious Lieutenant Ramirez. *Guess that lab guy from the Las Cruces isn't showing up for this meeting,* he inferred, still wondering how a particle physicist fit into this byzantine puzzle.

Morton did not waste time with pleasantries or small talk. "Is that it?" he demanded, spotlighting the lieutenant with the beam of his flashlight. He clumsily lurched his heavy body off the boulder he had been using as a seat, then pointed at Ramirez's briefcase with the muzzle of his pistol. The braying sound of his voice sent a fresh eruption of white-hot wrath through Max's body, but he bit down hard on his lip and merely kept watching. "Have you got it?" Morton challenged Ramirez.

Max wished he knew what "it" was. *To hell with pronouns,* he thought furiously, *tell us what's in the stupid briefcase!* Snatching the binoculars off the ground, where they had fallen during the altercation with the rattlesnake, he pressed the viewpieces against his eyes and tried to get a closer look at both Ramirez and his coveted case.

It took him a few seconds to get either of the clandestine pair in the binoculars' sights, during which time his eyes were treated to highly magnified views of cacti, yucca, and gravel, until, all of a sudden, he abruptly found himself staring into Morton's scowling, ill-shaven face and blood-shot eyes. The gunman's hated and hateful visage gave Max a momentary start, but then, using Morton as a guidepost, he managed to shift the view to the other participant in this midnight conference.

Ramirez looked just as clean-cut and well-groomed as he'd been described. He also looked extremely unhappy and distraught. Sweat beaded on his bronzed forehead, and a stray muscle twitched spasmodically beneath his cheek. Max could practically hear the man's teeth grinding together convulsively as the lieutenant climbed the last few yards to the cave's entrance. *I'd be worried, too,* Max thought, *if I had to deal with Morton, especially in a lonely canyon late at night.* No wonder Ramirez looked so troubled.

"Well," Morton repeated, shining his flashlight directly in the lieutenant's face. He glared at the other man irritably. "Have you got the merchandise?"

"Yes, damnit," Ramirez said, squinting through the glare of the harsh white beam. He held up his hand to shield his eyes. "I've got it all right, although I wish to heaven I didn't."

Sounds like the lieutenant is having second thoughts, Max guessed. He lowered the binoculars so as to examine Ramirez's attaché case more closely. Unfortunately, the matte-black finish of the case provided absolutely no clue as to its contents.

"Quit whining," Morton barked at the lieutenant, "unless your superiors at White Sands find out what you've been up to." He sneered sadistically, clearly enjoying his hold over the officer, and spat another mouthful of tobacco juice onto the trail. "You'd be looking at court-martial for sure, I figure, so don't go having any last-minute changes of heart now. You're in way too deep, flyboy."

Sure, Max thought restlessly, *but too deep into* what? Temporarily taking off the binoculars, he exchanged a frustrated look with Michael, who looked equally in the dark. All they could tell for sure was that Morton was somehow blackmailing the lieutenant.

"Fine, okay!" Ramirez conceded. He ran an agitated hand through his bristling military crew cut and looked away from Morton's blinding spotlight. "Just turn off that damn light!"

Having established who had the upper hand, Morton clicked off his flashlight. The crescent moon shining overhead provided sufficient illumination to complete their shadowy transaction. He placed the inactive flashlight on the flat-topped boulder and nodded toward the black leather case in the lieutenant's grip. "Hand it over," he ordered. "The key, too."

His cheek muscle twitching like a Mexican jumping bean, Ramirez surrendered both the briefcase and a small metal key to Morton, who plopped the case down on top of the boulder and unlocked the latch. Max peered intently through the binoculars, fiddling compulsively with the focus in his determination to get a glimpse of what was lurking inside the case. To his frustration, however, Morton's expansive back blocked his view completely. He looked over at Michael, offering him the binoculars just in case Michael had a better view, but the other teenager shook his head glumly. *Damn!* Max thought. If only he and Michael had set up shop on the opposite side of the canyon!

"You see," Ramirez said bitterly. His arms hung at his sides, his fingers uselessly clutching at the empty air, as though wishing that the precious briefcase was still in his possession. He swallowed hard, forced to digest the sour taste of treason. "Where's my money?" he demanded.

Satisfied with what he saw, Morton slammed down the lid of the attaché case and locked it shut, then stowed the key in the front pocket of his plaid flannel shirt. "Oh, that's right, your money," he said snidely. His Smith & Wesson remained pointed at the lieutenant. "You're not so proud and guilt-stricken, I see, that you don't want to get paid for delivering the goods and committing a major breach of national security."

Ramirez's cheek jumped as though an alien was about to burst from his skin. "Just give me the cash, Morton, and get out of here." His eyes hungrily focused on the canvas backpack resting on the ground near Morton's feet. "I never want to lay eyes on your ugly face again."

But Morton was in no hurry to finish their business. "About that money, Lieutenant," he taunted Ramirez maliciously. "You only get half now, and the other half after I have this merchandise"—he patted the top of the closed briefcase—"authenticated by an expert."

A-ha! Max thought, finally guessing how one piece of the puzzle fit into the whole. *That must be what the science guy back at the motel is for, to verify that the "merchandise," whatever it is, is the real deal.* Now all he needed to do was figure out what kind of classified contraband needed an expert physicist to give it a seal of approval. *So much for the idea that this was just some sort of mundane drug deal…*

"What?" Ramirez shouted resentfully. He took an angry step toward Morton, who brandished his semi-automatic menacingly. The infuriated lieutenant backed off, physically, but seemed no less outraged and upset. "That's wasn't the deal, and you know it!"

"Sorry," Morton said with a blatant lack of sincerity. His cocky attitude implied that he found the pilot's predicament amusing. "There's no chance you're getting the rest of the money, not until I'm one hundred percent certain that you're not pulling a fast one on me." His expression darkened, and menace crept into his voice, as he considered the mere prospect of deceit. "And you'd better hope, for your sake, that you've handed over the genuine article. Nobody cheats Joe Morton, at least not more than once."

Ramirez shook with barely-contained fury. He pointed fiercely at the case he had so unhappily relinquished to Morton. "But you saw it yourself, right there in that briefcase! That's no fake! It's just what I promised!" His voice sounded hoarse, and increasingly desperate. "You can't do this to me! I came through with my side of the deal, I want my money—now!"

"Tough luck, flyboy," Morton said, not at all bothered by the lieutenant's indignant protests. Keeping the muzzle of his gun aimed squarely at Ramirez's chest, he took hold of one of the backpack's straps and carelessly lobbed the pack at the profoundly unhappy test pilot. The bundle landed with a thud at Ramirez's feet. "Sure, what's in the case looks kosher to me, but what do I know? I'm no rocket scientist, just a guy who has what it takes to make a buck or two." He reached over and picked up the briefcase by its handle. "Once my handpicked PhD signs off on the merchandise, *then* you'll get the rest of the cash, not before."

His anguished face slick with sweat, Ramirez snatched the backpack from the rocky trail and fumbled with its flaps, in a panicky rush to check its contents. Finally getting the pack open, he balanced the canvas parcel on his knee as he groped inside the pack with his free hand. "It's not fair," he muttered sullenly. "I did my part!"

Using the binoculars, Max zeroed in on the open backpack just in time to see Ramirez's trembling hands pull out a wad of hundred dollar bills bound together with rubber bands. He riffled the stack of green paper bills with his thumb, making sure there was cash all the way through, then tossed it back in the bag and pulled out another wad. He eyed the bundled hundreds lustfully, like an addict hungry for a fix, or a Skin in need of a fresh husk. "It has to be here," he croaked hoarsely. "All of it..."

"Don't fool yourself, Ramirez," Morton scolded the other man smugly. "You can count it yourself, if you like, but I'm telling you, there's exactly half of your payment in that pack." He spat tobacco juice in the perturbed lieutenant's direction. "The rest of the cash isn't even here tonight. I've got it stowed away miles from here, where you can't possibly get at it."

The Motel 6, I'm guessing, Max thought. *Across the street from where Liz and the others are staying.* Ironically, he knew more of Morton's recent movements than Ramirez did, but *not* what all this wheeling and dealing was about. *We've got to find out what's in that briefcase,* he realized, *but how?*

"Damn you, Morton," Ramirez cursed his back-stabbing partner. Finally realizing that he had lost this battle, he gave up counting the loot and crossly threw the first few bundles of bills back into the pack. "Can't you at least tell me who you're working for, then?" he pleaded pathetically. "I don't know about you, Morton, but I'd sleep better nights knowing that I haven't turned that so-called merchandise over to any terrorists or enemy nations, that this is just industrial espionage, and not anything that really damages America's security?" A sob caught in his throat; he sounded like a man trapped in his own private hell. "If I can't have all the money now, at least give me something for my conscience!"

Morton shrugged. "Not my problem, Ramirez. I don't

give a flying saucer how you sleep, and the people I work with pay me good money to keep their names out of it."

Like whom? Max fretted. Without even knowing what Ramirez was so reluctantly selling, he couldn't help worrying about whom Morton was representing in this illicit and unsavory business. China? Libya? Iraq? The Skins?

His paranoid suspicions weren't all that was bothering him, however. After crouching in the same position for several minutes, his legs were killing him. He felt his arching limbs going numb as his static vigil cramped their circulation. Handing the binoculars to Michael, he tried to quietly shift his weight, but shooting pains made him gasp involuntarily at his first modest attempt at movement. *Ouch, that hurts!* he thought. *Too bad there's no top secret alien trick to waking up your legs after they've fallen asleep.* Wincing, he braced himself against the stone outcropping and laboriously attempted to lift first one leg, then another, despite the excruciating sensations that resulted as the blood started rushing into his inert lower limbs.

And then it happened: The dusty rock upon which he had placed the bulk of his weight came loose without warning. Max tumbled forward, losing his balance, while the dislodged boulder rolled down the side of the ridge, precipitating a mini-avalanche of falling rocks and rubble that noisily descended on the canyon below while throwing up a cloud of dust and sand.

Oh, crap! Max thought, throwing himself flat against the ground, then rolling quickly until he was safely behind one of the surviving boulders, only inches from where Michael looked on, aghast. Holding on tightly to the binoculars, Michael gulped and ducked beneath the ledge he had been peering over. "Oh, man, we're in trouble now," he predicted.

The cacophonous rockfall interrupted the tense, unequal confrontation between Morton and Ramirez. "What?" Morton shouted fiercely. "Who's that? Who's up there?"

Looking about nervously, Ramirez hastily slung the cash-filled backpack over his shoulders. "Maybe it's just some animal," he said hopefully, sounding like he was ready to bolt at any moment.

Morton, on the other hand, sounded more offended than anxious. "Show yourself, damnit! I'll teach you to spy on me, you sneaky bastards!"

Facedown against the gravel, holding his breath, Max found himself wishing desperately that he possessed Tess's gift for warping human perceptions. If only he could project a realistic illusion of a coyote, or maybe a couple of mule deer, into the minds of the two men below!

Alas, he had yet to master that trick.

"Oh God," Ramirez moaned, facing imminent exposure and ruin. "We've gotta get out of here!"

But Morton wasn't listening to him. "Show yourself!" he demanded again. Max heard the heavy man climbing toward the ridge, his feet slipping and sliding in the loose rubble. "Give yourself up, or I'll blow you to pieces!"

Wordlessly, Max and Michael looked at each other, both hoping that the other knew what to do next. Max was torn; part of him wanted to throw Morton's threats back at him, pitting scathing psychic energy against hot lead, but the lifelong imperative to conceal his powers helped him resist that reckless impulse. *But what else can I do?* he agonized. *Keep low and hope Morton doesn't find us?*

Michael had another, crazier idea. Throwing back his head, he cupped his hands around his mouth, and let out a feeble imitation of a coyote's howl. Max stared at his friend in disbelief, but Michael merely shrugged in return, his defiant expression plainly asking if Max had any better ideas.

The intent, clearly, was to trick Morton into thinking there was nobody up on the ridge except maybe a harmless coyote or two. It might have worked, too, if Michael had been able to pull it off convincingly; unfortunately, to Max's ears, Michael's heartfelt howl had sounded just like what it was: a desperate teenager trying unsuccessfully to mimic the real thing. *Nice try,* Max thought, *but, geez, Michael, Wile E. Coyote sounds more believable than that!*

Morton wasn't fooled for a second. "Yeah, right!" he laughed nastily; apparently all Michael had succeeded in doing was insult the hot-tempered gunman's intelligence. "Take this, smart guy!"

Gunshots rocked the night, and bullets slammed into the stony crags, chipping off bits of stone and dusting the two teenagers' heads with pulverized rock. Instinctively, Max threw up a force field between them and the disintegrating outcropping; a concave bowl of shimmering green energy blocked the bullets while casting an uncanny emerald radiance upon the hillside.

Max heard Morton's heavy tread stomping up the ridge toward them. More gunshots sounded, provoking semi-hysterical cries of protests from Ramirez. "Are you crazy?" the jittery, guilt-stricken lieutenant shouted. "Put away that gun! Someone will hear!"

Max could have told Ramirez, from personal experience, just how trigger-happy Morton could be once he lost his temper. If the hotheaded crook could draw his pistol in the middle of a crowded diner in broad daylight, what was going to stop him from opening fire alone in the wilderness well after midnight? *He's not going to give up,* Max realized. His brow was furrowed in concentration as he tried to think while simultaneously maintaining the force field. *We have to get away. We can't let him see us.*

"Get ready," he warned Michael tersely. He placed his palms against the side of the ridge and closed his eyes. This was going to take careful timing.

"Get ready?" Michael echoed in confusion. The lambent glow of the force field cast greenish shadows upon his face, making him look more, well, alien than usual. "Ready for what?"

"This!" Flexing his mental muscles, Max converted his defensive shield into a battering ram of psionic force that smashed into what was left of the outcropping, sending another avalanche of rocks tumbling toward Morton, who fired wildly, the unblocked bullets ricocheting off the hillside behind, one of the stray shots ripping apart a cactus only a few feet away from Max, who grabbed onto Michael's arm and leaped to his feet. Pins and needles stung his stiff legs, but Max ignored the pain in his eagerness to escape from Morton's murderous gunfire. Another ricochet shattered the Tabasco bottle, staining the soil red and filling Max's nostrils with its hot, spicy smell. "Run, coyote-boy, run!" he shouted to Michael. "Follow me!"

Running uphill would have slowed them down too much, not to mention presented Morton with a pair of easy targets, so instead Max took a chance, clearing the ridge and taking off down the hill, passing by Morton, who had thankfully been knocked off his feet by the rockfall Max had just triggered. Half skidding, half sliding, Max reached the floor of the canyon in seconds, with Michael right behind him. To his relief, Ramirez was nowhere to be seen; Max guessed that the gun-shy test pilot had decided to make tracks before any cops or park rangers showed up, drawn by the sound of gunfire. *Not a bad idea,* Max decided.

He sprinted down the trail, away from Slaughter Canyon Cave. Mercifully, the crescent moon provided enough illumination to see by, so he didn't need to risk generating any additional light on his own. He kept his gaze glued to the rough trail ahead, watching out for obstructions and pitfalls, even if that meant that he couldn't look back to see if Morton had regained his footing yet. Michael's racing footsteps smacked against the uneven ground behind him, letting Max know that the other teen was keeping up with him.

Suddenly, gunshots erupted from the top of the trail. "Come back here, you sons of bitches!" Morton hollered, having obviously recovered from the landslide. "Come back here!" he yelled irrationally, like anyone was really going to turn around and run back toward the crazed lunatic shooting at them. "Who the hell are you stupid kids? Where did you come from? How much did you see?"

Not enough, Max thought gloomily, putting on another burst of speed in hopes of evading Morton's blistering fusillade. This entire midnight excursion had turned into a disaster, and they hadn't even learned what was in that blasted attaché case. Bullets pelted the steep mountain trail, throwing up agitated plumes of sand and dirt. *What's the range of one of those pistols anyway?* Max worried. The ferocious cascade of bullets nipped at his and Michael's heels, and he realized that he never had learned why this particular corner of the park was known as Slaughter Canyon. He hoped and prayed that the name would not prove prophetic.

I'm sorry, Liz! More than anything else, he feared leaving her alone in a world that still held the threat of Joe Morton. *I tried to protect you! I should have killed him when I had the chance!*

10

It was Maria's turn to use the phone.

"Yeah, Mom. I know it's late. I just wanted to let you know that we ended up spending the night here at Carlsbad, so we can do some more hiking in the park tomorrow. Yes, Mom, we rented *two* rooms at the motel, one for the chicks and one for the guys. Uh-huh, Liz and Alex and the others are all staying over. Yes, Michael, too… That's right, Mom, you've seen right through me, I confess: We're eloping, all six of us, over the Mexican border for a group wedding in Tijuana. I'll be sure to send you a Polaroid." Maria sighed and rolled her eyes heavenward, inviting sympathy from the rest of the teenagers in the cramped motel room. "Don't worry, I'll be fine. Yeah, we're having a good time…."

That's stretching the truth a bit, Isabel Evans thought. She sat at the foot of one of the room's twin queen-size beds, pressing one of her favorite CDs against her ear. Paula Cole's "I Don't Want to Wait," from the *Dawson's Creek* soundtrack album, failed to drown out entirely Maria's one-sided discussion with her mother, nor did it ease Isabel's growing concern for Michael and her brother, who had been away for far too long now.

She looked at the cheap plastic alarm clock sitting on the end table between the two beds. It was almost 1:25 in the morning. The rest of them had already contacted their respective parents hours ago, notifying them of their overnight stay at the Days Inn, but apparently Maria's mom had been working late, or out on a date, or something. Fortunately, none of their parental units had raised too much of a fuss over the kids' plans, knowing that you really couldn't do all the Caverns in one day.

If only that were the worst of our problems, Isabel thought morosely. Not for the first time, she wished she could have a normal life, with normal teenage dilemmas, instead of the fraught existence she seemed doomed to live. Mentally increasing the volume of the music playing in her ear, she surveyed the scene around her, taking stock of their latest sorry situation.

Although they had indeed rented two rooms, for propriety's sake, everyone was crowded into the girls' room for the moment, waiting in unbearable suspense for Max and Michael to get back from Slaughter Canyon. Maria sat at the head of the same bed as Isabel, dutifully placating her mom, while Liz rested in the next bed over, her back against the headboard, her knees tented beneath the frayed cotton sheets. Aside from a brief call to her folks, which she had somehow managed to garner enough composure to fake her way through, the shell-shocked brunette had barely said five words all evening, still locked in what Alex had labeled post-traumatic stress disorder. Unable to sleep, Liz just sat up in bed, her arms locked around her knees in a quasi-fetal position, while her haunted brown eyes watched the front door, counting the seconds until Max's return. Her face was ashen, and dark purple shadows collected beneath her eyes, making her look positively gaunt and spectral, like the crazy wife in some old Brontë novel.

She needs a makeover, big time, Isabel thought, but she knew that Liz's troubles ran much deeper than that. A pang of sympathy pierced Isabel's heart. If truth be told, Liz Parker was not always her favorite person; through, admittedly, no fault of her own, the loose-lipped, lovestruck human girl had severely complicated Isabel's life by discovering the Big Secret, and broken her brother's heart on more than one occasion. Even still, it was impossible to look at Liz now, so frail and washed-out, and not feel sorry for her. Besides, Isabel kept looking at the front door, too; if nothing else, she and Liz were united by their common love for Max.

"I don't believe this," Alex griped close by. He squatted cross-legged at the end of Liz's bed, channel-surfing with the aid of a remote he had found on the end table. "Eighty-plus channels, and nothing decent to watch. Just infomercials and movies that were bad the first ten times you watched them." He leaned toward the unimpressive twelve-inch screen provided by the motel, his thumb relentlessly working the remote. "Have you ever noticed how *Earth Girls Are Easy* always seems to be playing on cable somewhere?"

"Speaking on behalf of Earth girls everywhere," Maria quipped, finally putting down the phone, "I object to that characterization, no matter what Michael might have told any of you." She yawned and looked at her watch. "Ohmigosh, they're not back yet?" The blond teenager joined Liz and Isabel in the Door-Watchers Club, her glib repartee failing to conceal that she was just as scared and worried as the rest of them. "What could they possibly be doing all night in a place called Slaughter Canyon? On second thought, don't answer that."

Catching the somber vibe in the room, Alex felt obliged to do something. "Hang on," he said, putting aside the remote and hopping off the bed. "Let me take another look outside."

"Be careful, Alex," Isabel urged him once more, putting down her CD. Alex had no special powers to protect him if that Joe Morton character, or even Lieutenant Ramirez, somehow managed to trace Liz to this motel room. *I'm giving Max and Michael until 2 A.M.*, she resolved, *then I'm going after them in the Jetta.* The only reason she let Alex act as lookout here at the motel was because the danger seemed minimal, and she knew that Alex needed something to do. As is, his ardent need to be of use to her and other women was, to be honest, already getting on her nerves.

"Never fear," he told her, stepping out of the room. A gust of warm air penetrated the air-conditioned motel room. "I'll be back right away."

In fact, he was gone less than ten minutes before the door swung open again and he lunged back into the room. She could tell by the look on his boyish face that he had something to tell them. She took a deep breath, bracing herself for the worst. "What is it?" she asked in a whisper.

Alex hesitated, unsure where to begin. "Well, the good news is that Morton's blue Chevy is back at the Motel 6, parked outside his room." He tapped one foot repeatedly against the floor, full of nervous energy. "The bad news is, I don't see any sign of the Jeep."

What does this mean? Isabel wondered. Making a deliberate effort to curb her fears, she forced herself to think through the implications of Alex's discovery. "Max and Michael wouldn't leave the park until Morton did," she speculated, "so maybe they're just hanging back now, putting a little time and distance between them and Morton."

"You really think so?" Liz asked plaintively, desperate for reassurance. Her journal rested on the bed next to her, next to a ballpoint pen. Isabel hoped that writing down her turbulent thoughts had helped Liz get some perspective on the traumatic memories and feelings eating away at her. Judging from her hollow eyes and pitiful tone, however, her private scribblings had provided Liz with little relief so far.

"Sure, that sounds right," Maria chimed in promptly. She uncapped a tiny brown vial and treated Liz to a therapeutic sniff of cyprus oil. "I'm positive they'll be back any minute."

Unless something terrible has happened to them, Isabel thought silently. Worst-case scenarios rose unbeckoned from her wayward imagination. *For all we know, Max and Michael might already be buried in the desert somewhere; with all these caverns and uninhabited wilderness around here, it could be years before anyone found their bodies. . . .*

"No," Isabel said softly, not allowing herself to succumb to such nightmarish imaginings. Max sometimes accused her of being too pessimistic, of always seeing the Tabasco bottle as half-empty, but she refused to give up hope just yet. "Come on, Max, Michael. Where are you?"

Over fifteen excruciating minutes later, there was still no sign of their missing friends. "That's it," Isabel declared, rising from the bed and extending an open hand toward Maria. "Give me the keys to the Jetta, I'm going to look for them."

"I'm going with you," Alex insisted, a little too hastily. He sprang to his feet and hustled to Isabel's side. His determined eyes and stubborn expression virtually dared her to leave him behind.

This isn't about us, Alex, she thought, with a flash of irritation. *It's about locating Max and Michael.*

On the other hand, she really didn't want to do this alone. "Okay," she said, recognizing that, deep down inside, she could use the company. "Thanks." Taking the car keys from Maria, she paused by the door long enough to look back at the other two women. "Will you be okay on your own?"

"Sure," Maria pledged. Moving over to the other bed, she draped her arm over Liz like a mother hen, then stared up at Isabel with anxious green eyes. "Find them, okay?"

I'll do my best, Isabel thought, uncomfortable with the thought that everyone was depending on her. Before she and Alex could embark on their possibly hopeless mission, however, a sudden knock at the door electrified everyone in the room.

Could it be? "Oh, thank goodness!" Isabel exclaimed, rushing to the door and placing her eye against the security peephole. To her vast relief, the minuscule spyglass presented a fish-eye view of both Max and Michael, apparently alive and well. Expelling a grateful sigh, she quickly undid the chain and let the returnees stagger in, sweaty and disheveled but each, thankfully, still in one piece.

"Where have you been?" she asked eventually, after heartfelt hugs and greetings all around. She paced back and forth between the TV and the beds, too keyed up and adrenalized to sit down, like she was still strapped into some sort of emotional roller coaster. "We were so worried!"

While Michael helped himself to a glass of cold water from the bathroom sink, Max told them all about what had taken place in Slaughter Canyon. Twigs and tiny flecks of gravel clung to his jeans and T-shirt, which also bore large, reddish-brown dirt stains. Isabel lovingly passed her hand in front of her brother, miraculously cleansing him of the most obvious evidence of his adventure even as he continued his exhausted account of his and Michael's close call.

"...after we finally got out of range of Morton's pistol, we left the trail and ended up hiding in the scrub overlooking the canyon. Then, unfortunately, we had to keep out of sight until Morton gave up hunting for us and drove out of the park. Just to play it safe, we decided to hide a little while longer before hiking back to the parking lot ourselves." Max sat down on the edge of Liz's bed and gratefully accepted a glass of water from Maria. "We also took the long way back here, off the main highway, just in case Morton was waiting in ambush somewhere between the park and Carlsbad." He cast a concerned look at Liz, no doubt seeing the emotional strain written on her face. "Sorry to keep you in suspense so long."

"I'll say," Maria blurted, speaking for the rest of the Door-Watching Club. "They also serve, who only sit around in cheap motel rooms, you know." Michael emerged from the bathroom and she patted the bed beside her, welcoming him back. "Although it beats dodging bullets, I guess."

"Oh my God, Max," Liz moaned, the death-defying details of the two boys' perilous expedition sinking in. "You could have been killed."

"But we weren't," Max stressed. He took Liz's hand to comfort her, but his own eyes remained darkly intent and troubled. "And the worst part is, we still don't know what Morton and the lieutenant were doing there tonight, besides arguing about the price of whatever was in that briefcase."

He lifted his gaze toward his sister. "That's where you come in, Iz. I have a really big favor to ask."

Isabel gulped, knowing already what Max wanted from her. *I have a bad feeling about this,* she thought.

11

A one-hour photo shop in Whites City had already processed the pictures Alex had shot while trailing Joe Morton through the caverns. Isabel stared at a slightly blurry snapshot of Morton and made a face; even from several yards away, it was clear that Liz's shooter was no Ricky Martin. *Ordinarily, I wouldn't even want to get near him,* she decided, wrinkling her nose at the overweight hoodlum's slovenly appearance, *let alone go inside his head.*

Unfortunately, that was exactly what she had to do.

"I really appreciate this, Isabel," Max said. For privacy's sake, they'd moved over to the guys' motel room, next door to the one where Liz, Maria, and Michael were waiting. Only Max and Alex had accompanied her here, to watch over her while she attempted to slip into Morton's dreams, which were almost certainly bound to be sleazy and disgusting. *I can hardly wait,* she thought sarcastically.

"You know I'd do this myself if I could," Max continued, sitting across from her on the next bed over, "but, of all of us, you've always been the best at dreamwalking." This was not meant as manipulative flattery, merely a statement of fact. "You're the only one who can find out what's in that briefcase, and whether he recognized Liz from the Crashdown this morning."

"Lucky me," she intoned bleakly. Despite her misgivings, which she felt were perfectly reasonable, she knew that Max was right; not knowing how much Morton knew about them, and the Crash, was arguably worse than whatever she might find poking around in the gunman's subconscious. And, boy oh boy, did she ever have plenty of experience when it came to waltzing through other people's sleeping minds. "Practice makes perfect, I guess."

She took another look at the 3×5 color photo of Morton pacing in front of a large, gnarled stalagmite. His ill-shaven jowls and sagging beer belly repulsed her; the last thing she wanted to do was make an intimate connection to the man in the photo. "What if he's not asleep right now?" she stalled. "You know how hard it is to get into someone's mind when they're still awake. Especially someone I've never even met."

Standing over by the window, Alex drew back the closed curtains and peered through binoculars at the motel across the street. "No lights on in #19," he reported. "In fact, no signs of any activity at all."

"It's almost two-thirty in the morning," Max reminded her gently, aware of her trepidations. He reached across the narrow gap between the beds to take her hand, while staring at her with that stoic, responsible expression she knew so well. "He's probably asleep, Iz."

So much for that excuse, she sighed inwardly. "Okay then, let's get this over with." Taking a deep breath, she placed her fingertips against Morton's picture, feeling tentatively for a link to his identity. At first, she didn't feel anything, and was extremely tempted to give up right there and then, but she closed her eyes and pressed further, her own genetically-engineered mind prowling like some sort of telepathic search engine through the tangled web of psychic vibrations hanging over Carlsbad and vicinity like so much mental smog. Still clutching Morton's unflattering photo between her manicured fingers, she laid back on the neatly-made bed, resting her head on the soft foam pillow. Alex thoughtfully dimmed the lights as she reached out with her mind, searching for the unique cerebral landscape that belonged exclusively to Joe Morton.

Was it Yoda or Obi-Wan Kenobi who said that the Force connected all living things, binding them together? Either way, Isabel knew that *Star Wars* had it wrong. It wasn't the Force that connected us; it was dreams. Dreams were the secret tapestry that linked her mind to everyone else's, even Joe Morton's.

She kept his image, as depicted in the photo, locked in front of her, while her subconscious compared it against the blur of dream-images and impressions that raced through her mind at the speed of thought. After only a second or two, a match was made and, bracing herself for what was to come, she followed the thread back to the slumbering mind where Morton's loathsome persona also dwelled. *Oh joy*, she thought caustically. *The things I do for my friends…*

To her surprise, she found herself standing in the middle of the Crashdown Cafe, back in Roswell. *Boy*, she thought, looking around at the tacky UFO art upon the walls, and at the cozy booths and counters where she had spent so many leisure hours, *this place must have really made an impression on Morton, if he's still dreaming about it two years later.* A chill gripped her heart as another, more compelling explanation occurred to her; maybe Morton was dreaming of the Crashdown because he had spotted Liz at the caverns earlier, and was worrying about his crime catching up with him. *That's not good,* she realized. Max might be right about Morton coming after Liz again, and maybe the rest of them as well.

She looked around for more clues to Morton's state of mind. Daylight shone through the large glass window at the front of the restaurant, facing Main Street, indicating that, in Morton's dream at least, it was broad daylight. Isabel spotted Maria waiting tables a few yards away, once again wearing the same short, faux Meg Ryan hairdo she had been experimenting with when she and Isabel had first gotten involved in each other's lives. *She looks better now,* Isabel concluded absently, *now that she's let it grow out some.*

Scanning further, her alert gaze fell upon Max and Michael, holding a whispered conversation in a booth near the front window. Drained bottles of Tabasco sauce littered the tabletop between them, and Michael's hair still had that moussed-up, spiky look that Maria had eventually convinced him to give up. Isabel wondered what Morton's unconscious mind thought they were talking about, feeling deeply disturbed that this violent stranger had remembered her friends with such uncanny detail. She suddenly felt very glad that she had not personally been present the last time Joe Morton had actually visited the Crashdown.

Loud, heated voices caught her attention, and she turned to see Morton himself arguing with another man at a nearby booth. Morton wore a plaid shirt and a blue cap, and his brutal features were flushed with anger, as were those of his companion, a large, bearded man wearing a black leather vest over a heavy metal T-shirt. Whereas Morton looked like a trucker, the other man struck Isabel as more of a biker type. His booming voice, impossibly loud, reverberated throughout the formerly peaceful diner as he shouted furiously at Morton. "I WANT MY MONEY NOW!" he thundered. An angry sweep of his brawny arm knocked both men's plates and glasses onto the floor, where they shattered noisily. "GIVE IT TO ME OR ELSE!"

Rising volcanically to his feet, the biker grabbed Morton by the collar and dragged him forcibly out of the booth. A gun, metallic and menacing, somehow appeared in Morton's free hand, the sight of the weapon hitting Isabel with the impact of a physical blow. "No!" she gasped, knowing what was about to happen but unable to halt the relentless chain of events. She looked around frantically for Liz, desperate to warn her, but could not spot the small brunette waitress anywhere. She racked her memory furiously, trying to remember where Max had said Liz was when she was shot. Over by the counter, wasn't it, in front of the kitchen?

Isabel struggled to orient herself, locating the counter immediately to her left. She glanced back over her shoulder at the swinging kitchen doors, realizing with growing horror that she herself was standing exactly where Liz should have been. *I don't understand,* she thought, paralyzed and panicky. *What's happening?*

The nightmarish scene played out in slow-motion, with Isabel unable to react any faster than the dream-figures around her, her mind and body seemingly mired in molasses. "GIIVVE MEEE MYYYY MONNNEEEY!" the biker bellowed, grappling with Morton for control of the gleaming blue-metallic pistol, which went off abruptly. Maria let out an endless scream as the muzzle of the pistol flared. *Liz, watch out!* Isabel thought, only seconds before an overwhelming impact struck her below the ribs. She fell backward onto the floor, searing pain setting her nerve endings on fire, and stared at the ceiling in shock and confusion, watching as gauzy black shadows crept over her vision until, just as the shadows threatened to eclipse the world entirely, her brother's face appeared above hers, staring down at her with anguished eyes. "Look at me, Liz," he pleaded hoarsely. "You have to look at me, Liz!"

Liz? Doesn't he mean Iz?

Isabel suddenly realized her mistake. This wasn't *Morton's* dream at all, it was *Liz's!* Max's traumatized girlfriend must have finally drifted off to sleep next door, and was now reliving the whole ghastly experience in her dreams. Searching for Morton's dream-image, Isabel had inadvertently stumbled into Liz Parker's own recurring nightmare. *Poor Liz!* she thought in a moment of heartbreaking empathy and insight. *Now wonder she's such a wreck right now!*

Making a deliberate mental effort, she disengaged her own consciousness from Liz's troubled awareness, stepping out of Liz's crumpled dream-self like a phantom and rising up from the blood-stained floor of the illusory Crashdown. For a few heartbeats, she stood there, looking down at Liz's bleeding form and at her brother crouching there beside the wounded girl. *So this is how it all began,* she reflected somberly. Funny, how certain events can change your life completely, even if you weren't even there in the first place....

Isabel peeked at her own stomach, making certain she had left the bullet wound behind, and considered what to do next. She wasn't done yet, she knew, turning to watch Liz's memory of Joe Morton, along with his equally panicked partner, run toward the diner's exit. *Stop,* she commanded mentally, freezing the entire scene in place, Morton included, while she pondered her next move. The fleeing gunman, along with all the other characters populating Liz's personal dreamscape, became as still as mannequins, frozen in position. All except for Isabel, who wandered over to the counter and helped herself to a refreshing sip of Tabasco sauce from the dream's imaginary inventory. The spicy draught tasted just like the genuine article, helping her put her borrowed memories of the shooting behind her.

I have to move on, she realized, placing the fictitious bottle back on the counter. She still had to track down Morton's own dreams and insinuate herself into them. But first, before exiting this unintended detour, she felt compelled to help Liz escape, if only for the moment, from this hellish nightmare.

She didn't want to wake Liz, who certainly needed the sleep, but maybe she could make her dreams a bit more pleasant. Isabel searched her memory again, trying to remember a time when she saw Liz laugh, when they had all been able to enjoy a brief respite from all the cover-ups and conspiracies. It was a depressing measure of just how stressful their lives had become that it took Isabel a moment or two to come up with a single occasion unmarred by danger, heartache, or the threat of exposure. That evening, after closing, when she and Liz and Maria had all danced in the diner to their favorite CDs? No, that had ended with Max, a bloody handprint upon his chest, bursting into the Crashdown to tell them that Nasedo had been murdered. Isabel's own surprise birthday party? No, that had been the night Tess was kidnapped, and Isabel had been forced to battle that Skin congresswoman to the death. "Why do we even bother?" she sighed.

Finally, though, her memory threw up a fleeting interlude that, she thought judiciously, just might do. *And it won't even take too much redecorating,* she noted approvingly:

Several months ago, before Tess arrived to complicate matters, when Max and Liz (and, indeed, Isabel and Alex) had, for once, had nothing better to do than savor each other's company and a blessedly uneventful night out. The four of them had caught the new James Bond movie at the cineplex, then relocated to the Crashdown to debate the abundant virtues and defects of the picture. She and Max had shared a custom-made hot fudge and Tabasco sundae (which, curiously, did not appear anywhere on the Crashdown's official menu), while Alex had consumed a small mountain of french fries while trying to convince them all that, really, Denise Richards was perfectly believable as a nuclear physicist. In retrospect, the whole evening had been perfectly frivolous and inconsequential, which may be why, thinking back on it now, Isabel felt a heartbreaking pang of nostalgia. *We were happy then, if only for an hour or two.*

Wiping her eyes, which had become unaccountably moist, she looked over at the booth they had all occupied that night. She closed her eyes for a second, re-creating the scene in her mind, and when she opened them again, dream-replicas of herself, Max, and Alex were seated around a table laden with sundaes, french fries, and other delectably unhealthy snacks. *Just like I remember,* she thought wistfully, experiencing another pang at the sight of the carefree smile on her own double's face. *I should do that more often,* she reflected, barely recognizing herself.

But this wasn't about her right now. Turning her back upon the reconstituted party at the booth, she helped Liz off the floor, erased her stomach wound with a pass of her hand, then escorted the dazed dreamer over to the booth, where she slid Liz in beside the dream-image of Max. "Here," she instructed the other girl while placing a spoonful of ice cream (sans hot sauce) in her hand. "I think you'll find this memory more appealing."

Liz's battered psyche took refuge in the revised dream with encouraging speed. "But, Alex," she laughed gaily, as her waitress uniform dissolved into something more casual and attractive, "you can't be serious! She couldn't even *pronounce* 'nuclear' correctly. . . ."

Isabel took a step backward to assess her work. The four teenagers chattered enthusiastically to one another, appearing completely oblivious to the fleeing felons who remained frozen in place at the entrance to the diner. All four kids, both human and hybrid, looked just as relaxed and stress-free as she recalled.

That's better, she thought, feeling surprisingly moved by her own generosity. *I'd better not let word of this get out, though, or it could completely ruin my reputation.*

Next door, a worried Maria watched vigilantly over the sleeping form of her troubled best friend. While she was glad that Liz was actually getting some sleep, it broke her heart to see that, even in repose, the traumatized young woman could not escape from the ghastly nightmare lurking in her memory. Liz moaned and whimpered as she slept, grimacing in fear and pain. She tossed and turned beneath the thin cotton sheets, frequently clutching at her stomach as if newly shot. *You don't have to be a creepy, Czechoslovakian dreamwalker,* Maria mused sadly, *to know exactly what Liz is reliving right now.*

Her hand hovered over Liz's shoulder, uncertain whether to wake her friend from her unquiet dreams. Lord knew Liz needed the sleep, but how much rest could she really be getting, suffering through such frightening nightmares? Asleep or not, Liz looked totally miserable, and Maria was on the verge of waking her, when, unexpectedly, Liz stopped making those pathetic little cries in her sleep and actually seemed to relax noticeably. A peaceful expression, accompanied by the tiniest of smiles, came over the sleeping teen's previously haggard face, and her body's restless contortions subsided as she sank mercifully into a deep, seemingly undisturbed slumber.

Thank goodness! Maria offered up a grateful prayer to whatever Higher Powers might be paying attention as she listened to the calm, measured breathing now coming from the bed; this evidence of tranquil hibernation struck her as just what the doctor ordered for her friend. *Pleasant dreams, honey,* she wished Liz from the bottom of her overflowing heart. *You sure deserve them.*

"How's she doing?" Michael asked, emerging from the bathroom. A quick shower had washed the dust and residue of Slaughter Canyon from the handsome alien teen and slicked down his perpetually unmanageable brown hair. Wearing a white terry cloth bathrobe, he toweled his head roughly as he checked on Maria and her dormant charge.

Maria appreciated his concern. "Better," she reported happily, contemplating Liz's serene smile and quiet stillness. "I think she's taking a break from all this, at least for now."

"Good," Michael said tersely, before wandering back toward the bathroom, toothbrush in hand.

Despite everything else going on, Maria couldn't help wondering if Michael was still mad at her for dragging him to the caverns against his will. They'd barely had a chance to talk at all since Michael took off with Max to tail Joe Morton. *Can't say I'd blame him if he was still ticked-off at me,* she thought guiltily, *considering the way this trip is turning out.*

12

Now then, Isabel thought, turning her attention to Joe Morton, whose dream-replica still lingered motionlessly at the Crashdown's exit. A frozen ribbon of gray smoke hovered about the muzzle of his upraised pistol. *Your turn,* she silently informed the gunman.

If dreams were indeed the unconscious corridors connecting the minds of humanity, perhaps she could use Liz's nightmare as a conduit to Morton's own depraved dreamland? If nothing else, it was certainly worth a try.

"Run," she ordered Morton's petrified figure, jolting the fleeing gunman and his accomplice out of stasis. Gun in hand, looking back worriedly at the scene behind him, Morton dashed out of the diner and into the street, only a few paces behind the other man. Isabel followed right behind him.

She chased them down the sunlit sidewalk of Roswell's main drag, past the UFO Museum, the Mexican folk art museum, and the rest of the tourist traps that sustained the town's struggling economy. Strolling sightseers, many of them in town for the upcoming UFO Festival, ducked out of the way in alarm as the armed criminals barreled through assorted clusters of pedestrians, pursued, inexplicably, by a tall blond girl in blue jeans. Behind her, back by the Crashdown, brakes squealed and a police siren blared as Sheriff Valenti arrived too late to apprehend the gun-wielding strangers.

Morton and his bearded accomplice got away in real life, Isabel knew. *But not this time,* she vowed, determined to track Morton all the way back to his own trigger-happy psyche.

Two blocks from the crime scene, Morton and the other man darted into a gloomy-looking side alley which Isabel was almost positive didn't exist in the real town. She hesitated at the entrance of the alley, fearful of the unknown. Shadows, surprisingly dense and impenetrable for such a sunny afternoon, shrouded the alley in darkness, hiding what lay ahead from the clairvoyant alien teenager. She heard Morton's lumbering footsteps retreating down the alley, getting farther and farther away from her, and realized she had no choice. Chewing nervously on her lip, she braced herself mentally and plunged into the murky alley.

It was like stepping into another world. The sun disappeared as the scene shifted abruptly from day to night. The temperature dropped ten degrees or so, making Isabel shiver despite her blue turtleneck sweater. As her eyes adjusted to the dim light, she found herself jogging uneasily through a dirty, squalid alley that stretched between the soot-blackened walls of two anonymous concrete buildings. Obscene graffiti defaced the walls further, while the broken pavement was littered with discarded cigarette butts, beer cans, broken glass, and syringes. Greasy puddles, which Isabel took care to step around, reflected the slivers of harsh white light that escaped from broken windows a few stories above her. The alley stank of spoiled garbage, spilled booze, and urine. Rats scurried between dented metal trash cans and Dumpsters, while, all around her, Isabel heard raucous laughter, racing police sirens, and loud honky-tonk music. *Somehow I don't think we're in Roswell anymore,* she thought nervously, feeling like a modern-day Dorothy who had just landed anywhere but Oz.

She doubted, too, that she was still in Liz's dream, unless Liz Parker, honor student and founder of Roswell High's Future Scientists Club, was leading a double life straight out of a David Lynch movie. *Where am I now,* Isabel wondered uncomfortably, *and do I really want to be here?*

Experiencing a failure of nerve, she paused and looked back the way she'd come. To her dismay, Roswell's safe, sun-drenched Main Street was nowhere to be seen, replaced by yet more of the grimy, disgusting alley, which now, impossibly, seemed to lead back only to more darkness, decay, and Dumpsters. Overturned trash cans, their rotting contents spilling onto the greasy pavement, served as barricades, blocking her escape route. Enormous rats, the size of porcupines, patrolled the scattered refuse, their black eyes glittering malevolently.

There was nowhere else to go but forward, she realized, after Morton. Straining her ears, she thought she still heard his ponderous footsteps ahead of her, farther down the slummy alley, and started after him again. *Guess I have to see this through to the end,* she thought less than enthusiastically, gingerly making her way through the garbage, broken glass, and stagnant, shining puddles of grease.

The alley had the kind of warped, irrational geography that only made sense in dreams. It twisted and turned without warning, leading Isabel through a confused, disorienting maze of broken pavement and dingy shadows. After several unnerving minutes of wandering through the maze, flinching every time a bottle rattled or a rat scurried somewhere nearby, she wasn't sure if she was still looking for Morton or just for a way out of these fetid back streets. She remembered the brief, idyllic moment she had re-created for Liz back at the Crashdown, and wished fervently that she'd had the good sense to stay there. *You owe me, Max,* she thought, scowling.

Then, just when she'd pretty much convinced herself that this entire dreamwalk had been a dreadful mistake, she heard Morton snarling up ahead, not very far away. Holding her breath, she tiptoed up to the next curve in the alley and cautiously peeked around the corner. Trying hard not to touch anything, she gazed in alarm at the frightening drama unfolding before her eyes.

Morton had cornered the other man, who was even larger than the beefy gunman, in what appeared to be a dead end. A flickering red neon light, shining over the back entrance of the building to the right, cast a crimson glow over the tense confrontation, which had the biker backed up against a graffiti-covered brick wall, looking scared to death. The red neon made the sweat on his face glisten like blood. "Hold on, Joe!" he pleaded, his Adam's apple bobbing like the dopey antennae the waitresses wore at the Crashdown. "Don't do anything crazy, man! We're all on the same side, you know?"

Morton loomed in front of the other man, his florid face only inches from his accomplice's, the muzzle of his pistol pressed up beneath the biker's bearded chin. "Shut up!" he barked savagely. "That was all your fault, back at that stupid sci-fi greasepit!" Isabel doubted that Liz or her parents would have appreciated Morton's sneering description of the family-owned diner. "What the hell did you think you were doing, going loco back there?"

"I just wanted my money," the muscular biker stammered. "I needed the cash now, you know. To cover my expenses." He squirmed against the unyielding brick wall. "I did my part, I hooked you up with that air force flyboy, the one with the expensive habits." Isabel guessed that was a reference to Lieutenant Ramirez, whom Morton apparently intended to bribe or blackmail. "All I wanted was the money you promised me, that's all!"

Morton jabbed the bigger man with his gun, forcing his chin up. "You would've got your money when your pilot buddy came through with the goods," he growled. Isabel frowned and dug her nails into her palms, frustrated by the gunman's overly cryptic references to whatever it was he wanted from Ramirez, but Morton was too busy ragging on the petrified biker to flesh out the details. "But not right away. I'm still working on getting that pilot over a barrel. You can't rush this sort of thing. I need to give him more time to dig himself an even deeper hole, get him good and ready to do what he's told—or else."

"Yeah, right! That's smart, Joe. I see what you mean." The big, bearded biker smiled weakly, trying to get Morton to put away his gun. He shrugged his apelike shoulders, in what he obviously hoped was an ingratiating manner. "I just wanted a little cash to tide me over, until you were ready to reel him in, you know?"

"So you almost blow the whole deal by blowing your top back at that space-case diner?" Morton snarled, outraged by the other man's stupidity. "Listen, jerk, you're playing in the major leagues now. My bosses have been trying for years to get their hands on this merchandise, and the last thing I need is some hotheaded punk messing things up, just when I'm about to make the biggest score of my life. You got that, butthead?"

"Hey, I didn't have to come to you with this deal," the bearded man reminded Morton defensively. He threw out his chest, attempting a show of bravado. "There are plenty of other people out there who'd pay good money for the dirt on that lieutenant."

Morton nodded slowly, thinking it over. "You're right about that," he said craftily. "And the only thing I need less than a moronic screwup like you is competition where Ramirez is concerned." He looked the biker over coldly. "You're a security leak, mister, that needs plugging up."

"What—?" Comprehension heightened the panic in his bulging eyes. "No, wait, I—!"

Blam! The pistol flared, and Isabel didn't look away in time as the gunshot blew away the top of the biker's head, splattering the dingy brown bricks with an explosion of blood and brains. Shocked by both the sudden blast and the bloodshed, Isabel thrust her knuckles into her mouth to keep from screaming and alerting Morton to her presence. She stared in numbing horror as the biker's body slid down slowly onto the pavement, leaving behind a gory trail on the crumbling brick wall.

Isabel had seen more death and violence in the past two years than any decent eighteen-year-old alien princess should ever behold—she had even been forced to kill in self-defense—but she still felt her stomach churn queasily, and she had to look away for a minute to keep from throwing up. *Okay,* she concluded, nauseous, *I'm well and truly in Morton's head now, since he's the only one who would know about this murder, unless Liz Parker has a really gruesome imagination.*

With a grunt of satisfaction, Morton stepped back from the grisly remains of his victim and, to Isabel's relief, put his handgun away. "That showed him," he congratulated himself smugly, before kneeling to rummage through the dead man's pockets. "Nobody shakes me down and gets away with it." He removed the biker's wallet, perhaps to make the killing look like a routine robbery, then kept searching until, grunting with satisfaction, he found a folded scrap of paper tucked in his victim's back pocket. *Morton's name and phone number?* Isabel speculated. *Or the lieutenant's?* In any event, the meticulous killer set the scrap on fire with a lighted match, stomped the spent match beneath his boot, then scowled and spit on the ground by the dead man's body. With a callous shrug, he stuffed the other man's wallet into his own back pocket. "So much for that loser," he muttered.

Leaving the biker's corpse bleeding on the pavement, Morton wiped his hands on his jeans and adjusted his cap. Then he swaggered over to the rusty metal door beneath the red neon light. Watching from around the corner, Isabel saw now that the fluorescent crimson letters spelled out the name of a bar: HANGER 18.

She gulped nervously. According to popular UFO lore, and confirmed by Michael after his meeting with that old air force vet several months ago, Hanger 18 at the Roswell

Army Air Field was where the authorities had originally stored the debris from the '47 Crash, including, briefly, before Nasedo rescued them from the inquisitive scalpels of the army scientists, the gestation pods holding the genetically-engineered fetuses of Max, Michael, Tess, and herself. *Why that name?* she worried anxiously. *Why here, in this creepy back alley of Morton's mind?*

Seemingly untroubled by the pseudo-historical implications of the name, Morton knocked arrogantly on the rusty door. Moments later, the door opened just a crack, spilling a jagged shard of bluish light into the alley. Isabel backed away from the light instinctively, but Morton wasn't looking in her direction. Instead he held a short, muttered conversation with someone on the other side of the door, who opened the door farther and let Morton in. Isabel heard loud music and harsh, strident laughter coming from within the building, until the door slammed shut, leaving her alone in the alley with a dead body and way too many rats.

She hesitated, uncertain what to do, where to go, next. More than anything else, she wanted to wake up, which would send her back to the motel room with Max and Alex, far from Morton's vile nightworld, but she also knew that she had not learned nearly enough yet about Morton's plot. What had the blackmailing gunman managed to extort out of Lieutenant Ramirez? She still had no idea.

Talk about a dreamwalk on the wild side! As much as she longed to exit this sordid nightmare, she realized she had to see what lay behind the flickering neon sign reading HANGAR 18.

Giving the grotesque corpse a wide berth, she crept up to the forbidding metal door. The fluorescent lights sputtered and hummed, as though the glowing glass tubes were filled with angry hornets instead of ionized gas. Isabel summoned up all her courage and rapped upon the door, timidly at first, then louder and more forcefully. *Let me in!* she thought feverishly. The sooner she got inside, the sooner she could escape back to the waking world. *Open up!*

She heard bolts being slid back and, moments later, the door opened a few inches. A sinister-looking guy, with greasy black hair and bad skin, leered at Isabel from the other side of a short length of chain that prevented the door from opening all the way. His leathery, mottled complexion hinted at too many years of drugs, booze, or both. Gaunt and emaciated, he wore a rumpled white tuxedo that hung slackly on his withered frame. "Yes?" he asked suspiciously, looking at Isabel as though she hardly belonged here. *Can't argue with that,* she thought.

"Er, can you let me in?" she asked, flashing an ingenuous smile. "I'm supposed to meet someone inside."

"Is that so?" Skeptical eyes looked her over, lingering longer than she liked on her chest and legs. His frayed, dilapidated white suit was nearly worn through at the knees and elbows. "How old are you? You got ID?"

Terrific, she thought acidly. *I'm getting carded in a dream.* In real life, of course, her actual driver's license was sitting in her purse back at the motel, but it took only a moment's concentration to produce a reasonable facsimile in this dreamworld. She already knew what date to cite as her birth year; if truth be told, she had sometimes been known to "adjust" the date on her real driver's license using her powers. This was just a variation on the same trick.

She handed the freshly-generated ID to the man behind the door, who inspected it dubiously before returning the card to her. "That'll do, I suppose," he declared, then scrutinized her again. A nasty grin revealed chipped, yellow teeth. "Now then, what's the password?"

Password? Isabel was stumped momentarily, then realized that the correct answer had to be lurking somewhere in the psychic framework of this dream. Maybe if she just left herself open to the vibrations, the password would seep from Morton's mind into her own? She glanced up at the flickering red glow of the HANGAR 18 sign.

"1947," she guessed, free-associating.

"Try again," the yellow grin taunted her.

"Roswell?"

"You're getting closer," he teased, his smirking tone making her innocent guesses sound dirty.

"Area 51?"

"Closer...."

Isabel racked her brain for more UFO lore. The correct password was on the tip of her tongue, she knew it. What was that other code name for the government's top secret UFO research program, the one mentioned in all those crazy pamphlets and TV specials? *Max would know this,* she thought, frustrated and wishing that she'd spent more time prowling that goofy UFO museum back home. It was something extremely appropriate, something like....

"Dreamland?"

"Bingo," the greasy scarecrow cackled, undoing the chain. "And the little lady wins admission to our humble establishment." The door swung outward and its revolting guardian stepped to one side. "Come on in."

Isabel gulped and inched over the threshold, part of her devoutly wishing that she had never hit on the right password. The dingy vestibule just past the door was dark and musty and smelled of cigarette smoke. She eased past the scuzzy doorman, contorting her body so as to avoid brushing against him. Was everything in Morton's dream smelly and disgusting? Isabel had to wonder how he managed to sleep nights. *Unless this is just how he likes things,* she thought, sickened and repulsed by the notion that anyone, even a cold-blooded killer like Joe Morton, could feel at home in a seedy environment like this.

"Step right up, miss," the doorman directed her, snickering at her obvious discomfort. "Just through the curtain there." Isabel flinched, and her skin crawled, as an overly friendly hand patted her from behind. "Hope you find what you're looking for."

Anxious to get away from the doorman's foul breath and dirty chuckles, Isabel ploughed blindly through a thick velvet curtain into...the bright, garishly-lighted interior of an enormous casino. Isabel blinked in bewilderment, taken back by the shocking, surreal disparity between the dank, musty vestibule and the sprawling, jam-packed, pleasure palace she had just rushed into. Flashing lights and candy-colored strips of neon outlined every angle and surface, while country-western music boomed from above, almost but not quite drowning out the clatter of rolling dice, the whir of spinning roulette wheels, and the constant *ka-ching* of innumerable slot machines. Showgirls wearing nothing but string bikinis, high heels, and tall, feathered headdresses promenaded through the crowd of jubilant high rollers, handing out free cigars and cocktails.

Giant, fifty-foot television screens, mounted high above the gaming area treated the paying customers to titan-size coverage of heavyweight boxing matches and high-stakes horse races. Drunken gamblers whooped it up, cheering every roll of the dice and spin of the roulette wheel. The overheated air smelled of cheap perfume, cigarettes, and spilled champagne.

So this *is Morton's idea of heaven?* Isabel thought, aghast, her eyes and ears adjusting to the sheer sensory overload of the imaginary casino, which seemed three times larger on the inside than it did from outdoors. She couldn't believe that he was willing to blackmail and kill to attain such a tawdry vision of the good life. *I'm not even from this planet,* she thought, *and I have better taste.*

Given the colossal scale of the casino, she briefly despaired of ever finding Morton again. Looking down the long red carpet in front of her, however, she realized that she needn't have worried; Morton was, naturally enough, the undisputed center of attention, the strutting star of his own vulgar Vegas spectacle, presiding over a mob of breathless admirers and hangers-on at the biggest and snazziest of the roulette tables. He was even dressed for the part, having traded in the workaday clothes he'd worn on the day of the shooting for glitzier, more ostentatious attire. An ivory-colored, ten-gallon hat perched on his head, above a fringed buckskin jacket that hung open to accommodate Morton's protruding gut. An enormous silver belt buckle, the size of a showy brass door knocker, was studded with polished turquoise, as was the clasp of his bolo tie. A showy gold-plated watch glittered on one wrist, and he lit a grotesquely large cigar by setting a hundred-dollar bill on fire with a monogrammed silver lighter. Clinging to his arms on both sides, giggly bleached-blond bimbos, wearing rhinestone-studded dresses two sizes too small, oohed and aahed appreciatively at his extravagance. Isabel looked up to see that Morton's jowly face, smirking in smug self-satisfaction, now occupied every one of the fifty-foot television screens towering above her.

She couldn't believe her eyes. *For this Liz Parker was almost killed?* Some of Isabel's apprehension faded as she found herself looking forward to the prospect of bringing Joe Morton down. *We'll see what a big man you are once you're safely behind bars,* she thought venomously. *Or maybe six feet under.*

Before heading in for a closer look, she took a second to consider her own costuming. While perfectly adequate for hiking through caves, the simple sweater and jeans combination she now wore seemed out-of-place amid the tacky glitz of the casino. *Better switch to something less conspicuous,* she decided, looking over the milling patrons of Morton's idealized gambling mecca. A scantily-clad showgirl, wearing only strategically-placed sequins and feathers, walked by at that moment and Isabel snorted huffily. *Uh-huh, right,* she thought, arching an elegant eyebrow. *Like that's going to happen....*

Unwilling to go quite that far to blend in, she contented herself to transforming her comfortable hiking garb to a stylish black sequined dress and high heels. Rearranging molecules in a dream was even easier than in real life, so it took next to no effort at all to spruce up her hair and makeup as well. Isabel checked her reflection in the polished silver casing of a nearby slot machine, nodded in approval, and marched confidently down the red carpet, casually joining the carefree crowd watching Morton try his hand at the roulette wheel. "Excuse me," she murmured, elbowing her way to the very edge of the gaming table, across from Morton.

On closer inspection, she was surprised to see that the spinning wheel had been done up to resemble a flying saucer. Silver glitter sparkled like stardust on the rotating disk while a green papier-mâché alien sat atop the hub of the wheel like the pilot of a cartoon spaceship. *That looks nothing like Nasedo,* she thought with a frown, disturbed to find alien imagery creeping into Morton's fantasies once again. Looking around, she now observed that the entire casino had an extraterrestrial motif, not unlike the campy, kooky decor of the Crashdown Cafe. Model rocketships and flying saucers hung from the ceiling. Painted ray-guns and bug-eyed monsters decorated the sides of the slot machines, while many of the strolling showgirls now looked like extras from *Barbarella,* complete with fishbowl helmets, pointed ears, or silver antennae, just like the waitresses at the Crashdown wore.

Where did all this come from? Isabel wondered, somewhat baffled. Had she somehow missed all this sci-fi kitsch before, or had the casino just been completely redecorated by some tremor in Morton's sleeping consciousness? In dreams, almost anything was possible, she recalled, but why did the slumbering Morton, immersed in his private fantasyland, still have aliens on the brain? *I don't like this,* Isabel thought, chewing on her newly painted lips. *Where's this space-age symbolism coming from?*

The spinning roulette wheel slowed to a halt, causing the rolling ball, which was painted to resemble the planet Earth, to bounce from wedge to wedge before coming to rest in Black Eighteen. A roar of approval rose from the crowd of awestruck spectators as Morton chortled triumphantly and, gripping his cigar between his jaws, scooped up an appallingly large pile of bright plastic chips into his corner. He magnanimously threw a handful of chips into the air and laughed as his adoring entourage scrambled madly after the flying chips, one of which landed directly in front of Isabel, who felt obliged to grab for it in order to avoid attracting attention. She snatched up the blue plastic disk, which bore a printed sticker reading $100, and smiled weakly across the table at Morton, trying to look appropriately avaricious. His gleaming, carnivorous eyes made contact with hers, and Isabel had to repress a shudder. "Do I know you?" Morton asked, winking lecherously.

Thankfully, the bimbos flanking Morton, unable to secure any of the flung $100 chips on their own, chose that moment to raise a fuss, pouting and complaining, and Morton had to look away from Isabel to appease them, eventually buying their smiles and sloppy kisses with a handful of chips for each of them. "Help yourselves, ladies. My ship has definitely come in, or should I say my flying saucer? Hah!" He took a deep puff on his cigar, then reached for a crystal goblet sitting at one corner of the table. He raised the glass to his lips, then scowled as he discovered it was empty. "Ramirez!" he shouted, snapping his fingers.

The crowd of spectators and sycophants parted to reveal Lieutenant David Ramirez, in full dress uniform, standing at attention only a few feet away. Isabel's eyes widened as she spotted a black leather attaché case resting upright on the red carpet next to Ramirez's black military boots. *That has to be the case Max and Michael saw at Slaughter Canyon!* she thought in excitement. *The one with the unknown "merchandise."*

"Excuse me." Slowly, inconspicuously, she started working her away around the circular table, toward the lieutenant and the briefcase. She almost left her $100 chip behind, but, at the last minute, remembered to hang onto it. "Excuse me, excuse me...."

"Get me some more whiskey!" Morton bellowed at Ramirez, as though he were a servant. The obnoxious gunman blew a mouthful of smoke into the lieutenant's face, then patted his own corpulent belly. "And get me a roast-beef sandwich while you're at it, with plenty of mayonnaise!"

"Yes, sir!" Ramirez saluted Morton smartly, then executed a crisp about-face and started to march away, briefcase in hand. *No!* Isabel thought in dismay, afraid that the dream-lieutenant would depart with the case before she could get close enough to follow him.

Turned out Morton wanted to keep an eye on the case, too. "Hold on!" he gruffly ordered the departing soldier. He pointed with his cigar at the floor by his feet. "Leave that here with me."

Ramirez obediently deposited the briefcase next to Morton before goose-stepping away to fetch the bullying killer's refreshments. Isabel took this as more evidence that, in the real world, Morton had some really prime dirt on the actual lieutenant. She was less interested, though, in what Morton had on Ramirez than in what was in the attaché case, which she slowly but surely drew nearer to. Was there any chance that she could snatch the case with-

out Morton noticing? That seemed unlikely, but she was at
a loss for what else to try. *What I really need*, she realized,
eyeing the mysterious case covetously, *is a good distraction.*

"Ohmigod, that's him! That's the man who shot me!"

The shocked cry caught both Isabel and Morton by surprise. Spinning around, the dreamwalking teenager was
amazed to see Liz, with her original brown hair and all,
staring in horror at the high-living gunman. Behind her,
Carlsbad Caverns's underground gift shop now appeared
to occupy one corner of the casino. At first the dream-Liz
seemed to be clad in the same outfit she had worn to the
caves that morning, before Isabel gave her a molecular
makeover, but then Isabel blinked and rubbed her eyes as
Liz's casual attire was suddenly replaced by her Crashdown
waitress uniform, complete with a gaping, bloody hole just
above the silver apron. "There he is!" Liz shouted to all
concerned, pointing accusingly at Morton. "That's him!"

His cigar drooping from his lower lip, Morton glowered
at Liz, his good mood replaced by anger with pathological
speed. Snarling, he shoved his flunkies and bimbos aside,
then reached into his buckskin jacket and drew out his pistol, which now looked as large as a bazooka. Fire erupted
from the muzzle of the handgun and a cascade of hot lead
slammed into the displaced gift shop, blowing apart shelf
after shelf of souvenir plates, mugs, ashtrays, and snow
globes. Gamblers and showgirls ran for cover, shrieking in
fear, but every shot missed Liz, who continued to point an
accusing finger at the gun-wielding felon.

Obviously, Isabel realized, cringing at the repeated blasts
from the oversize pistol, Morton's unconscious mind had
finally made the connection between the brown-haired

girl at the gift shop and the waitress he had shot at the Crashdown two years ago. *This is just what Max was afraid of,* she thought in dismay. *Morton's figured out that Liz can expose him.*

As distressing as this development was, Morton's maniacal attempt to blow away the dream-Liz left the crucial briefcase momentarily unguarded. Seizing the opportunity, Isabel pushed her way through what was left of Morton's entourage, tossing a peroxide blonde to one side, and grabbed onto the handle of the attaché case. Without missing a step, she yanked the case from the carpet and ran like mad away from the roulette table. *Got it!* she thought triumphantly.

But the theft had not gone unnoticed. "Hey! What the——?" Morton exclaimed angrily. Forgetting Liz for the moment, he hollered and aimed his massive artillery at Isabel. "Come back with that, you bitch!"

The pistol boomed and a slot machine exploded only a few inches away from Isabel, showering silver dollars in all directions. Isabel's heart missed a beat, and she dropped her $100 chip, but she kept on running, trying to put as much of the casino as possible between her and Morton. The high heels slowed her down, so she kicked them off as she ran, preferring to sprint barefoot upon the springy red carpet. She ducked to the right, down a corridor of clattering one-armed bandits, all of which seemed to feature spinning UFOs and oval-eyed E.T.s instead of lemons and jokers and such.

Morton chased behind her, firing his gun wildly. Bullets smashed into gamblers and gaming tables alike, turning the lavish casino into a scene of bloody pandemonium. Frightened screams filled Isabel's ears, yet, bizarrely, no police officers or security guards made any attempt to stop the amok gunman from chasing an apparently unarmed high school girl through the crowded edifice. *Sometimes dreams can be just too darn weird,* she thought irritably.

Fortunately, the alien teen wasn't nearly as defenseless as she looked, not as long as she still possessed her special powers. Halting long enough to spin around and look back the way she had come, she raised her open palm and concentrated. An entire row of slot machines, jolted by an unseen telekinetic force, toppled forward, blocking Morton's path. Then, to retard his progress even further, she concentrated again, transmuting a stretch of velvety red carpet into gooey black sludge instead. She watched, with a smirk of satisfaction, as Morton's expensive-looking snakeskin cowboy boots bogged down in the thick, viscous muck. "What?" he growled in frustration. "Where did all this goddamn goo come from?"

Good, Isabel congratulated herself. *That buys me a little time.* Darting out of range of Morton's pistol, she hurriedly looked around for someplace where she could inspect the stolen briefcase in privacy. Her gaze immediately fell upon the entrance to the ladies' room, which was identified as such by the silhouette of a space woman wearing a fishbowl helmet and Judy Jetson skirt. *Perfect,* she decided.

The rest room was conveniently empty, except for a coin-operated robot dispensing toiletries, so Isabel wasted no time throwing the briefcase down on the counter by the sinks and tugging at its lid. The case was locked, of course, but that was no problem; a single touch of her fingertip undid the lock, which came open with a click. Taking hold of the sides of the lid with both hands, she paused in hushed anticipation for only a single heartbeat. *Okay,* she thought gravely, *let's see what the big deal is.*

She lifted the lid and a blinding silver glare escaped from inside the case, forcing Isabel to blink and look away, her eyes watering. The unearthly glow faded after a moment, though, and she cautiously shifted her gaze back toward the case's exposed interior, eager to see what the initial burst of light had concealed.

To her surprise, she saw that the bottom of the case had turned into a kind of window, through which she saw a gleaming silver saucer cruising through space toward a bright blue sphere that she quickly identified as the planet Earth. A frown twisted her lips as, mystified and disappointed, she tried to make sense of what she was seeing. *This can't possibly be the literal contents of the case!* she theorized in a rush, based on equally surreal experiences on other dreamwalks. *More like some freaky symbolic metaphor.*

Before her bewildered brown eyes, the spinning saucer entered Earth's atmosphere, glowing brightly red as some sort of protective aura shielded the alien spacecraft from the searing heat of entry. The saucer sped downward, approaching the surface of the planet at a precipitous angle, and Isabel gasped out loud as she swiftly guessed what she was witnessing. She recognized the blue skies and arid terrain of southeastern New Mexico only seconds before the shining saucer collided violently with the ground, throwing up a cloud of flying dust and debris. *I knew it,* she thought, her appalled eyes aflame with realization. *It's the Crash!*

A lump formed in her throat as she waited for the smoke and dust to settle, revealing all that was left of the space-faring vessel after it disintegrated on impact. Part of her didn't want to see the twisted wreckage and broken, inhuman bodies, but she couldn't look away either. This was, after all, the same fateful accident that had stranded her and Max and the others on a planet where they could never truly fit in. *Is this what the Crash really looked like*, she wondered, *or just how Morton imagines it?*

There was no way to know for sure, but the inexplicable, eyewitness coverage of the alien craft's earthshaking demise stirred powerful emotions in Isabel, so that she was completely caught off guard when the door banged open and Joe Morton barged into the ladies' room, tracking sticky black tar onto the tile floor. "There you are!" he snarled, thrusting his immense gun in Isabel's face while his free hand slammed the lid of the briefcase shut. "Who the hell are you anyway?" he demanded, standing so close to Isabel that she could see the tobacco stains on his teeth. He grabbed onto her arm and shook her roughly. "Who are you working for?"

Heat radiated from the red-hot muzzle of Morton's firearm. The smoky smell of gunpowder, like Fourth of July fireworks, filled her nostrils. She heard the gun cock ominously. *Okay*, she decided. *Enough is enough. Briefcase or no briefcase, I'm getting the heck out of here.*

"Spill it, you witch!" Morton barked at her, spraying saliva in her face. His beefy fingers dug painfully into her arm. "Who are you, and how did you pull that stunt back there, with the tar and the slots? Tell me, you thieving slut."

"In your dreams," Isabel replied. She spit directly into

his fuming, beet-red face, and he pulled the trigger at the very split second that she—

—woke up back at the motel room, the deafening boom of Morton's gun still ringing in her ears. She sat up in bed, shaking and soaked in sweat, provoking gasps from both Max and Alex, who hurried to her side instantly. "Iz! Are you okay?" they asked almost simultaneously.

She nodded woozily, too breathless to speak right away. Tremors shook her from head to toe, and her own blood pounded in her ears, making her dizzy. "Just give me a minute," she murmured finally, as she struggled to readjust to reality. Exhaustion, both emotional and physical, washed over her body, which felt as though it had actually run for its life across the length of the imaginary casino. Despite the air-conditioning, the room felt unbearably hot and stuffy, so she peeled off her heavy sweater. *That's a little better,* she thought, although the short-sleeved silk blouse underneath felt soiled and sticky with sweat.

Glancing at the clock radio by the bed, she was startled to see that less than thirty minutes had passed since she had first lowered her head onto the cheap motel pillow. *Is that all?* she marveled; it felt as if she had been stalking Joe Morton for half the night.

"What happened?" Max asked insistently, kneeling beside the bed next to her, his dark, serious eyes searching her face for clues to what had transpired during her exploratory dreamwalk. "What did you see?"

Isabel started to answer, but her mouth was as dry as the desert. "A glass of water, please," she croaked pitifully, massaging her throat, "with maybe a couple drops of Tabasco in it?"

Alex sprang at once to secure her tonic. "I'm on it!" he announced eagerly, while Max stayed to watch over Isabel, waiting tensely until Alex returned from the bathroom with a glass of clear water faintly tinged with red. Isabel reached gratefully for the cup, but was startled when Alex reacted with shock and surprise. "Isabel!" he blurted, eyes wide with dismay. "Your arm!"

She followed his own horrified gaze to where five ugly purple bruises defaced the toned white flesh of her upper arm, exactly where Joe Morton's brutal fingers had squeezed her arm so mercilessly. "Oh, that," she said archly, regarding the telltale bruises with icy disdain. "Nothing to worry about. Just a little souvenir from our friend with the gun, not to mention anger-management issues."

"Here, let me fix that," Max offered. His fingertips brushed over her arm, removing the bruises by healing the injured tissues beneath her skin.

"Thanks," Isabel murmured. She sipped the Tabasco-flavored tap water, which soothed her throat and helped steady her nerves. Slowly, haltingly, she told her brother and her (sort of) boyfriend everything that she had experienced while exploring Morton's memorably nasty dreamscape, while also trying to interpret the dream's occasionally surreal symbolism. She didn't understand everything she'd seen and felt in the dank alley and lurid casino, but a few things seemed obvious.

"Whatever he's got in that briefcase," she said with utter certainty, "it has something to do with the Crash." In her memory, the soaring UFO once again dived into the unforgiving Earth, and she started to choke up. Another gulp of cool water was required before she could deliver one more piece of bad news. "And that's not all, Max," she said, swallowing hard because she knew that her brother wasn't going to like what she was about to tell him. "Morton *knows*. He knows about Liz!"

13

*B*oy, we couldn't look more hungover, Maria thought, *than if we'd actually spent all of last night drinking.*

Breakfast was the morning buffet at the Denny's next to the Days Inn. Except for Liz, who was still recuperating in her motel room, and Max, whose turn it was to keep watch over Morton's temporary residence at the Motel 6, the rest of the vacationing teens were refueling with various combinations of coffee, orange juice, scrambled eggs, bacon, fruit, and breakfast pastries. An aspiring vegetarian, with occasional lapses, Maria had eschewed animal products in favor of toast, cantaloupe, grapefruit, and a plate full of melon balls, but her healthier diet failed to spare her from the subdued, enervated atmosphere at the table. Worn out by all their intensive snooping the night before, nobody was talking much, aside from Alex, who kept making sporadic attempts to get a smile or a laugh out of Isabel, who still seemed to be recovering, emotionally, from her nocturnal trek through Joe Morton's psyche.

"So how was the food at that imaginary casino last

night?" Alex asked her with forced levity. He dipped a rather soggy piece of toast into some scarily homogenous-looking scrambled eggs. "Better than this, I hope."

"I don't know, Alex," Isabel replied humorlessly. She stared distantly at her plate, absently soaking a chocolate donut in a pool of Tabasco sauce. "I didn't eat anything."

"Oh," he said, obviously hoping to generate a bit more conversation momentum than that. An awkward silence followed, making Maria wince inside, until Alex adopted another tack. "How are you doing, Iz?" he asked solicitously, his guileless green eyes beseeching her to open up to him about whatever was troubling her.

That, clearly, wasn't going to happen. "I'm fine, Alex. Really." A touch of exasperation entered her dull monotone, and Isabel got up from the circular wooden table at which they were all sitting. "I'll be right back," she said, excusing herself as she headed for the ladies' room.

Alex watched her depart with a stricken expression, and Maria decided to take advantage of Isabel's absence to offer her friend some much-needed advice. "You're trying too hard, Alex," she informed him in a low voice, leaning over the table toward the wiry young man. "Just give her a little space, okay, before you really piss her off."

"But I'm just trying to help," Alex protested. Frustration was written all over his adolescent face. "I hate seeing her all broody and depressed like this."

"I know," Maria sympathized. This was none of her business, of course, but she couldn't just sit by while Alex let his good intentions lead him astray where his dream girl was concerned. She'd seen this vicious circle play out before, and not just between Alex and Isabel: Person A won't leave Person B alone, forcing B to withdraw, which just makes A redouble his or her efforts to overcome B's defense, thus driving B even further away, and so on. "Look," she said compassionately, "I don't pretend to understand all the intricacies of your relationship with Queen Amidala, but I do know that you can't *force* somebody to be happy or to open up emotionally, and they'll probably just resent you if you try."

Had she managed to get through to him? Maria wanted to think so. Maybe she couldn't cure Liz of her debilitating post-traumatic whatsit, but that didn't mean she still couldn't play a positive role in her friends' lives. She considered offering Alex a bracing whiff of rosemary or cyprus, but then recalled that, along with every other guy she'd ever known, Alex probably considered aromatherapy irredeemably girly. *Their loss,* she thought, sighing inwardly.

"I guess you're right," Alex said glumly after a couple of minutes. Obviously, leaving Isabel alone right now was the last thing he wanted to do, but he appeared to have taken Maria's advice seriously. He threw up his hands in frustration. "It's just so hard, you know."

"Tell me about it," Maria said, considering the laconic alien rebel sitting directly to her right. Michael had maintained a discreet silence during her heartfelt romantic strategy session with Alex, sulkily attacking his bacon and eggs instead. Was that because he was simply disinterested in such mundane, mushy matters, she pondered, or was his own bizarre sister/lover relationship with Isabel sufficiently complicated that he felt uncomfortable discussing her with Alex? *Or maybe,* she admitted to herself, *he's still ticked-off at me for forcing him to come along on this fun-filled road trip in the first place.*

Between taking care of Liz and dogging Morton's every move, she and Michael had not had much time to talk since their carefree weekend excursion had turned into a film by Quentin Tarantino. She kept expecting Michael to say "I told you so," and couldn't quite figure out why he hadn't done so yet. Unless he'd been too busy dodging bullets, that is.

Maybe I should take some of my own advice, she thought. "Say, Michael, can I talk to you for a minute, in private?"

His lean face immediately took on a wary expression, the universal male response to the prospect of a serious conversation with their significant other. "Sure, I guess," he said dubiously. "Where?"

Maria pointed toward an empty booth at the back of the coffee shop. After apologizing to Alex for abandoning him, she and Michael transferred their plates and cups to the other table and settled in. "Okay," Michael asked once their relocation was complete, already sounding defensive. "What's this all about?"

This isn't going to be easy, she thought, downing a gulp of fresh orange juice as she gathered her thoughts. "I want to apologize," she said finally.

Michael blinked in surprise. Usually, he was the one she expected to apologize. "Umm, what for?"

"For making you take a vacation when you didn't feel like it, and then giving you a hard time about not enjoying yourself." She poked at melon balls with her fork while she tried to explain what she meant. "It's like I just told Alex. You can't force someone to have a good time when they're worried about something else. You and Max and Isabel have a lot on your minds these days; it wasn't fair of me to twist your arm like that just because I wanted to pretend you and I were an ordinary couple for one weekend." She glanced out the window at the Motel 6 across the highway, and rolled her eyes. "And, boy, did this little brainstorm of mine turn out to be a complete fiasco!"

"No, no," Michael insisted. "It was a good idea, even if I was too stubborn to admit it. We *were* all stressed-out and needing a break." He reached across the table to pat her hand clumsily, an almost astonishingly demonstrative gesture by Michael's standards. "It's not your fault that Liz bumped into the shooter by accident."

"Yeah, but now look at her!" Guilt snuck up on Maria and whacked her over the head. "She's practically having a nervous breakdown, and all because I wanted to get out of Roswell for a while." Overcome with emotion, she told Michael about everything he had missed while trailing Morton, about Liz's panic attacks and post-traumatic flashbacks. "I'm really worried about her, Michael. I've never seen her like this."

As edgy and guarded as he often was, Michael sometimes surprised her by revealing his true feelings. This was one of those moments. "I know what you mean," he confided in her. "Max is acting really strange, too. I don't know what's with him." He quickly brought her up to speed on all of Max's bizarre behavior, including the way he had almost lost control while spying on Morton last night in Slaughter Canyon. "It's gotten so that I'm almost afraid to leave him alone," Michael said, "for fear of what he might do without thinking."

Maria suddenly wished that they had compared notes

earlier. "Ohmigod," she gasped in realization. Her olive eyes lit up and she clutched her head with both hands. "Don't you see what's happening? Max has got it, too. The post-traumatic stress disorder!"

Michael looked confused. "But Max wasn't shot."

"No," Maria admitted, still convinced that she had ze-roed in on the truth, "but he mind-melded with her right afterward, while he was healing her." A vivid memory of Max, crouched over Liz's perforated body, flashed through Maria's mind. "Liz told me all about it, about how they shared their memories, and saw each other through the other's eyes." Even now the concept sent a shiver through Maria. *Talk about romantic!* "Don't you get it? Max must have absorbed everything Liz felt when she was shot by Morton, that's why he's reacting this way, too!"

Michael nodded thoughtfully. "Yeah, that makes sense, sort of." She could practically see the wheels turning in his head as he digested her brilliant diagnosis. "But how come Max is on this whole bloodthirsty vengeance kick, while Liz ended up afraid of her own shadow?"

"Testosterone?" Maria speculated. She shrugged her shoulders, not feeling obliged to fill in *all* the blanks in this particular theory. "Alex said that post-traumatic you-know-what affects different people different ways, depend-ing on their backgrounds, personalities, etcetera. The point is, both of them are having a delayed reaction to what hap-pened at the Crashdown that day."

"Which means neither of them is exactly thinking straight," Michael concluded, sounding convinced at last. He hastily gulped down the dregs of his coffee and jammed one last piece of bacon into his mouth as he slid out of the booth at top speed. "Sorry to ditch you like this, but I've gotta talk to Max right away." He pulled out his wallet and threw down a twenty to cover his share of the check. Before running out, though, he paused long enough to give Maria an irresistible grin that made her feel like a million dollars. "Good thinking, babe," he said warmly. "And don't beat yourself up about that whole vacation thing. Nobody's blaming you for anything."

Good to hear, Maria thought, smiling to herself as she watched Michael hurry out of the coffee shop. *Especially from Michael Guerin, of all people.*

14

Sunday, June 3rd.

I don't know who I am anymore. Am I the Liz Parker who successfully coped (more or less) with the discovery that human-alien hybrids lived among us, even right next to me at school, or am I the Liz Parker who, all of a sudden, can't get past the fact that I was shot by accident two years ago?

Alex says that it's "post-traumatic stress disorder," and he's probably right. Alex was always more interested in psychology than I was; I'm more of a hard sciences kind of girl, at least I was before I ran into Joe Morton again, eight hundred feet beneath the ground. Now I feel more like a test animal than a laboratory scientist, like a frightened white mouse being forced to take part in some cruel psychological experiment, which I suspect I'm flunking. Why, I don't even have enough strength to run through any mazes, which must be terribly disappointing to whomever's conducting this experiment.

I'm rambling, I know, but I don't know what else to do. I was hoping that writing in this journal would help me make sense of things, maybe put my traumatic memories behind me, but it doesn't seem to be working. I'm all alone here in this gloomy motel room, with the curtains drawn and the blankets pulled up to my armpits so that I don't have to look at that silver handprint again. I want to be with Max and the others, but I'm afraid to even step outside, for fear that Joe Morton will find me again.

Which is irrational, I realize. Morton wasn't even trying to kill me in the first place. It was all one big stupid accident, like you hear about on the news all the time. "Innocent Bystander Hit by Stray Gunshot." No big deal.

But I almost died. For good. And that's the part that I can't forget anymore, even when I try to close my eyes and go to sleep. (Except for one weird moment last night, when, right in the middle of that same awful nightmare about the shooting, I suddenly found myself reliving a completely different incident: that time when Max and I double-dated with Alex and Isabel, after that silly James Bond movie. Where did that come from?)

So what do I do now? Talking to a psychiatrist wouldn't do any good. Last fall, after that whole mess with Tess and Nasedo and the Special Unit, Max's parents made him see a shrink for a couple of sessions, but it was a big waste of time because Max couldn't tell the doctor anything about what had really happened to him. I'd just run into the exact same problem. How can I discuss what happened at the Crashdown when I can't even mention being shot? And how do I explain to an ordinary shrink where this weird glowing handprint came from?

I guess I have to cure myself somehow, but how can I do that when I don't even know who I am? When I look in the mirror, I can barely recognize myself, and not just because Isabel turned me into a redhead. Who's that pale, trembling, pathetic, little mouse I see where my own reflection should be? That's not who I want to be. That's not who I am.

Alex said I have to confront my fears, so I guess that's what I'm going to have to do, no matter how terrified I feel. One way or another, I have to stop feeling like a victim.

Even if it kills me.

15

"Maxwell, we need to talk."

Perched in the back of the Jeep, keeping watch over Morton's motel room and convertible, Max lowered his binoculars as Michael approached the parked vehicle. He scowled impatiently, squinting against the intense morning sunshine. "Have I ever told you how annoying I find that nickname?" he grumbled.

"Trust me, you've got bigger problems, bro," Michael informed him as he clambered into the front seat of the Jeep, then twisted around so he could speak to Max directly. Although it wasn't even eleven yet, the temperature in the quiet motel parking lot was already climbing toward the upper nineties; Michael wiped his sweaty brow with the front of his T-shirt and put on a pair of shades to protect his eyes from the glare. *It's way too hot out here,* he decided. *Lousy weather for a stakeout.*

"Like what?" Max asked skeptically. Dark circles shadowed his eyes and Michael noted other signs of strain in his friend's face and manner. His face looked gaunt and sunburned, while his whole body seemed noticeably tense and jittery. He fidgeted with the binoculars in his lap and kept looking away from Michael to check on the Chevy parked on the other side of the busy highway. Was Max's ragged state caused by simple lack of sleep and concern for Liz, Michael wondered, inspecting his friend carefully, or was Maria right that something more serious was going on?

"Tell you the truth, Max, you've looked better." Not wasting any time with chitchat, Michael confronted Max with Maria's theory that the young alien leader had picked up a bad case of post-traumatic stress disorder via his intimate connection with Liz. "Kind of like catching mono, if you know what I mean."

Max responded with instant denial. "So what are you saying, Michael, that I'm suffering from the emotional equivalent of secondhand smoke or something? Don't be ridiculous." He sneered at the notion. "And since when are we taking psychiatric advice from Maria DeLuca of all people? I mean, no offense, Michael, Maria's a sweet person and all, but she's definitely a bit on the flaky side."

As opposed to your girlfriend, who freaks out when a flock of bats fly overhead? Biting down on his tongue, Michael resisted the temptation to spring to Maria's defense. "That's not the point," he argued. The sun was baking his brains, but he knew he had to get through to Max somehow. "You and I both know that you've been acting weird ever since Liz spotted Morton at the caverns."

"Not at all," Max insisted defensively. "I'm just taking seriously a serious situation, the same way I always do. You heard what Isabel said; not only is Morton's crooked deal mixed up with the Crash somehow, but he also knows about Liz, which puts her in genuine danger. Excuse me if that makes me a little uncomfortable." He turned his back on Michael and placed the binoculars back over his eyes, once more aiming the lenses across the street at the closed door to room #19. "Now then, if your little one-man intervention is over, I'm kind of busy here."

But Michael wasn't about to be dismissed so easily. "Bullshit," he told Max bluntly. He leaned back between the Jeep's front seats and roughly snatched the binoculars away from Max's face. "I want to keep Liz safe, and find out what Morton's up to, as much as you do, but that's what we're talking about here. You look me in the eye and tell me that you weren't on the verge of completely losing control last night up on the ridge. I *saw* your hand heating up like an acetylene torch last night, Max, and don't tell me you did that on purpose!"

His face flushed with anger, Max grabbed wildly for the stolen binoculars, which Michael defiantly held up above his head, out of Max's reach. "Give me those, Michael!" he growled, clenching his fists at his sides. "I don't have time for this psychobabble garbage."

"No way, Max!" Michael stood up on the Jeep's front floorboard, making sure Max couldn't get his hands back on the binoculars. "Not until you admit that there's something seriously wrong with you, that you're not acting like yourself." The blazing sun beat down on Michael's head and shoulders, toasting the back of his neck and making him even more in a hurry to make his traumatized friend see sense. "Look at me, Max!" he challenged. "Tell me everything's okay with you. I want to hear you say it!"

"Damnit, Michael!" Max roared, the veins in his neck

standing out like hydraulic cables. He threw up his hand and unchecked power burst from his open palm. A blinding flash hit Michael like a tidal wave, sending him tumbling backward over the Jeep's windshield and onto the vehicle's hot metal hood. The impact knocked the wind out of him, and the binoculars flew out of his fingers, crashing to the pavement several yards away. After sitting in the sun all morning, the Jeep's army-green hood seared his bare arms where they came in contact with the overheated metal. Still somersaulting backward, Michael managed to use his own momentum to roll awkwardly off the Jeep onto the blacktop below, landing with a thud upon the baking asphalt. *Ouch,* he thought, wincing in pain. *Did someone get the license number of that ballistic missile?*

Fortuitously, the Days Inn parking lot wasn't terribly active this late in the morning, most of the visiting tourists having already gotten an early start on the day's sight-seeing and outdoor activities. Even still, Michael felt obliged to leap instantly to his feet, ignoring his bruised and battered flesh, and call out to whomever might be listening, "I'm cool! Nothing to worry about! Just a little fall, clumsy me!"

A pair of slow-moving senior citizens, wearing matching Hawaiian shirts and straw hats, regarded Michael uncertainly from the sidewalk in front of the motel. *How much had they seen?* he worried, hoping that the entire incident had happened much too quickly for any eyewitnesses to really grasp what Max had done. "Sorry for the excitement, folks," Michael said loudly, brushing the dust and grit of the parking lot from his arms and clothes. "A flashbulb went off by mistake," he improvised, despite the absence of any visible camera. "Gave me a bit of a start, I guess, but

I'm okay now. Just a couple of bumps and scrapes, that's all."

In fact, his ribs felt like they had just been pounded on with a sledgehammer, making him flinch with every breath, and there was a suspicious black scorch mark on the front of his T-shirt which, quickly turning away from the two apprehensive retirees, he quickly made disappear. *Is anyone buying this?* he wondered, fully aware of just how lame his impromptu explanations sounded. *Or am I ending up on the front page of the* Weekly World News *or maybe on "American's Most Incriminating Alien Videos"?*

He held his breath as the elderly couple shook their heads disapprovingly and muttered darkly among themselves, but then they continued on their way to the coffee shop, apparently not wanting to get any more involved in whatever suspicious activity the two teenage boys were involved in. *Thank God,* Michael thought, expelling a sigh of relief once it became obvious that the two old folks were not about to start screaming "Alien!" *That was a close one,* he realized.

The crisis averted, Michael turned toward Max, who stood frozen at the back of the Jeep, staring in dismay at his own open hand. He looked utterly crestfallen, a mixture of shock and remorse written all over his face, which had gone pale beneath its outer layer of sunburn. "Oh my God, Michael!" he exclaimed, hopping out of the Jeep and rushing across the pavement to where Michael stood, grimacing in pain. "Are you all right?"

"Well, I'm going to think twice about getting between you and a vendetta again," Michael said wryly. After furtively looking around to make sure no one was watching, he peeled up his T-shirt to inspect the damage, which turned out to consist of a nasty black-and-purple bruise concentrated over his breastbone. Most of his chest was sore and sensitive to the touch, but, thankfully, nothing felt broken or seriously injured. "I'll live," he stated.

The sight of the ugly bruise caused Max's face to collapse. "God, Michael, you've got to believe me, I never meant to—I mean, I didn't want...." Guilt and horror rendered Max momentarily speechless, and his hands drooped limply at his sides, as if he was afraid to raise them at all. "I'm so sorry, Michael...."

"I know that, man," Michael said, letting Max off the hook. *I don't know what's more amazing,* he marveled, *that Max would use his powers against me, or that he would do so in public, and in broad daylight, no less.* Michael leaned against the side of the Jeep, taking some of the load off his feet. "Maybe now, though, you'll admit that you've got a problem." He gave his friend a knowing look. "The Max Evans I know does not go around blasting his buddies in motel parking lots."

Max nodded soberly. He stared at the pavement, unable to meet Michael's gaze. "Yeah, maybe you're right," he admitted after a moment or two. "There have been a couple of times this weekend when, okay, I felt like maybe I was losing control." He looked up at last, letting Michael see the anguish in his eyes. "I can't help it, though. Whenever I see Morton, or even think about him, it's like I'm back at the Crashdown, watching Liz slip away right before my eyes."

"That's textbook, man." Despite his aching ribs, he smiled wolfishly, thinking that maybe a bruised chest was a small price to pay to get Max to listen seriously to what he had to say. "According to Maria, who learned about all this from Alex, who read about it in a book somewhere, you've got yourself a classic case of post-traumatic stress disorder."

Max frowned, disliking anything that impaired his ability to take care of his responsibilities, which included protecting both Liz and his fellow alien hybrids. "So what do I do about it?"

"Well, maybe you listen to your friends when they tell you that you're losing it. Let us provide a reality check for you whenever those Crashdown flashbacks start getting a little too intense. Beyond that,"—Michael shrugged his shoulders—"do I look like a shrink to you?"

"More like one-hundred-and-fifty pounds of freshly pounded ground chuck," Max joked, sounding more like his old self for the first time in over twenty-four hours. He nodded at Michael's black-and-blue torso. "Let's head back to the room and get that healed right away," he suggested.

"Aren't you afraid that Morton will sneak away while you're not looking?" Michael asked him pointedly. He looked past Max at the Motel 6 across the way.

Max hesitated, looking back over his shoulder at the hated gunman's current lair. Clashing priorities warred behind his eyes as indecision caused his lips to twitch. Then he shook his head and turned his attention back to Michael. "Maybe if we hurry right back," he proposed uneasily.

Now it was Michael's turn to shake his head. "Not so fast," he said firmly. "I appreciate the thought, Max, old pal, but want to find out what's inside that damn briefcase, too." Moving slowly, to minimize the wear and tear on his sore ribs, Michael retrieved the binoculars from where they had fallen, a few yards away from the Jeep. One lens had cracked, but a moment's concentration repaired the glass, making the instrument as good as new. Next, he gingerly climbed into the back of the Jeep, gritting his teeth against the pain, and turned the binoculars on Morton's door, which appeared not to have budged an inch during the time Michael had knocked some sense into Max by letting Max knock the wind out of him. "Go get Alex or Isabel or somebody to take over the stakeout," he suggested, "and then we can apply some old-fashioned alien healing techniques to my ribs."

Morton must be sleeping late, Michael deduced, *after his late night hunting us through Slaughter Canyon.* "So," he asked Max, before the other youth could go for reinforcements, "do you have a plan for getting at that case?"

"Of course," Max declared, as if that went without saying. "What do you think I've been thinking about out here, besides wanting to teach Morton what an alien abduction really feels like." His voice still held a trace of seething malice and resentment. "Don't worry, though, I'll run the details by you, just in case I've completely lost my mind, you know."

"Thanks," Michael said. "I'll let you know about that, *after* I've heard your plan."

16

"Okay, what we need is a good distraction," Max declared. "Then, after Morton and the science guy have been lured away, I'll slip into their room to check out that briefcase."

With the exception of Alex, who had volunteered to monitor Morton's hangout from the Jeep, the gang had crowded into a single motel room to work out the details of Max's plan. Liz sat at the foot of one of the unmade beds, determined to take part in the proceedings, despite the monster-size butterflies in her stomach and the panicky feeling that came over her every time Morton's name was mentioned. *I can't let the others solve this problem for me,* she resolved, *not if I want to stop feeling like a helpless victim.*

"The question is," Max continued, "what kind of distraction?" He sat next to Liz on the bed, his arm around her shoulders. An air conditioner hummed steadily in the background, beneath the curtained windows that kept out the late morning sun while also hiding their conference from prying eyes.

Slouching against the wall, her arms crossed atop her

chest, Isabel sighed dramatically. "Just leave that to me," she suggested with a definite air of noblesse oblige, her weary tone implying that this was just one more burdensome task that only she was fully equipped to handle.

Maria snorted and rolled her eyes. "Let me guess, you're planning to bat your eyelashes and flirt them into a state of total submission." Seated on the other bed, next to Michael, she gave Isabel a trenchant look. "Is that, like, your only plan—ever?"

Max's sister was unfazed by Maria's sarcasm. "It's never failed yet," she said with a smirk.

Liz saw a pithy retort forming on Maria's lips, but Max interrupted the two women's verbal sparring before it could escalate further. "No offense, Isabel," he stated diplomatically, "but I think we need something more ambitious, that's certain to keep Morton and his accomplice occupied long enough for me to make a thorough search of their motel room."

"Why you?" Michael objected. He exchanged a meaningful look with Max, which left Liz wondering what exactly she had missed. "Remember that little talk we had earlier this morning, Max? Under the circumstances, I'm not so sure that you're the one who should be taking point on this operation."

To Liz's slight surprise, Max didn't seem to mind having his strategy questioned by Michael. "I see where you're coming from," he replied reasonably, "and I appreciate your concerns, but I really think this is something I ought to do." His tone was firm, but conciliatory. "Besides, in theory, I won't be the one dealing with Morton; that will be the rest of you, which is probably just as well."

Why wouldn't Max want to meet up with Morton? Liz thought, puzzled. Yesterday he had been almost too anxious to confront the hated gunman. Once again, she had the distinct impression that she was missing something, maybe that "little talk" Michael had alluded to. *Maybe I should ask Max about that later, when we have a little more privacy.*

"Okay," Michael agreed, nodding unenthusiastically. "But somebody should go with you, as backup," he insisted, clearly intending that he be that person.

A reasonable assumption, Liz conceded, except that she had other ideas. "I'll go with Max," she blurted quickly, before she had a chance to chicken out.

Her terse announcement caught everyone in the room off guard. No surprise, considering that she'd barely been able to string a coherent sentence together for the last day or so. "What?" Max exclaimed, shocked and appalled by the mere idea. He held onto her tightly, searching her face with dark, troubled eyes. "You can't be serious, Liz," he said softly.

"Max is right," Maria added forcefully. "You really don't have to do this, honey. We can take care of this on our own, I promise."

Liz was tempted to give in, especially if it meant not leaving the relative safety of the rented motel room, but knew that she had to resist that impulse if she ever wanted to feel like herself again. "No, you don't understand," she spoke out, trying, with mixed results, to keep her voice from quavering. "I *have* to do this, myself. It might be the only way I can put this whole, awful nightmare behind me." A thin cotton blouse concealed the glowing handprint on her belly, but Liz could still feel it tingling against her skin, a tangible reminder of her inability to escape her traumatic memories. "I need to face my fears directly, just like Alex said."

"Are you sure, Liz?" Max asked gently. She sensed that, somehow, he understood what she was going through, and why it was so important that she take an active part in this investigation. "It could be dangerous," he reminded her.

Liz nodded slowly. "I know."

"Okay, then," Max said decisively, sounding very much like the deposed ruler of an alien planet. "Liz and I will search Morton's room, while the rest of you create a sure-fire distraction." He took Liz's hand and gave it a reassuring squeeze. "We'll get through this together," he promised her.

Michael looked uncomfortable with this arrangement, but must have realized that Max's mind was set. Instead of arguing, he just shrugged his shoulders and muttered, "Fine. Sure. But we still haven't figured out what kind of distraction."

A sneaky smile came over Max's handsome face as an idea occurred to him. "I think I know just what will do the trick." He leaned toward the others as he whispered conspiratorially. "Listen...."

"Yes, can I have room #19, please?" Michael said into the cell phone. He waited with sweaty palms for the Motel 6 operator to connect him with Morton's room. Isabel sat next to him in the back of the Jeep, chewing nervously on her lower lip as she looked with obvious trepidation. They were on their own now, the rest of the gang having already moved into position, per Max's plan. Michael felt uncomfortable making this call out in the open, in the Days Inn parking lot, but they had finally been forced to check out of their twin rooms, which, with any luck, they wouldn't need anymore after Max and Liz discovered what Morton was hiding in that black attaché case. *This had better be worth it,* he thought.

"Hello?" Morton answered crossly. Michael recognized the gunman's raspy voice at the other end of the line. "Who is this?"

"My name doesn't matter, Mr. Morton," Michael stated in a hushed, conspiratorial tone. "The point is what I can do for you."

"Wait a second," Morton barked, sounding increasingly agitated. "How do you know my name? Where did you get this number from?"

The temperature in the parking lot was unbelievably hot, but Michael kept his voice cool. "I believe we have a mutual acquaintance, Mr. Morton. A Lieutenant David Ramirez?"

"Ramirez!" Michael could easily imagine Morton's shocked expression. "That's impossible. I never gave Ramirez this number!"

Oops, Michael thought. Still, the mention of the compromised test pilot's name had definitely caught Morton's attention. "Perhaps you've underestimated Lieutenant Ramirez's resources," Michael hinted ominously.

The alien teen thought he heard another voice babbling worriedly in the background. No doubt the unnamed lab technician, wondering what was going on. "Shut up!" Morton snapped at his roommate before speaking over the phone again. "What's this all about?" he demanded savagely.

"I understand you're interested in certain 'merchandise,' related to a certain 'aviation accident' that occurred fifty-some years ago." Michael hoped his vague allusion to the Roswell Crash would pique the gunman's curiosity. *Two can play the cryptic references game,* he thought vindictively; such seeming discretion helped him to pretend that he knew more about Morton's mysterious business than he actually did. "Isn't that so, Mr. Morton?"

Michael deliberately mentioned the killer's name at every opportunity, the better to unnerve Morton. *Anything to keep him from hanging up,* he resolved.

"Maybe," Morton said suspiciously. "But we shouldn't say anything about that, not now. This isn't a secure line." His gruff voice grew even more menacing. "Don't call this number again, you got that?"

"Sure," Michael said, "whatever." He refused to be intimidated. "Meet me at the Denny's across the street, ASAP. I'll be waiting." Morton started to protest, angrily refusing to be dictated to by an anonymous voice, but Michael silenced him by dropping yet another incriminating name. "Bring that science guy with you, the one from Las Cruces."

Michael heard Morton gulp nervously. "Hey, how do you know about that?" he practically shouted. All of Michael's inside information was clearly getting to the paranoid gunman. "Who the hell are you?"

Morton's flustered tone brought a smirk to Michael's lips. Figuring he'd baited the trap sufficiently, the youthful alien issued his invitation one more time. "Both of you. Denny's. Right now," he insisted. "Don't keep me waiting."

He hung up the phone before Morton could argue any further. The minute the line went dead, a rush of relief washed over him; he hadn't realized how tense he'd been until the high-pressure call was over. Adrenaline still coursed through his veins, leaving him hyper and on edge. "Whew!" he exclaimed. Although he'd never admit it, he found himself wishing he could borrow one of Maria's silly aromatherapy bottles. *Talk about performing without a net!*

Isabel watched him with wide, worried eyes. "Was that him?" she whispered hoarsely. "Is he coming?"

"Oh, yeah," Michael said with complete certainty. Morton couldn't pass up a meeting with a stranger who seemed to know so much about his illicit arrangement with Lieutenant Ramirez. "He's coming, all right."

Okay, Max, he thought, taking a deep breath to come down from his adrenaline high. *I've done my part. Now it's your turn.*

17

Max and Liz waited, hiding behind the ice machine, until Morton and the unnamed scientist hurried out of their motel room, looking nervous and sweaty. They piled into the blue Chevy and zoomed away from the parking lot, presumably heading for the Denny's on the other side of the highway. Michael's anonymous phone call had obviously done the trick, just as they'd planned. Max counted softly to five, then looked at Liz with concerned, caring eyes. "Ready?" he asked her tenderly.

As I'll ever be, Liz thought, nodding once. Her heart was ticking faster than a Geiger counter at Los Alamos, and she felt another panic attack scratching at the back door of her mind. The memory of the shooting tormented her, so that she could practically smell the gunpowder again, hear the two men's dishes crash to the floor only heartbeats before Morton's wild gunshot left her bleeding on the floor. *Not again,* she prayed, reliving the dreadful moment for maybe the thousandth time. *Please don't let it happen again!*

"You can always wait with Maria and Alex," Max reminded her, giving her one last chance to back out. Their friends were parked in the Jetta several yards away, at the far end of the Motel 6's parking lot, ready just in case she and Max had to make a speedy getaway.

"No," she told him, shaking her head. A tremor in her voice betrayed her unsettled emotions. "Let's go."

She closed her eyes to compose herself, then looked up at Max as he rose behind the ice machine and hustled toward room #19. She followed close behind him, focusing on Max's comforting presence as an antidote to the violent specters plaguing her memory. *The shooting wasn't a completely negative experience,* she reminded herself as they scurried together down the walkway in front of the motel. If not for that alarming brush with death, Max Evans would have never entered her life in such a profound and unforgettable way. *We turned that near-fatal moment into a new beginning,* she remembered. *I just have to have faith that we can do that again.*

A DO NOT DISTURB sign hung on the door to #19, but that didn't stop Max, who only had to lay his hand upon the doorknob to release the lock. The two teens looked around quickly, to ensure no one was watching, then slipped into the room, closing the door rapidly behind them.

The curtains were closed, to hide Morton's nefarious dealings from the world, so the room was dark and murky. Liz reached automatically for the light switch, but Max grabbed her wrist, shaking his head. Instead he raised his right hand and concentrated for a second; within moments, a silver glow emanated from his outstretched fingers, illuminating the modest motel room.

"Look," he whispered, pointing toward the corner table, where a portable laboratory had been assembled, complete with test tubes, slides, graduated cylinders, Bunsen burner, microscope, laser apparatus, titration setups, ammeter, spectroscope, bottles of chemical catalysts, and even a Geiger counter. Max headed straight for the table, throwing his personal spotlight onto the impressive array of equipment. "This has to belong to that science guy," he assumed. "The one from Las Cruces."

Liz inspected the miniature lab, feeling a twinge of envy. All the instruments were state-of-the-art, and in much better condition than Roswell High's well-worn and frankly antiquated lab supplies. "Looks like he's conducting some sort of chemical analysis," she guessed from the arrangement of the equipment. She looked over the hardware curiously, being careful not to break or rearrange anything. "Probably metallurgical or mineralogical."

Max gave her an admiring gaze. "Good thing you came along," he said. "As a bona fide space alien, I should be embarrassed that you know more about science than I do." They exchanged amused smiles before getting back down to business. "Last night at the canyon, Morton told Ramirez that he needed to authenticate the 'merchandise' before he gave the lieutenant the rest of his payment." He nodded at the tableful of lab equipment. "That must be what this is all about."

Makes sense, Liz agreed. "But where exactly is the merchandise?" Although all the scientific instrumentation was on full display, there was no sign whatsoever of what was being tested. *Funny,* she thought, *you'd think there would be some samples of the test subject lying around.*

"Good question," Max said. Turning away from the mini-lab, he swept the rest of the room with a wide beam of lambent silver light. Liz kept her eye out for the infamous black attaché case, but all she saw was the ungodly mess that Morton and his cohort had managed to make of the motel room. Beer cans, Domino's pizza boxes, and empty two-liter bottles of Coke littered the carpet, while the ashtrays were overflowing with stubbed-out cigarette butts. Sleazy porno magazines, some of them looking unbelievably gross, were piled on the end table between the two beds, which looked like they hadn't been made in days. The air-conditioned atmosphere, although pleasantly cool compared to the torrid heat outside, reeked of tobacco and dirty laundry. DO NOT DISTURB, Liz recalled, guessing that no maid had seen the inside of the room since Morton and his techie buddy moved in.

Guess they take their privacy seriously, she concluded. *No surprise.* Apparently such concerns extended to hiding the briefcase, too; Max's searchlight probed every cluttered corner of the trashed motel room without falling upon the luggage they sought. *Hmm,* Liz thought, *if I was a briefcase full of extraterrestrial contraband, where would I be?*

Playing a hunch, she got down on her hands and knees and peeked under the nearest bed. At first, all she saw was darkness, but then Max crouched behind her, flooding the space between the bed and the floor with his incandescent ray of light. Liz's eyes lit up as well when she spotted a matte-black case right in front of her. "Oh my God, Max, there it is!"

Eagerly, she yanked the attaché case out from beneath the bed and dropped it onto the dirty, disheveled sheets. It was surprisingly light; whatever was hidden inside obviously didn't weigh very much. The clasp was locked, naturally, so Liz stepped aside to permit Max to perform his telekinetic magic. The lock came open with a click and Liz held her breath, half-expecting to find frozen alien embryos within the mysterious case.

Instead they found several torn and ragged sheets of a strange, silvery metal foil, folded meticulously to fit within the shallow confines of the case. Carefully, almost reverently, Max removed one sheet from the case and spread it out atop the bed, where it was revealed to be about the size of a large pillow case. Once laid flat, each and every crease in the foil disappeared completely, so that it looked as though it had never been folded at all. Max tugged on one corner of the sheet, experimentally trying to tear off a small piece, but the exotic material resisted his increasingly strenuous efforts, remaining stubbornly intact and unrumpled. Liz had to marvel at whatever cataclysmic forces must have been required to have torn apart these sheets in the first place.

"Liz," Max whispered in an awestruck tone. "Do you realize what this is?" The metallic sheet reflected the starry radiance shining from his upraised hand, casting an effulgent glow over the entire scene. "This is the same unbreakable stuff that Captain Carver found at the Crash site in '47, that he showed to Michael back in October."

Liz nodded, understanding. The retired air force pilot, now deceased, had given Michael an eyewitness report of the Crash and its hectic aftermath, and had shown him a much smaller sample of a very similar material, which Carver had covertly pocketed at the debris field over fifty years ago. She gazed at the unearthly material in wonder. It was amazing to realize that, more likely than not, they were looking at an actual piece of the alien spacecraft that had brought Max and the others to Earth so many years *ago. How many light-years had this ragged leaf of foil traveled?* she marveled.

To confirm his suspicions, Max picked up the sheet and crumpled it into a small ball, about half the size of his fist. He placed the ball back atop the bed, and he and Liz watched in amazement as the compressed wad of foil automatically unfolded itself, so that, within seconds, the sheet once more laid flat upon the bed, looking as pristine and unwrinkled as before.

Max and Liz exchanged knowing looks. This tendency to reassume its original form, even when folded or compacted, was highly characteristic of the unearthly materials found after the Crash, according to Michael, Carver, and any number of alleged witnesses from '47. "It's true," Max gasped, delicately touching the silver foil as though it were a sacred relic. "This is from the Crash!"

No wonder there were no test samples over by the lab equipment, Liz realized, impressed by the alien material's preternatural resilience and durability; *the poor science guy probably hasn't been able to break off a single piece of the sheet for testing purposes.* "The air force must be experimenting with this stuff at White Sands," she deduced. Although the details were top secret, everyone knew that the Pentagon tested new aircraft and missile systems at the nearby base. "That must be how Lieutenant Ramirez managed to get his hands on this stuff."

"But what does Morton want with it?" Max wondered, sorting quickly through the rest of the samples in the black briefcase. There were also fragments, Liz saw, of an almost weightless tan substance, as smooth as plastic, that, based on Max's tentative attempts to bend or break them, were just as invulnerable as the silver foil. These smaller frag-

ments were embossed with cryptic pink and purple hiero-
glyphics that bore a striking resemblance to the obscure
petroglyphs she and Max had once found in a cave outside
River Dog's Indian reservation, markings made by Nasedo
decades before Max and the other human-alien hybrids
emerged from their pods. The tan-colored fragments, Liz
knew, also gibed with testimony given by others involved
in the Crash investigation back in 1947. (You didn't grow
up in Roswell, New Mexico, without picking up a thorough grounding in basic UFO lore.)

"He probably intends to sell it to the highest bidder," she
guessed. "Even without the Roswell connection, which
might appeal to wealthy UFO enthusiasts, materials like
these—lightweight, indestructible—would be worth millions if they could be duplicated. We could be talking industrial espionage here, never mind foreign governments
that might want to find out what the U.S. is up to at White
Sands." She couldn't resist wadding up the sheet herself,
just to watch it unfold miraculously once more. "One way
or another, Max, we're talking big money here."

Money enough to kill for, she thought somberly. A shiver
ran through her as she realized that the huge potential payoff inherent in these artifacts was almost surely what must
have ignited Morton's violent outburst in the Crashdown
way back when. *I almost died for these fragments,* she ac-
knowledged, but, for once, she managed to keep the post-
traumatic flashbacks at bay; it helped somehow to be using
her brain to unravel the mystery. The mad, unreasoning
panic was still there, prowling around at the back of her
mind, poised to overwhelm her sanity and intellect once
more, yet she felt a little less like a victim now that she was

finding out for herself what the shooting had been all about. It was no longer just a random, meaningless act of violence, but part of a larger conspiracy whose outline was rapidly becoming clearer.

She peeked quickly at her watch, unsure how much longer Maria and the others would be able to keep Morton and his pet PhD occupied. Almost ten minutes had passed already, so she and Max had to be running out of time. "We've got to go," she warned Max, whose fascination with the alien wreckage, however understandable, might have conceivably overcome his instinct for self-preservation. "And we've got to take this stuff with us."

"Are you sure?" Max asked, even as he refolded the silver sheet and placed it back in the briefcase with the rest of the debris. "Morton will know we've been here if his so-called 'merchandise' disappears."

"I don't care, Max," she stated, feeling more decisive and certain of her judgment than she had since running madly out of that underground gift shop the day before. "What if Morton really is planning to sell these samples to a hostile country?" She touched Max's hand gingerly, hoping she could make him understand. "I know you and Michael and Isabel have little reason to trust the federal government, especially after the way they tortured you in that white room, but I'm still an American, Max, and I can't just let Joe Morton sell our secrets to gods know who!"

To her relief, Max did not challenge her patriotic concerns. "That's fine, Liz," he told her without hesitation. He closed the lid of the attaché case and locked the clasp. "You're right. I don't like the idea of this technology falling into the wrong hands, either." He gave her a joking smile as he lifted the case by its handle, easily managing its weight. "Just don't ask me to personally hand-deliver this package back to the army boys at White Sands."

"I was thinking maybe Area 51 instead," she teased him right back. She couldn't believe how good it felt to smile again, to indulge in a bit of playful repartee with the boy she loved. Suddenly, she was very glad that she had summoned the courage to break-and-enter along with Max. This was just what she'd needed to get over her pathological fear of Joe Morton and his gun.

Now we just need to get out of here, she decided, heading for the door, *before he gets back.*

18

Morton and his anonymous partner made good time. Less than ten minutes after Michael hung up on the murderous outlaw, the two men entered the Denny's, looking about avidly for the unknown party who had lured them here. *Michael must have done a good job of planting doubts in Morton's mind,* Isabel concluded, repressing a shiver at the very thought of the killer's warped psyche. She knew from firsthand experience what an ugly place that was.

Neither man was carrying the infamous black attaché case. *Good,* Isabel thought, assuming that the case was back at Morton's motel room; at least that part of Max's scheme had gone off as planned.

Michael raised a hand to catch Morton's eye, just in case their disguises didn't attract his attention. To bolster their assumed identities as associates of Lieutenant Ramirez, both she and Michael had transmuted their street clothes into reasonable facsimiles of U.S. Air Force uniforms. Mirrored sunglasses further concealed their actual origins, while Michael had even gone so far as to give himself a military-style crew cut to complete the deception. It didn't look bad on him, actually.

An ugly scowl upon his face, Morton marched over to the booth the two bogus officers had occupied. His unknown associate followed him, looking nervously around the restaurant as though deathly afraid of being recognized. He seemed ready to bolt and run at the slightest provocation.

That's no good, Isabel thought. They needed to keep *both* men occupied, so that Max and Liz would have time enough to search their room at the Motel 6. She gave the scrawny Asian guy a friendly smile, hoping to put him more at ease.

Without ceremony, Morton planted himself down in the booth, across from the disguised teens. "All right, I'm here," he growled sourly, his blood-rimmed eyes wishing them off the face of the Earth. "Who are you and what do you want?" His palpably uncomfortable companion slid into the booth next to Morton. "And make it quick."

That's the one thing we can't *make it,* Isabel fretted. Morton's close proximity made her skin crawl, remembering the vile sights, sounds and smells she'd experienced while slumming in his unconscious mind. She could still see the biker's brains splattering the walls of that dismal alley, feel Morton's beefy fingers digging into her arms moments before she'd finally escaped the nonstop greed and violence that filled the loathsome killer's nocturnal fantasies. Max had thoughtfully erased the bruises Morton had inflicted on her, but she still had her memories of being chased like a hunted animal through that gaudy, ghastly casino.

"Well?" Morton demanded. His real-life attire was a good deal less flashy than what he had worn at the height of his imaginary glory and success. An open pack of cigarettes was stuck in the top pocket of a faded flannel shirt, while his hunter's cap covered what Isabel suspected was a balding scalp. She craned her neck, trying to look inconspicuously for the telltale lump of a gun beneath the bottom of his untucked shirt; the tabletop, alas, blocked her view of Morton's waistband. "Speak up!" he snapped at Michael. "Let's hear what you have to say."

Michael had already agreed to handle most of the talking, since Morton had already heard his voice. Isabel had only come along, despite the risk of Morton recognizing her from last night's dream, to help out with the special effects they had in mind.

"Hold your horses," Michael stalled. He took a long, slow sip of coffee before continuing. "Anyway, as I previously informed you, my friend and I are associates of Lieutenant David Ramirez, whom I believe you are acquainted with."

"Stupid son of a bitch!" Morton spat, unable to contain his aggravation. "Can't keep his big mouth shut." He shook a meaty finger in Michael's face. "You tell that cowardly excuse for a soldier that I don't appreciate him blabbing about our business. I don't care who you are. He's going to regret this, believe me!"

Isabel winced, hoping that this scam of theirs didn't get the poor lieutenant killed. He hadn't seemed like *that* bad a sort back when she'd flirted with him by the Bottomless Pit. She suddenly imagined Ramirez in that alley, his blown-apart brains joining the biker's on the blood-stained wall. Then she remembered that Ramirez's crooked deal with Morton had already put Liz in danger, and threatened to expose all of Roswell's alien secrets. *We're just doing what we have to, I guess.*

"That's between you and Ramirez," Michael said diplomatically, responding to Morton's vehement threats against the blackmailed pilot. "We're interested in striking our own deal with you, as well as your employers."

"Oh yeah?" Morton said. A waitress swung by to see if the two newcomers wanted to order anything, but Morton chased her away with a dirty look and a snarl. The science guy just squirmed and sweated next to Morton, trying to hide his face behind a menu. "What kind of deal?" Morton snarled.

Isabel held her breath as she waited tensely to see how Michael was going to finesse that particular query. *This would be easier,* she thought, *if we actually knew what Morton had extorted from Ramirez.* Thinking back, she remembered what she had found within the dream-version of the black briefcase: that disturbing peek at the Crash itself. Unfortunately, that kind of visual symbolism, no matter how powerful and emotionally devastating, was of limited use in the present circumstances.

Still, Michael did his best with what they'd managed to glean from Morton's dreams. "Again, as I believe I stated on the phone," he said long-windedly, "this concerns a certain controversial incident that occurred several miles north of here, over fifty years ago."

"Yeah, yeah," Morton grumped irritably. "The Crash at Roswell. You don't need to be so cute about it." He toyed menacingly with a bread knife he lifted from the table; Isabel still couldn't tell if he was carrying a gun or not. "Cut to the chase, buddy. How do I know you jokers are on the level?"

Michael leaned forward, lowering his voice to a furtive

whisper. "Mr. Morton, you and I both know that what crashed at Roswell in 1947 was no top secret spy balloon, no matter what the authorities would now have us believe."

"Maybe," Morton said skeptically, "but UFO nuts and would-be con artists are a dime-a-dozen in these parts, like the clowns who sold that phony 'alien autopsy' video a few years back. What makes you two any different?"

That video gave me nightmares for weeks, Isabel recalled, *even though I knew it had to be fake.* She shuddered when she remembered how close Max had come, after the Special Unit captured him, to starring in a real-life alien autopsy. *Don't think about that now,* she told herself. *Concentrate on the task at hand, fooling Morton and his accomplice.*

"What makes us different?" Michael echoed, dragging out the discussion. "An excellent question." He maintained a cool, cocky expression as he strung Morton along. "Perhaps it's that we have access to certain 'souvenirs' left over from the Crash itself." He nodded at Isabel, letting her know that it was time to carry out the next part of Max's plan. "As we are fully prepared to demonstrate..."

Show time, she thought mordantly, retrieving a rumpled backpack from the floor by her feet. Reaching into the pack (which she had borrowed from Alex), she removed two curious items and placed them carefully on the table. The first item was a length of copper-colored wire twisted into a complicated rosette design, reminiscent of the crop circles famously found in England during the nineties. The second was a peculiar, futuristic-looking skullcap made from a silvery, iridescent material that reflected the fluorescent lights overhead, producing a prismatic dance of colors across the pliable surface of the cap.

In fact, the two items were, respectively, a wire hanger and a rubber shower cap, both filched from their rooms at the Days Inn, then cosmetically enhanced by a little creative molecular rearrangement. *Not bad work,* Isabel thought, admiring her craftsmanship, but would they really fool Morton and his scientific sidekick, at least long enough to keep the two men occupied awhile longer? Suddenly, she had her doubts.

"Well, gentlemen?" Michael said shamelessly, gesturing toward the two oddball artifacts. Isabel decided that she never, ever wanted to play poker against Michael. "Are you taking me a little more seriously now?"

The nerdy science guy was obviously impressed, peeking out from behind his menu for a better look, but Morton snorted disparagingly. "Are you kidding?" he snickered, sounding more amused than annoyed for the moment. "I've seen better props in carnival sideshows." Bushy eyebrows lowered balefully as his bad humor reasserted itself. "You better not be wasting my time, punk."

"I wouldn't dream of it," Michael insisted. He arched his eyebrows and waved theatrically over the two counterfeit items. "Watch this."

He delicately tapped the wire rosette with his index finger and the copper wire began to emit an eerie white glow that caused even Joe Morton to drop his jaw. Within seconds, the ornately-configured wire was glowing so brightly that Morton and his tremulous cohort were forced to look away. Michael then tapped the modified coat hanger again, and the glow faded almost immediately. He waited until the two men were once more gazing at the now-inert wire before lifting the ersatz alien artifact to reveal the flowery rosette design now burned into the polished wooden tabletop. "Holy cow!" the science guy exclaimed, while Isabel made a mental note to fix the table before they left.

Despite his hostile attitude, Morton appeared impressed as well. Looking about quickly to make sure no one else had witnessed the wire's miraculous illumination, he slid a paper placemat over the burned impression of the wire. "Okay," he said grudgingly, settling back into his seat. He nodded at the silver skullcap. "What does that one do?"

Somehow Michael managed to keep a straight face as he explained that, "We believe that this unique item may be some manner of extraterrestrial crash helmet." He lifted the sparkling shower cap from the table and handed it back to Isabel. "As you'll see, it possesses a number of unusual properties, as my colleague will be happy to demonstrate."

Feeling more like a magician's beautiful assistant than an undercover alien, she held up the rubber cap and, using both manicured hands, tore it down the middle until the two halves were held together by less than an inch of silvery material. She then laid the bisected "crash helmet" back on the table and gently smoothed it out upon the flat wooden surface. As she did so, the cap magically reknitted itself, the severed parts joining back together seamlessly until the headpiece was completely intact once more. *Voilà!* she thought sarcastically, holding up the restored cap for the two men's inspection.

"Is that all?" Morton asked, eyeing both the cap and the wire emblem greedily. Isabel imagined she could see the dollar signs forming in his bloodshot, piglike eyes.

"Not at all," Michael said boldly. He nodded at Isabel again. "If you please, lieutenant."

She resisted a snarky impulse to salute, instead placing the glittering shower cap over her own sandy-blond hair. Closing her eyes behind her mirrorshades, she concentrated intently on the effect she aimed to achieve. Both Morton and the nerdy guy gasped out loud as, chameleon-like, the rubber cap morphed to match the tawny color of her tresses, becoming all but invisible. "As you can see," Michael announced, sounding like the host of some cheesy, late-night infomercial, "the helmet is endowed with astounding camouflage capabilities."

Michael seemed to be enjoying himself, in a perverse sort of way, but Isabel felt extremely uncomfortable using her powers so openly in front of Morton and the other man, even with the fig leaf of plausible deniability provided by the supposed alien technology. Unable to avoid a morose scowl, she peeled the shower cap off her head and slapped it back onto the tabletop, restoring its futuristic silver coloration as she did so. Morton reached out to inspect the cap and the wire personally, but Isabel snatched them up before he could grab onto them, and placed them back in Alex's pack in an impressive display of brisk, military efficiency.

Morton grunted brutishly and tried for the pack itself, but Michael blocked him by leaning across the table between Morton and Isabel. "Whoa there, pal," he discouraged the overeager gunman. "Show and tell is over." Michael assumed a tough, hardball attitude. "Time to talk a little turkey." He coldly appraised the mismatched pair sitting across from him. "We've proven we're legitimate. What do you two bring to the table?"

"Watch the lip, punk," Morton rasped, bristling. Giving up on the pack for now, he crossed his arms atop his chest, regarding the two "officers" with open distrust. "Don't get smart with me. As far as I'm concerned, I still don't know you from Adam." He cocked a beefy thumb at Isabel. "What's her story anyway," he groused. "How come she never says anything?"

Isabel's stomach did a nervous somersault, but Michael handled Morton's aggressive challenge with aplomb. "My colleague prefers to let me handle the verbal aspect of our negotiations," he said smoothly. "That's our own business, though. I don't see where that concerns you." He subjected the furtive scientist to a scornful stare. "After all, I don't see you volunteering the name of your silent partner there."

Morton stiffened, picking up on something Michael had just said. "You don't know his name?" the startled gunman said. A suspicious edge entered his voice. "Not at all?"

Oh no! Isabel thought. On the phone, she recalled, Michael had hinted that he knew all about the nameless technician from Las Cruces. Now his minor slipup seemed to have Morton reevaluating his prospective new business partners.

Cunning, red-rimmed eyes narrowed as Morton looked them both over one more time. "Just how much did Ramirez tell you anyway? And how did you find out where I was staying? I never told Ramirez that."

"Er, we have our own sources of information," Michael improvised vaguely, trying to recover from his careless slip of the tongue. "Like I said, that's none of your concern."

Morton wasn't buying it. "No dice," he blustered. "I don't deal with anybody unless I know a hell of a lot more about them than they do about me." With surprising speed, he reached out and yanked Isabel's sunglasses off her face.

Shocked, she flinched and threw herself backward, into the far corner of the booth. For a fraction of a second, she felt like she was back at the Hangar 18 casino, staring down the barrel of the heartless killer's oversize pistol. Fearful brown eyes, suddenly exposed to Morton's scrutiny, stared in alarm at the gunman's bestial features.

For himself, Morton looked almost as stunned as the young woman he had so roughly unmasked. "You!" he blurted, crushing the stolen shades inside his fist. "You're the witch who stole my case last night." Outright fear and confusion came over his coarse, ill-shaven face as he realized that he was remembering a dream. "What the hell?" he exclaimed, loud enough to attract scandalized looks from the staff and patrons of the restaurant. "What kind of freaky head game are you playing?"

Next to him, the scrawny scientist panicked. "What's the matter?" he squealed, shrinking into his seat. "What's happening?"

Morton shoved the techie out of the booth in his haste to get away from Isabel. Lurching to his feet, the frothing gunman pulled out a handgun and waved it in front of Isabel and Michael. "Gimme that pack!" he roared. "Now!"

Terrified shouts and screams greeted the surprise appearance of Morton's weapon. "Watch out! He's got a gun!" someone shouted as cashiers, waitresses, and customers ducked for cover. "Someone call the police!" another voice yelled.

It's the Crashdown all over again, Isabel realized, flashing on her borrowed memories of the shooting. Horror melded with déjà vu as, her heart pounding, she gladly surrendered the backpack and its worthless contents to the volatile hoodlum. Morton snatched the pack by its taut straps and tossed it over to the science nerd, who clutched it against his chest. "Nobody follow us!" he shouted for all to hear, firing a bullet into the ceiling for emphasis.

Leaving the disguised aliens alone in their booth, Morton and his accomplice ran for the exit. "Oh my God," Isabel gasped. What if the two men went back to their motel room to reclaim the vital briefcase? "We have to warn Max and Liz!"

Her hands shaking, she found the cell phone in her purse and somehow managed to dial the number for the Motel 6. Meanwhile, Michael stood up and, exploiting his phony uniform for all it was worth, tried to calm the upset denizens of the Denny's. "Everyone remain calm," he ordered with mock authority. "Remain in your seats. We'll be taking statements shortly."

"C'mon, c'mon," Isabel muttered fervidly, waiting for the motel operator to pick up. Standing up in the booth, she watched through the restaurant's clear glass windows as Morton and the other man plowed through an approaching party of tourists, shoving the startled bystanders aside in their headlong flight from the restaurant. She listened anxiously to the ringing of the cell phone, knowing there wasn't a minute to lose. They couldn't let Morton catch Max and Liz in his room!

"Hello, Motel 6 here," a voice said chirpily into her ear, on about the fourth or fifth ring. "How can I help you?"

Finally! Isabel thought. "Connect me with room #19, right away, please! It's an emergency!"

The operator obligingly transferred the call, but, to her

intense distress, nobody answered. The cell phone gripped in her sweaty palms, Isabel waited in an agony of suspense to hear her brother's voice at the other end of the line. *Come on, Max! Pick up the damn phone!* Michael gazed at her with a worried, mystified expression, obviously wondering what was taking so long, while the phone continued to ring maddeningly. "I'm sorry," the operator broke in after a minute or so. "There seems to be something wrong with that line. May I take a message for you?"

Isabel hung up the phone. "I can't get through to them," she told Michael, scared to death. "Something's gone wrong."

"Damn!" Michael swore, fully aware of the danger their friends were in. "Come on," he said, grabbing onto her hand and pulling her out of the booth, onto her feet. "We've got to get over there!"

They ran, hand in hand, for the exit. "Wait!" someone shouted after them. "What about those reports?" A hefty male cashier tried to block their escape, but Michael knocked him aside with a blast of concussive force. Isabel hoped to heaven that their disguises were still working.

Dashing out the door, into the full heat of the afternoon, they saw Morton and the science guy pile into the blue Chevy and speed out of the parking lot. Horns honked and brakes squealed as the Chevy recklessly cut straight across the highway, causing pileups and rear-end collisions in both north and south lanes of traffic. The nerve-jangling thunder of crashing metal only heightened Isabel's acute feeling of dread as she watched Morton's convertible roar into the parking lot of the Motel 6, where her brother and his girlfriend were about to be caught snooping by a psycho with a gun.

Get out of there, Max! she thought, climbing into the driver's seat of the Jeep as fast as she could. Michael buckled himself into the seat next to her, staring furiously through the windshield as Isabel started the ignition and pulled out after the Chevy. Even with her foot flooring the gas pedal, she knew she couldn't catch up with Morton in time.

Now, Max! Get out of there now!

19

Max let the light from his hand dim as he followed Liz toward the door of Morton's messy motel room. They wouldn't need any artificial illumination once they were back outside; Max just hoped that Michael and Isabel were still keeping Morton and his scientific consultant occupied. *Liz is right*, he thought apprehensively. *The sooner we ditch this place, the better.*

Liz was reaching for the doorknob when they suddenly heard footsteps and angry shouting right outside the door. Morton's gruff, raspy voice sent Max's heart racing. "Hurry up, will you?" the gunman bellowed impatiently as someone rattled the doorknob from the other side. Max and Liz looked at each other in alarm, frozen in place with nowhere to run. The teenage alien stared in confusion at the phone on the end table. *Why didn't Michael and Isabel warn us Morton was coming back?* Suddenly, he noticed that the phone cord was no longer attached to the back of the cheap plastic phone. "No!" he whispered out loud, realizing that Morton must have unplugged the phone before leaving the disorderly motel room. But why?

"Oh, crap!" another voice exclaimed outside, with audible shock and dismay. "The door's unlocked."

The science guy, Max guessed. Instinctively, he extinguished his silver glow, throwing the room into murky darkness.

"What!" Morton snarled. The door slammed open, almost hitting Liz, who had to jump backward to avoid being whacked by the swinging door. The intense New Mexican sunshine flooded the room, exposing Max and Liz to the two men who now crowded through the narrow doorway, blocking their escape route. The scientist barely preceded Morton, who shoved his learned accomplice out of the way in order to charge at Liz like a wild boar, his florid face a mask of malevolence. "What the hell is going on?" he shouted, spittle flying from his lips, then did a double take when he got a better look at Liz's face. "Wait a second," he muttered, confusion briefly supplanting rage upon his porcine features. "I know you." He grabbed onto Liz's arm and pulled her closer, struggling visibly to place where he'd seen her before. "Where...?"

Max raised his hand, aiming his open palm at Morton's broad frame. A faint silver aura outlined his fingers as he summoned the concentration to blast Morton to kingdom come. At the last minute, though, he remembered the rattlesnake he had so thoroughly obliterated the night before, and Michael's disturbing warnings regarding Max's current lack of control—and the awful consequences of taking a human life. The rattler's smoking remains sprang from his memory, superimposed on Morton's repugnant face, and Max hesitated before unleashing his psychic energy.

He paused just long enough, in fact, for the overlooked lab worker to tackle Max from the side, knocking him to the floor amidst a clatter of upset beer cans and plastic Coke bottles. Max landed hard, the bone-jarring impact causing him to grunt out loud. He almost lost his grip on the attaché case, but he held onto the handle with all his strength, unwilling to let go of the precious alien artifacts. The surprisingly aggressive techie kicked viciously at Max's head, and Max barely managed to roll out of the way in time to avoid the blow. Reaching out desperately from his position on the floor, he succeeded in catching hold of his attacker's sneakered foot with his right hand, forcing the techie to hop precariously on one leg while Max, still lying on his side, used his other arm to swing the briefcase like a club, smashing the case into his opponent's hip. *Too bad the contents are so insubstantial,* he thought; ironically, the amazingly lightweight nature of the alien technology undermined his use of the case as a weapon.

Nevertheless, the off-balance scientist tottered backward, leaving an empty sneaker in Max's grasp. The flailing teenager tossed the shoe aside and scrambled to his feet. Concentrated mental energy flowed into his fingertips, turning them into instruments of death. *If I have to,* Max realized, *I'll gladly burn my handprint into Morton's heart to stop him from hurting Liz again. The techie, too, maybe.*

"Not so fast, Bruce Lee," Morton snarled, before Max could put his lethal intentions into action. To his horror, he saw that Morton now had one arm around Liz's waist and the muzzle of a semi-automatic pistol pressed to her head. Her beautiful face was white as a cadaver's, while pure, unadulterated fright filled her glistening brown eyes. "Stay right where I can see you, or your pretty little girlfriend is history."

Max went still as a statue, his left hand poised at his side as though reaching for his gun. Morton nodded at the briefcase clutched in Max's other hand and barked at his hapless cohort. "Get the case!"

The techie approached Max hesitantly, glowering at the paralyzed youth through the thick lenses of his wire glasses. "Don't give me any trouble, kid," he spat, although his threats were a lot less convincing than Morton's. "Just hand over the bag."

Max hated to surrender such valuable links to his native world to the likes of Morton and his geeky accomplice, but he wasn't about to sacrifice Liz for pieces of a broken flying saucer, no matter what planet it came from. "Take it," he said coldly, his dark eyes fixed on Morton and his scared hostage. The lab guy snatched the briefcase from Max and scurried away. "Now let her go."

The gunman ignored Max's urgent plea. He glared at his partner instead. "Make sure the merchandise is still inside," he ordered the scientist while keeping his gun pressed against Liz's temple.

The techie placed the case atop the closest bed and rapidly inspected its contents. "It's all here," he reported a moment later. He was sweating profusely and kept looking at the door, as though he ardently wanted to be anywhere but here.

"Good," Morton grunted. "Pack it up. We're getting out of here."

"But my equipment...," the distressed lab worker objected, locking the briefcase shut once more.

"Leave it!" Morton snapped. Still holding onto Liz, he backed toward the door. "Let's go!"

"Wait!" Max shouted, afraid to move an inch for fear of inciting Morton's eager trigger finger. "You don't need her! Take the briefcase, sure, but let her go!"

Morton sneered cruelly. "Sorry, kid, she's coming with us." He waited until his nerdy partner had slipped out of the door behind him, carrying the crucial samples, then swung the muzzle of his handgun toward Max. "Tough luck."

The gun fired, its jarring report almost deafening in the close quarters of the motel room. Acting on instinct, Max threw up his hands and a shimmering emerald force field instantly formed between Max and Morton, shielding him from the oncoming bullet, which ricocheted off the protective energy bubble, slamming into the ceiling instead. Pulverized plaster rained down on Max, only to slide harmlessly off the verdant force field.

"Wha—!" Morton's jaw dropped and his bloodshot eyes bulged from their sockets. He fired again, this time out of panic, but the radiant green barrier once again shielded Max from the gunfire. Visibly freaked-out, his blubbery jowls quivering, the berserk felon turned his gun back on Liz, shouting hoarsely at Max as he dragged Liz out of the dingy motel room. "Keep away from me, you freak! Stay back!"

Trembling with fear and frustration, Max ground his

teeth behind the translucent green energy, which added a bizarre emerald tint to the awful sight of a terrified Liz being carried off by the gun-wielding killer. His alien powers had saved him from almost certain death, but what about Liz?

Morton had her!

20

"**O**hmigod, Alex! What are we going to do?"

Maria was beside herself, sniffing rosemary oil like it was the elixir of life, to absolutely no effect. Beside her in the front seat of the Jetta, parked outside the Motel 6, Alex looked just as horrified and helpless. The whole plan was falling apart right before their eyes!

First, Morton's blue Chevy had come squealing back into the parking lot, taking Maria and Alex by surprise. Then the two criminals had charged back into room #19, before either of the teens in the Jetta could do anything to warn Max and Liz that they were about to be caught in the act.

And what could we do anyhow? Maria realized, paralyzed with shock and uncertainty. Neither she nor Alex was armed with anything more potent than a half dozen miniature vials of scented oils, all of which she would have gladly traded at this moment for a working Uzi and the skill to use it. How were a couple of ordinary teenagers, like her and Alex, supposed to rescue their friends from a trigger-happy felon like Joe Morton?

As they watched impotently, the other man—the lab tech from the university—rushed out of the motel, clutching what had to be the legendary black attaché case. Gunshots sounded from within #19, causing Maria to almost jump out of her skin. *Two shots,* she counted, going pale. *One each for Max and Liz.* She clasped her hands over her mouth, holding back a scream, and looked hopelessly at Alex, to make certain that she wasn't hearing things, but the anguished look on his face made it clear that he'd heard the shots, too. Tears welled in her eyes as she imagined Liz and Max lying bleeding and dying on the floor of room #19.

Where are Michael and Isabel? she wondered desperately, looking frantically for the Jeep, which she thought she spotted parked across the street, which was now filled with the noise and confusion of a multi-car pileup. *It's not fair!* She and Alex were both one percent human; neither of them had the power to heal Liz and Max if they'd really been shot. *There's nothing I can do to save them.*

So convinced was Maria that her friends had been gunned down that it came as an actual relief when Joe Morton backed out of #19, his meaty arm around Liz's squirming waist. *She's alive!* Maria rejoiced, then noticed the gun in Morton's free hand. *But what about Max?*

The gunshots, along with the crashes on the highway, attracted plenty of attention. Numbered wooden doors opened up all along the length of the motel, as potential witnesses poked their heads out of their rooms to see what was happening, then ducked back inside at the sight of Morton and his smoking pistol. The imposing gunman fired a shot into the air to keep any onlookers at a distance as he tossed Liz into the backseat of the Chevy and, gun in hand, clambered in after her.

With the cowardly-looking science guy at the wheel, the blue convertible burned rubber out of the parking lot, passing the Jeep as Michael and Isabel suddenly arrived on the scene. Morton fired repeatedly at the Jeep, clipping one corner of the windshield and forcing the army-green vehicle to swerve across the parking lot, almost colliding with the parked Jetta. Sticking to the shoulder of the road, to avoid the accident blocking the highway, the Chevy sped away in a cloud of dust and gravel, taking Liz Parker with it.

Maria gripped the steering wheel in front of her, uncertain whether to take off in pursuit or to check on Max first. Her dilemma was solved when Max himself came running out of Morton's motel room, seemingly unharmed. A desperate look upon his face, he dived into the backseat of the Jetta, breathing heavily. "Max!" Maria shouted, twisting around in her seat. "Are you all right?"

"I'm fine," he gasped, "but you have to follow them!" His voice was ablaze with urgency. "They've got Liz!"

"I know!" Maria told him. Afraid of losing her best friend forever, she fired up the Jetta even as Michael and Isabel, side-by-side in the Jeep, still wearing their faux military uniforms, pulled up beside them. Maria shuddered at the sight of the bullet hole in the Jeep's windshield. *That could've been Michael's head,* she realized.

In ten words or less, Max updated his fellow hybrids on what had just happened. "We can't lose that Chevy!" he stressed passionately. "We can't let Morton hurt Liz again!"

Sirens sounded nearby, growing louder by the second. "The police," Maria realized, drawn by the gunshots, the auto accidents, or both. "Hang on!" she warned Max and Alex as she threw the Jetta into drive and peeled out of the parking lot, going from zero to sixty in a matter of seconds. With any luck, she hoped, the cops would be too tied up with the big highway pileup to chase after them right away. In the rearview mirror, she saw the Jeep zooming right behind her. Michael had already used his powers, she saw, to repair the damage to their windshield. *Hold on, Liz,* she thought, following Morton's escape route along the shoulder of the highway. *We're coming for you!*

Pouring on the speed, they came within sight of the blue Chevy before long. At first, Liz and her kidnappers were heading north on 180, toward Carlsbad proper, but they quickly veered off the main highway, turning left onto a less-populated side road that led west toward the mountains. Motels, souvenir shops, and fast-food restaurants soon gave way to flat, barren, desert scenery. Cacti and yucca provided sparse decoration to the arid landscape whizzing past them on both sides of the road. Keeping one eye on the road and the other on the speeding convertible carrying away her friend, Maria tried to figure out where Morton and his accomplice were heading. Geography wasn't exactly her forte, but she didn't remember much in this direction except the mountains and maybe the northern tip of the park.

Okay, she recalled, there was always Las Cruces, where the university was, but that was almost 150 miles away, on the other side of the Guadalupe Mountains. Surely the science guy wasn't planning to take a shanghaied teenage girl all the way back to his snazzy labs and academic colleagues? *They must be planning to hide out in the mountains somewhere,* she guessed, pushing the speedometer needle up to eighty and beyond. *Not if I have anything to say about it!*

Morton knew they were chasing him, of course, especially after they followed him off the highway into the desert, where pretty soon they were the only cars on the road. He glared back at them from the back of the convertible, holding onto his cap with one hand and his gun with the other. Maria glimpsed the back of Liz's head, bizarro red hair and all, but she was too far away to tell how Liz was holding up. *First the shooting, now this!* she agonized silently, trying to imagine what her friend was going through now. *This must be like her worst nightmare coming true.*

"Can't you just blast him or something?" she asked Max in desperation. She had the air conditioner turned all the way up, but still felt covered in sweat. "Some sort of Czechoslovakian tractor beam maybe?"

Max shook his head. "It's not that easy," he explained succinctly, "not at these speeds." Shunning seat belts, he perched on the very edge of the backseat, leaning forward between Maria and Alex, his head and shoulders straining to bring him as close to the fleeing Chevy as possible. "If that car crashes, Liz could be killed."

So much for that brilliant idea, Maria thought. She desperately wanted to close the gap between them and the convertible, just so she could get a better look at Liz, but knew that she had to keep a safe distance between the Jetta and Morton's gun. He had already fired at them a couple of times, but without much success, the wild shots ricocheting off the asphalt ahead of the Jetta or whizzing by overhead. *Don't take too many chances,* she warned herself, knowing that Liz was depending on her. Morton had to run out of gas and bullets eventually. *If I have to, I'll chase him all the way to Tucson.*

The wail of a solitary police siren, coming from several miles behind them, complicated her plans. She couldn't see any flashing lights in the mirror yet, but the siren definitely sounded like it was getting closer. "Do you think they've got our description?" she asked uneasily, sharing an anxious look with Alex. There was no way they could rescue Liz if they had to cope with the police, too. *Too bad we're way out of Sheriff Valenti's jurisdiction,* she thought.

"Don't worry about that," Max said grimly, dropping back into his own seat. He rolled down the window and shoved his arm outside, placing his palm against the outside of the door. "Just keep driving," he said, his brow knitting in concentration.

What in the world—? She gulped, nearly losing control of the wheel, as the Jetta's cherry-red paint job changed before her eyes, a new metallic-green color spreading out from the right side of the vehicle, where Max's hand was, until the entire exterior of the car resembled some giant, glittering, green bug.

"Hey, pretty cool!" Alex enthused, impressed by the Jetta's instant makeover. "You ever consider a career in grand theft auto, Max?" he joked in an obvious attempt to relieve some of the tension in the car. "You'd be a natural."

"I changed the license plates, too," Max replied dryly. He sounded winded, as though the large-scale transformation had taken a lot out of him. "Just to be safe."

Maria had mixed feelings about this whole thing. "Um, you can change it back, right?" She glanced sheepishly back at Max. "Otherwise, my mom is going to freak."

"Keep driving," Max repeated, unconcerned with anything except Liz's safe recovery. He sank back into his seat, exhausted.

Peering in the mirror, she saw that Michael and Isabel had apparently been inspired by Max's ingenuity; within seconds, the olive-green Jeep had acquired a spanking new black paint job. She wondered briefly whether Michael or Isabel had selected the color, then blinked her eyes as the numbers and letters on the Jeep's front license plate rearranged themselves. *Wow,* she thought, amazed at how adept her alien friends were getting with their powers. *Instant, automotive dyslexia.*

She had to wonder what Joe Morton thought of the pursuing cars' uncanny metamorphoses. Tearing her gaze away from the mirror, she looked ahead—and saw the no-good gunman staring back at the Jetta with a totally flabbergasted expression on his ugly face. *Hah!* Maria gloated, enjoying his extreme confusion and discomfort. Maybe the Jeep and the Jetta's unnatural transformations would put the fear of God—or, at the very least, little green men—into the slimeball.

A flashing blue light appeared in her mirror, ruining the moment. Looking back out her side window, she saw a black-and-white State Patrol car zooming up fast behind them. Instinctively, she put her foot on the brake, slowing down to something closer to the legal speed limit. A few car lengths back, behind the wheel of the Jeep, Isabel obviously did the same.

"Hey, what are you doing?" Max shouted, watching in horror as Morton's blue Chevy pulled farther ahead of them, disappearing toward the not-so-distant mountains. "They're getting away!"

"You want those cops to pull us over?" she snapped back at him, fully aware that Liz was speeding farther away from them with each passing second. "You want to try explaining to the police what's going on?" She knew there was no other choice but to slow down and hope the cop car passed them by. "If you've got a better idea, Max, lay it on me!"

Despite his all-consuming desire to rescue Liz from Morton's clutches, Max couldn't argue with Maria's trenchant assessment of their current predicament. Hissing in frustration, he slammed his fist into his palm as his anguished eyes watched the Chevy shrink toward the horizon.

Lights flashing, siren blaring, the State Patrol car drew up behind the two slowing vehicles. "Okay, everyone put on their Not-Guilty faces," Maria said, swallowing hard. A horrible thought occurred to her and she suddenly prayed that Michael and Isabel had been shrewd enough to transmute their bogus air force uniforms into something less incriminating. That was all they needed now: for the pair of disguised aliens to get busted for impersonating an officer (or two).

The cop car cruised up alongside the Jetta and a stone-faced state trooper, peering through the passenger side window, scanned the metallic green vehicle and its occupants. Maria slowed down cooperatively, letting the officer take a good long look. "These aren't the 'droids you're looking for," she whispered under her breath, feeling a cold sweat glue the back of her shirt to her suddenly sticky skin. *Here's where we find out,* she thought, *if Max's magic paint job did the trick.*

Paranoia made the next few seconds stretch out torturously, but, finally, the wary trooper looked away from the Jetta, back toward the road ahead. Putting on a sudden

the Jeep and the Jetta were acquiring new paint jobs before their eyes, the surprising new hues flowing the cars' old colors like a high tide washing over a dy shore. Liz felt a stab of guilt, knowing that Max and others must be frantic to rescue her if they were willing use their powers so flagrantly in broad daylight.

"Holy cow!" Okada exclaimed. For a moment, he sounded more intrigued than panicked, his scientific curiosity piqued by the two automobiles' inexplicable transformations. "How is that possible?"

The switch occurred in seconds; only moments later, the red Jetta and olive Jeep had been completely replaced by their green and black counterparts. Infuriated by his inability to comprehend what he had just witnessed, Morton turned on Liz, jabbing his semi-automatic pistol under her chin. The steel muzzle felt hot against her tender skin. "Who are you kids?" Morton demanded, spittle flying from his blubbery lips. His face was so close to hers that she could taste his sour breath, see his yellow, tobacco-stained teeth. "*What* are you?"

The blaring police siren, growing louder by the minute, spared Liz any need to reply immediately. "Oh crap!" Okada screeched, his voice cracking. Flashing blue lights were now visible behind them, passing the transformed Jeep and Jetta to chase after the speeding convertible and its passengers. "It's the State Patrol!"

"Later," Morton promised Liz ominously, before giving the cop car his full attention. "Faster!" he ordered Okada, yanking his face and gun away from his frightened hostage. "Give it everything you've got!"

The Chevy shot like a rocket down the lonely desert road, leaving the Jeep and the Jetta far behind, but the

burst of renewed speed, the flashing cop car accelerated away from them in pursuit, Maria assumed, of the fleeing blue Chevy.

Letting her forehead droop onto the steering wheel, Maria let out a fervent sigh of relief, and wondered if she was ever going to get used to being on the run from the authorities. *I'd better get used to it,* she mused, *if I'm going to keep hanging out with Michael and the rest of the Pod Squad.*

They had gotten away with it this time, but at an excruciating cost. Maria stared straight ahead at the disappearing lights of the patrol car. Morton and his convertible were nowhere to be seen, already long gone. She heard a brokenhearted groan from the backseat, but found herself afraid to turn around and look Max in the eyes.

They had lost Liz.

21

"Shoot-outs. Kidnapping. Chases. This is more than I bargained for!" the science guy shouted over the wind blowing in their faces. Behind the wheel of the blue convertible, he sounded positively hysterical. "You just said that you needed a couple of tests done, that there was no danger, damnit! Now look at us. We're fugitives!"

"Shut up and drive!" Morton ordered from the backseat, where he kept guard over Liz while glaring back at the vehicles doggedly pursuing them. He fired again, *bang, bang,* then swore venomously as his shots missed their targets. "Who the hell are these kids?"

Trapped in the back of the Chevy with the enraged gunman, Liz flinched every time the gun went off, throwing her hands over her ears. Morton's unhappy curses came as a relief to her, since they meant his bullets had not yet found her friends. *Be careful!* she silently urged Max and the others, deathly afraid that someone she cared for might be hurt or killed while trying to rescue her. She felt like she was caught in an endless, recurring nightmare, one that

had started two years ago in the Crash first risked everything to save her. *How m* spaired, *is Joe Morton going to make my frie selves in jeopardy for my sake?*

A siren cried shrilly somewhere behind th didn't know whether to welcome or dread the the police. She was being kidnapped, true, but she way too many secrets of her own, secrets that, at a needed to be hidden from any and all official attenti

The driver's reaction to the distant siren was a good less ambiguous. "Oh, God," he moaned. "I'm going to ja He peered, ashen-faced, into the rearview mirror, watchin for the inevitable appearance of a police car in hot pursuit. "This can't be happening! I'm a scientist, not an outlaw!"

"Stop whining!" Morton berated the terrified techie. "Hit the gas! Faster!" He looked like he wanted to strangle the driver and take the wheel himself. "No one's locking me up now, not this close to the big payoff!" Liz knew he was talking about the briefcase full of alien hardware, now resting on the passenger seat beside the self-proclaimed scientist. "Hit the gas or I swear I'll blow your head off right here and now!"

The Chevy sped up dramatically, the sudden acceleration throwing Liz back against the padded seat cushions. "That's better," Morton muttered, twisting around to check out the road behind him. "What the—!"

His florid, bloodthirsty features went pale and slack as he witnessed something that shocked him to the core. "Okada!" he called hoarsely to the science guy, whose name Liz finally learned. "Look behind us. Am I going crazy or are those cars changing color?"

Liz risked a peek back over her shoulder. Sure enough,

black-and-white police car continued to gain on them. "ATTENTION: YOU IN THE BLUE CHEVROLET," an amplified voice addressed them sternly. "THIS IS THE STATE PATROL!" Liz heard Okada whimper pathetically; the distraught scientist was definitely not cut out for a life of crime. "SLOW DOWN AND PULL OVER AT ONCE. I REPEAT: SLOW DOWN AND PULL OVER!"

"The hell I will!" Morton snarled, aiming his pistol at the oncoming police vehicle. "Nobody's taking my merchandise away from me now!"

He opened fire, unleashing an ear-splitting salvo of gunshots against the cops, who must have gotten nearer to the Chevy than the Jeep or the Jetta ever did, because Morton's bullets inflicted a lot more damage this time around. One shot perforated the hood of the police car, causing an eruption of steam and smoke from the engine below, while another shot tore apart the besieged car's right front tire. Morton chortled with vicious glee as the injured vehicle lost control and swerved off the road into the desert, bulldozing through a stand of thorny mesquite before coming to rest amid a miniature sandstorm generated by the car's own bumpy landing.

"Hah!" Morton gloated. "Serves them right!" Liz crossed her fingers, praying that the officers were okay. She stared intently, hoping to see the troopers emerge unscathed from their wrecked vehicle, but the gritty cloud obscured her view, and the Chevy literally left the crash scene in the dust as they made their getaway, Okada still whimpering quietly to himself.

Liz searched the empty roadway stretching out behind them. She spotted no sign of either the Jeep or Maria's

Jetta. Had the police car chased them off? She didn't need extrasensory perception to appreciate the dilemma her friends must have been in. *I'm on my own,* she realized, numb with horror. No cavalry was coming, not right away, leaving her alone and helpless with a man who had already come close to killing her once before. *Maybe this time,* she thought, *my luck has run out.*

Consumed by a crazed desire to get as far away from the stranded State Patrol vehicle as possible, Okada kept his foot to the gas pedal, not slowing until they were well into the foothills of the looming Guadalupe Mountains. "I don't believe this! This can't be happening!" Okada kept repeating over and over, apparently unable to believe that his career as a legitimate scientist had led him to this bullet-strewn flight from justice; Liz would have felt sorry for him if her own future career prospects, along with her life, weren't also hanging by a thread.

"I've been thinking," Okada said, glancing nervously back at Morton. "Maybe we should just turn ourselves in, before anybody gets hurt." The Chevy slowed to under fifty mph, so that the reluctant fugitive could concentrate on persuading his volatile partner. "I mean, this whole thing is getting way out of control. Testing some spacy metal you liberated from the feds is one thing, but taking hostages, shooting at police cars—that wasn't part of the deal!"

"Forget it!" Morton said forcefully. "Nobody's talking to the police about anything." He gave Liz a murderous look. "Let me worry about the girl."

But Okada wasn't taking no for an answer. "I'm serious, Morton. You're going to get us both killed, in a police shoot-out, probably!" Mustering all his courage, the rebel-lious scientist tried to lay down the law. "Well, no way. I'm a PhD, not a desperado. My life is worth more than that!"

"Why, you——!" Morton lunged from the backseat, losing his temper, but stopped himself before actually attacking the man driving the car. He took a deep breath, regaining control, then contemplated his mutinous accomplice with a calculating look upon his ruddy face. "Okay," he said eventually. "Pull over to the side so we can talk this over."

Liz didn't like the sound of this, but she kept her mouth shut. If there was any chance that Okada could talk Morton into letting her go, she was all for it, even though that prospect struck her as extremely unlikely. *Stay out of this,* she told herself prudently. *You don't want to get between two desperate men, especially when one of them is armed.*

Coming to a halt next to some desert shrubs, Okada parked the Chevy, then turned to confront Morton. "About time you started seeing sense," he said, wiping the perspiration from his forehead. "Things are bad enough already. We don't want to let this disaster escalate into a full-fledged bloodbath!"

"Yeah, whatever you say," Morton grunted. He shoved Liz down into her seat. "Don't move a muscle!" he threatened her before swinging open the back door and stepping out of the convertible, where he then yanked open Okada's door as well. "Get out," he ordered the scientist.

"What? I don't understand?" Okada peered up fearfully at Morton, suddenly very reluctant to surrender the wheel. His Adam's apple bobbed up and down like a sine wave as he made another stab at reasoning with the stocky gunman. "I thought we were going to talk about this...."

"Get out, I said!" Morton bellowed. He plucked Okada's

glasses off the shocked scientist's nose and hurled them into the gravel at his feet. Liz heard glass and plastic shatter beneath the gunman's cowboy boot. "Talk time's over," Morton snarled, grabbing hold of Okada's collar and dragging him out of the parked convertible. He spun the smaller man around so that Okada's back faced the desert scrub, then pushed him away. Sneering coldly, Morton raised his gun. "Guess I don't need you anymore, professor."

"No, wait!" Okada cried out, trying to ward off death by throwing up his hands. He stumbled backward, almost tripping over a patch of plump cacti. "Let's work this out!"

Liz knew she should look away, but all she could do was cover her ears as a single gunshot permanently ended Okada's scientific career. His crumpled body lay amid the cacti, a crimson stream irrigating the sun-baked soil. Morton gave the body a savage kick that sent it rolling into a deep ditch beside the road. "How much is your life worth now, Mr. PhD?" he remarked snidely.

"You—you killed him," Liz stammered, the callous execution nearly triggering another post-traumatic flashback to her own shooting. She clutched her stomach protectively, but, with considerable effort, forced her tumultuous thoughts to stay firmly rooted in the present. *I have to keep my wits about me,* she realized, *if I want to get out of this alive.*

The odds of that were looking slimmer and slimmer, though. Liz knew that Morton would not have shot Okada right in front of her if he had any intention of letting her go. The only reason she wasn't dead yet, she figured, was that Morton still wanted to know how she and her friends were connected to all this, not to mention how they man-

burst of renewed speed, the flashing cop car accelerated away from them in pursuit, Maria assumed, of the fleeing blue Chevy.

Letting her forehead droop onto the steering wheel, Maria let out a fervent sigh of relief, and wondered if she was ever going to get used to being on the run from the authorities. *I'd better get used to it,* she mused, *if I'm going to keep hanging out with Michael and the rest of the Pod Squad.*

They had gotten away with it this time, but at an excruciating cost. Maria stared straight ahead at the disappearing lights of the patrol car. Morton and his convertible were nowhere to be seen, already long gone. She heard a brokenhearted groan from the backseat, but found herself afraid to turn around and look Max in the eyes.

They had lost Liz.

21

"Shoot-outs. Kidnapping. Chases. This is more than I bargained for!" the science guy shouted over the wind blowing in their faces. Behind the wheel of the blue convertible, he sounded positively hysterical. "You just said that you needed a couple of tests done, that there was no danger, damnit! Now look at us. We're fugitives!"

"Shut up and drive!" Morton ordered from the backseat, where he kept guard over Liz while glaring back at the vehicles doggedly pursuing them. He fired again, *bang, bang,* then swore venomously as his shots missed their targets. "Who the hell are these kids?"

Trapped in the back of the Chevy with the enraged gunman, Liz flinched every time the gun went off, throwing her hands over her ears. Morton's unhappy curses came as a relief to her, since they meant his bullets had not yet found her friends. *Be careful!* she silently urged Max and the others, deathly afraid that someone she cared for might be hurt or killed while trying to rescue her. She felt like she was caught in an endless, recurring nightmare, one that had started two years ago in the Crashdown, when Max first risked everything to save her. *How many times,* she despaired, *is Joe Morton going to make my friends place themselves in jeopardy for my sake?*

A siren cried shrilly somewhere behind them, and Liz didn't know whether to welcome or dread the advent of the police. She was being kidnapped, true, but she also had way too many secrets of her own, secrets that, at all costs, needed to be hidden from any and all official attention.

The driver's reaction to the distant siren was a good deal less ambiguous. "Oh, God," he moaned. "I'm going to jail." He peered, ashen-faced, into the rearview mirror, watching for the inevitable appearance of a police car in hot pursuit. "This can't be happening! I'm a scientist, not an outlaw!"

"Stop whining!" Morton berated the terrified techie. "Hit the gas! Faster!" He looked like he wanted to strangle the driver and take the wheel himself. "No one's locking me up now, not this close to the big payoff!" Liz knew he was talking about the briefcase full of alien hardware, now resting on the passenger seat beside the self-proclaimed scientist. "Hit the gas or I swear I'll blow your head off right here and now!"

The Chevy sped up dramatically, the sudden acceleration throwing Liz back against the padded seat cushions. "That's better," Morton muttered, twisting around to check out the road behind him. "What the—!"

His florid, bloodthirsty features went pale and slack as he witnessed something that shocked him to the core. "Okada!" he called hoarsely to the science guy, whose name Liz finally learned. "Look behind us. Am I going crazy or are those cars changing color?"

Liz risked a peek back over her shoulder. Sure enough,

both the Jeep and the Jetta were acquiring new paint jobs right before their eyes, the surprising new hues flowing over the cars' old colors like a high tide washing over a sandy shore. Liz felt a stab of guilt, knowing that Max and the others must be frantic to rescue her if they were willing to use their powers so flagrantly in broad daylight.

"Holy cow!" Okada exclaimed. For a moment, he sounded more intrigued than panicked, his scientific curiosity piqued by the two automobiles' inexplicable transformations. "How is that possible?"

The switch occurred in seconds; only moments later, the red Jetta and olive Jeep had been completely replaced by their green and black counterparts. Infuriated by his inability to comprehend what he had just witnessed, Morton turned on Liz, jabbing his semi-automatic pistol under her chin. The steel muzzle felt hot against her tender skin. "Who are you kids?" Morton demanded, spittle flying from his blubbery lips. His face was so close to hers that she could taste his sour breath, see his yellow, tobacco-stained teeth. "*What* are you?"

The blaring police siren, growing louder by the minute, spared Liz any need to reply immediately. "Oh crap!" Okada screeched, his voice cracking. Flashing blue lights were now visible behind them, passing the transformed Jeep and Jetta to chase after the speeding convertible and its passengers. "It's the State Patrol!"

"Later," Morton promised Liz ominously, before giving the cop car his full attention. "Faster!" he ordered Okada, yanking his face and gun away from his frightened hostage. "Give it everything you've got!"

The Chevy shot like a rocket down the lonely desert road, leaving the Jeep and the Jetta far behind, but the black-and-white police car continued to gain on them. "ATTENTION: YOU IN THE BLUE CHEVROLET," an amplified voice addressed them sternly. "THIS IS THE STATE PATROL!" Liz heard Okada whimper pathetically; the distraught scientist was definitely not cut out for a life of crime. "SLOW DOWN AND PULL OVER AT ONCE. I REPEAT: SLOW DOWN AND PULL OVER!"

"The hell I will!" Morton snarled, aiming his pistol at the oncoming police vehicle. "Nobody's taking my merchandise away from me now!"

He opened fire, unleashing an ear-splitting salvo of gunshots against the cops, who must have gotten nearer to the Chevy than the Jeep or the Jetta ever did, because Morton's bullets inflicted a lot more damage this time around. One shot perforated the hood of the police car, causing an eruption of steam and smoke from the engine below, while another shot tore apart the besieged car's right front tire. Morton chortled with vicious glee as the injured vehicle lost control and swerved off the road into the desert, bulldozing through a stand of thorny mesquite before coming to rest amid a miniature sandstorm generated by the car's own bumpy landing.

"Hah!" Morton gloated. "Serves them right!" Liz crossed her fingers, praying that the officers were okay. She stared intently, hoping to see the troopers emerge unscathed from their wrecked vehicle, but the gritty cloud obscured her view, and the Chevy literally left the crash scene in the dust as they made their getaway, Okada still whimpering quietly to himself.

Liz searched the empty roadway stretching out behind them. She spotted no sign of either the Jeep or Maria's

Jetta. Had the police car chased them off? She didn't need extrasensory perception to appreciate the dilemma her friends must have been in. *I'm on my own,* she realized, numb with horror. No cavalry was coming, not right away, leaving her alone and helpless with a man who had already come close to killing her once before. *Maybe this time,* she thought, *my luck has run out.*

Consumed by a crazed desire to get as far away from the stranded State Patrol vehicle as possible, Okada kept his foot to the gas pedal, not slowing until they were well into the foothills of the looming Guadalupe Mountains. "I don't believe this! This can't be happening!" Okada kept repeating over and over, apparently unable to believe that his career as a legitimate scientist had led him to this bullet-strewn flight from justice; Liz would have felt sorry for him if her own future career prospects, along with her life, weren't also hanging by a thread.

"I've been thinking," Okada said, glancing nervously back at Morton. "Maybe we should just turn ourselves in, before anybody gets hurt." The Chevy slowed to under fifty mph, so that the reluctant fugitive could concentrate on persuading his volatile partner. "I mean, this whole thing is getting way out of control. Testing some spacy metal you liberated from the feds is one thing, but taking hostages, shooting at police cars—that wasn't part of the deal!"

"Forget it!" Morton said forcefully. "Nobody's talking to the police about anything." He gave Liz a murderous look. "Let me worry about the girl."

But Okada wasn't taking no for an answer. "I'm serious, Morton. You're going to get us both killed, in a police shoot-out, probably!" Mustering all his courage, the rebel-lious scientist tried to lay down the law. "Well, no way. I'm a PhD, not a desperado. My life is worth more than that!"

"Why, you—!" Morton lunged from the backseat, losing his temper, but stopped himself before actually attacking the man driving the car. He took a deep breath, regaining control, then contemplated his mutinous accomplice with a calculating look upon his ruddy face. "Okay," he said eventually. "Pull over to the side so we can talk this over."

Liz didn't like the sound of this, but she kept her mouth shut. If there was any chance that Okada could talk Morton into letting her go, she was all for it, even though that prospect struck her as extremely unlikely. *Stay out of this,* she told herself prudently. *You don't want to get between two desperate men, especially when one of them is armed.*

Coming to a halt next to some desert shrubs, Okada parked the Chevy, then turned to confront Morton. "About time you started seeing sense," he said, wiping the perspiration from his forehead. "Things are bad enough already. We don't want to let this disaster escalate into a full-fledged bloodbath!"

"Yeah, whatever you say," Morton grunted. He shoved Liz down into her seat. "Don't move a muscle!" he threatened her before swinging open the back door and stepping out of the convertible, where he then yanked open Okada's door as well. "Get out," he ordered the scientist.

"What? I don't understand?" Okada peered up fearfully at Morton, suddenly very reluctant to surrender the wheel. His Adam's apple bobbed up and down like a sine wave as he made another stab at reasoning with the stocky gunman. "I thought we were going to talk about this...."

"Get out, I said!" Morton bellowed. He plucked Okada's

glasses off the shocked scientist's nose and hurled them into the gravel at his feet. Liz heard glass and plastic shatter beneath the gunman's cowboy boot. "Talk time's over," Morton snarled, grabbing hold of Okada's collar and dragging him out of the parked convertible. He spun the smaller man around so that Okada's back faced the desert scrub, then pushed him away. Sneering coldly, Morton raised his gun. "Guess I don't need you anymore, professor."

"No, wait!" Okada cried out, trying to ward off death by throwing up his hands. He stumbled backward, almost tripping over a patch of plump cacti. "Let's work this out!"

Liz knew she should look away, but all she could do was cover her ears as a single gunshot permanently ended Okada's scientific career. His crumpled body lay amid the cacti, a crimson stream irrigating the sun-baked soil. Morton gave the body a savage kick that sent it rolling into a deep ditch beside the road. "How much is your life worth now, Mr. PhD?" he remarked snidely.

"You—you killed him," Liz stammered, the callous execution nearly triggering another post-traumatic flashback to her own shooting. She clutched her stomach protectively, but, with considerable effort, forced her tumultuous thoughts to stay firmly rooted in the present. *I have to keep my wits about me,* she realized, *if I want to get out of this alive.*

The odds of that were looking slimmer and slimmer, though. Liz knew that Morton would not have shot Okada right in front of her if he had any intention of letting her go. The only reason she wasn't dead yet, she figured, was that Morton still wanted to know how she and her friends were connected to all this, not to mention how they managed to generate force fields, change the color of moving cars, etc. *Couldn't hurt to remind him of all those unanswered questions,* she judged, just in case he was thinking of disposing of her at the same time as Okada.

"You know, my friends are going to keep looking for me," she warned him, crouching in the backseat of the Chevy. "They're very talented. They can *do* all sorts of things." It felt weird to hint, even obliquely, at the hybrids' special abilities to such an untrustworthy character, but at this point, Liz reasoned, the paranormal cat was pretty thoroughly out of the bag. "You don't want to make them too angry."

Was that a flicker of fear in Morton's bloodshot eyes? "Yeah? Well, you don't want to get *me* mad, little lady." He placed a fresh clip into his handgun and lumbered toward the front seat of the convertible. Before he could sit down, however, another siren wailed nearby. *The same patrol car,* Liz wondered, *or reinforcements?* For her friends' sake, she hoped Max and the others were keeping a low profile.

"Damn!" Morton cursed. He eyed the Chevy dubiously, suddenly seeing it as a liability. He checked the dashboard and grunted. "Almost out of gas anyway," she heard him mutter, moments before he grabbed the attaché case from the passenger seat and picked up a canvas backpack from beneath the glove compartment. He tossed the backpack, which she recognized as the one Alex had donated to Michael and Isabel's con routine, at Liz, hitting her in the chest. "Take that," he ordered brusquely, taking a long, hard look at the arid wasteland and the ocher foothills beyond. "We're going for a hike."

22

The cave was dark and gloomy, the only light coming from a narrow entrance about twenty feet away. Liz squatted on the dank stone floor, her hands tied behind her back with duct tape, while Joe Morton checked to make sure the tape was secure. "Okay, that should hold you," he grunted, lurching to his feet behind her. He circled around so she could see the pistol tucked into his bulging waistband. "Don't try anything. I'm watching you."

They must have hiked a couple miles into the hills, before stumbling onto this primitive hideaway. *Must be one of those unexplored caverns I read about in the guidebook,* Liz guessed; it was even possible that they were back on the park grounds somewhere. Unfortunately, it didn't look like any tour guides would be coming along soon.

In search of better light, Morton trudged up to just within the cave's secluded entrance. Muttering irritably to himself, he dialed a number on the cell phone he had claimed from the glove compartment of the abandoned

Chevy. "Damnit," he grumbled, lifting the phone to his ear. "He'd better be there!"

Liz wondered whom he was calling, but not for long. "Ramirez!" the surly gunman barked into the phone. "This is Morton. What the hell were you thinking, sending those two air force clowns to surprise me?…Don't play dumb with me! They told me they worked with you, and they had the goods to prove it. Yeah, more leftovers from '47. Crazy stuff, too. An alien crash helmet and some kind of glow-in-the-dark antenna or something…What do you mean you've never heard of anything like that? I saw this merchandise with my own eyes!"

Liz realized he was talking about Isabel and Michael, and the phony alien gizmos they had whipped up at the Days Inn. She looked over at the canvas backpack, currently resting against the notorious attaché case on the floor of the cave, only a few feet away. She assumed the bogus artifacts were still in the pack. Why else would Morton have forced her to carry it all this way? Not that this was likely to do her much good; even if she managed to get her hands free, what could she do with a shower cap and a twisted wire hanger?

It took several minutes, but Ramirez somehow managed to convince Morton that he'd had nothing to do with the uniformed strangers at the Denny's. "Okay, okay, maybe you're on the level," Morton admitted reluctantly. "Something fishy's going on, though, and I don't like it." He scratched his ill-shaven jowls as he tried to figure out his next move. "Okay," he said finally, spitting a mouthful of tobacco juice onto the floor of the cavern. "Here's what we're going to do: You're going to meet me here, and I'll give you the rest of your cash in exchange for a ride to the Mexican border. Listen up...."

He gave the lieutenant detailed directions on how to find the cave, along with the number of his cell phone, just in case Ramirez got lost. He did *not* mention anything about transporting a teenage girl as well, which made Liz feel scarily expendable. *I have to give him a reason to keep me alive,* she realized, even as Morton wrapped up his call. "Make it fast," he warned Ramirez. "No one's going to find me here, but the sooner I get the merchandise out of the country, the better it will be—for you and me both."

He hung up on Ramirez and stuck the phone in his back pocket. "Okay, Red," he announced, leering at Liz from the top of the cavern's sloping floor. "Now it's your turn." He marched toward her, rubbing his meaty palms together in anticipation, until he was right in front of her, looking down at his hostage with cruel, bestial eyes. "We've got a couple of hours to kill, and I've got plenty of questions that need answers. Sounds doable to me, as long as you cooperate. Otherwise, things could get kind of ugly."

Yeah, right, Liz thought skeptically. *Like you're really going to let me live if I tell you everything I know.* She knew that her only chance was to make like Scheherazade and give Morton just enough info to keep him good and anxious to hear more. *Think of it as a challenge,* she thought, *something to keep my brain too busy to freak out.*

The fear—the blind, unreasoning panic—was still there, ready to reduce her to a trembling wreck once more, but Liz fought against the creeping terror, and was surprised to find herself coping. *Maybe it's because,* she speculated, *the only thing that can drown out those awful memories from my past is facing the very same threat in the present!* It was almost funny, in a blackly comic way. *Alex said I needed to confront my fears, but I don't think he meant quite this literally!*

"W-what do you want to know?" she asked, her voice quavering a little. Even if she hadn't been squatting on the floor, Morton would have been much taller than she; as is, he towered over her like a fairy-tale ogre or giant.

"First off, who are you?" Morton scrutinized her face, rubbing his chin. "The hair is different, but I've seen you before." He bent over to brush some newly-red tresses away from her face. Liz shuddered as his callused knuckles momentarily brushed her cheek. "Yeah, I got it now. You're the girl from the gift shop yesterday, the one I shot at Roswell a couple years back! At that dopey sci-fi diner."

Liz decided to play dumb, if only to buy time. "Diner? Roswell? I don't know what you're talking about." *Isabel would know how to wrap this guy around her little finger,* she thought mournfully, but all Liz could think to do was fake a vacant expression. "Trust me, I've never been shot!"

"No," Morton said, shaking his head. His rancid breath made her stomach turn. "I remember you now. I shot you by accident, while I was wrestling with that butt-headed idiot. The papers said you hadn't been hit, but I *know* I shot you."

Without warning, he knelt down and tore open Liz's blouse, looking for the bullet wound. Instead his eyes widened in astonishment as he discovered the silver handprint, still shining brightly upon her belly. In the murky gloom of the cave, the mark's eerie glow was even more apparent. "What in the world—?"

The luminous handprint, on top of everything else he'd witnessed today, actually seemed to frighten the brutal gunman. He sprang to his feet, jumping back from the glowing sigil as though it might be dangerously radioactive. "What the hell is that?" he hollered at Liz, pulling out his pistol and waving it wildly. "What does it mean?"

Her eyes nervously tracking every swoop of the lethal handgun, Liz tried to calm Morton. "It's just a tattoo!" she insisted lamely, wiggling her torso so that her sundered shirt fell more or less back into place, concealing the telltale handprint. "Everybody has one!"

"Don't give me that b.s.!" Morton shouted, his frenzied words echoing inside the cavern. An insane gleam came into his eyes, and Liz sensed that the volatile, trigger-happy gunman was on the verge of losing his cool altogether. *Not* an encouraging development. "What's going on here?" he ranted, his cowboy boots stamping against the floor of the cave. "What was that freaky light show your boyfriend put on back at the motel? And how did your friends pull that stunt with their cars?"

He paced back and forth across the cave, yelling like a lunatic. "Those *are* your friends, right? The guy in my room. That pair at Denny's. The girl in my dreams...!" He fell silent for a second, realizing what he was saying. Throwing his cap on the ground, he ran a shaking hand over his balding cranium. "Are you trying to drive me insane, is that it?"

"No, no!" Liz assured him. She looked up at him plaintively, trying to convince him of her sincerity. "It's nothing like that! We're just a bunch of kids, that's all."

"Like hell you are!" Morton accused. He tore open the backpack and pulled out the two counterfeit gadgets.

"How do you explain these babies?" He laid the wire rosette on the floor of the cave and tapped it hesitantly with a pudgy finger.

Nothing happened. Of course.

"Huh? What's the matter?" he wondered, looking utterly baffled. He savagely ripped the silver shower cap in half, then tried to get the two ragged pieces to merge together again, which was not about to take place. Frustrated and upset, unaware that he'd been conned by a bit of extraterrestrial sleight of hand, Morton flung the torn silver segments at Liz's lap. "What's wrong with them?" he demanded. "Why won't they work?"

"I don't know," Liz mumbled, uncertain what tack to take. What would rile Morton more, finding out his artifacts were fakes or thinking that they weren't? "Maybe they're broken?" she suggested meekly.

"Fix them!" he barked savagely. The muzzle of his gun pointed straight between her eyes. *Could Max heal me,* she wondered instantly, *if I was shot in the head?*

"I can't," she pleaded helplessly. "My hands…" If nothing else, the duct tape gave her an excuse to leave the phony gadgets alone. Morton looked unconvinced, though, so she tried something else. "Besides, repairs aren't my…area of expertise."

Morton's trigger hand dropped to his side as he gazed at her wide-eyed. "So you *are* one of Them." His booming voice dropped to a raspy hush. "I always knew You were out there—where else could the merchandise come from?—but I never thought I'd ever run into one of You for real." He wiped the sweat from his glistening, sunburned brow. His bald spot, Liz observed, was paler and less florid than the rest of his head. "I was just trying to make a buck, you know?"

He circled her warily, keeping his distance now that he thought she was a visitor from another planet. *This would be funny,* Liz thought, *if it wasn't so dangerous.* Pretending to be an alien was a risky game, but if it kept Morton away from her. . . .

"Is that your real form?" he asked apprehensively, looking her over from several feet away. He was still hanging onto his gun, but at least it wasn't aimed at her skull anymore.

"It is now," Liz said cryptically. *Keep him guessing,* she thought.

"Damn!" Morton exclaimed, getting over his initial fright. "This is incredible." He stared at her as if she had suddenly sprouted tentacles or something. "Where— where are you from?"

Liz raised her eyes heavenward, hoping she wouldn't be joining the angels soon. *Is he buying this,* she marveled, *and do I really want him to?*

"Good God," he exclaimed. "I wouldn't have believed it if I hadn't seen it with my own eyes." Liz assumed he meant Max's force field, the missing bullet wound, and everything else, not her nonexistent tentacles. She didn't think Morton was *that* much of a psycho.

"Please, you can't tell anyone!" she begged, mimicking Max, Isabel, and Michael. If there was one thing she knew about being an alien, it was that they didn't like their secrets revealed. "We come in peace. We mean you no harm!"

Was that too corny? she worried. *Maybe I should just speak when spoken to.*

"Tell anyone?" Morton laughed heartlessly. "I can't decide whether to kill you on the spot—or sell you to the highest bidder." He started pacing again, thinking out loud as he pondered the fate of his "alien" captive. "If those metal spaceship parts are worth a couple million, how much could I get for an actual alien?"

Bloodthirsty rage and confusion succumbed to calculating greed as the ruthless gunman considered his options. Dollar signs replaced the manic gleam in Morton's eyes, which started looking on Liz like she was just another piece of contraband salvaged from the Crash. Liz guessed that was an improvement, but she couldn't imagine that her alien act was a workable, long-term solution. *Somehow I've got to get away from Morton,* she knew, *before he figures out that I'm nothing more than a completely human eyewitness to Okada's murder.*

Her gaze shifted from the sunlit entrance of the cave to the impenetrable darkness farther within. Who knew how deep—or how far—this tunnel extended into the Earth? Liz didn't relish the idea of escaping into the lightless depths of the unexplored cave, but it might be her only option, provided Morton ever stopped watching her for a second. She wondered how far she'd have to descend before she'd be safe from his bullets?

"Listen up, spacegirl," Morton snarled, interrupting her desperate search for a way out. He planted himself on a squat rock formation between Liz and the exit to the desert outside. "I've thought it over, and here's what we're going to do. The way I figure it, you're too valuable to just throw away, even if you are some kind of spooky monster from outer space. I have contacts in Mexico who will pay good money to examine your alien carcass, so you're coming with me across the border."

He toyed with his loaded semi-automatic as his voice and expression grew deliberately threatening. "Here's the catch. A live alien is worth more than a dead one, but I'll settle for the lower price if you give me any trouble. Got that?"

Liz nodded, afraid to speak for fear of giving herself away. From the sound of it, she had just bought herself a few more hours of life.

"Good." Morton appeared satisfied with her response. Relaxing somewhat, as he settled in to wait for Ramirez, he regarded Liz with frank curiosity. "You have a name?" he asked brusquely. "What do I call you anyway?"

Liz went with the scariest alien name she could think of. "Tess," she said. "My people call me Tess."

23

"Yeah, Mom, we're having a little car trouble, so we might be getting home a bit later than planned." Max held the cell phone to his ear. "No, nothing serious. Thanks for the offer, but you don't have to send Dad down to pick us up. Don't worry, we'll definitely be back in time for school tomorrow."

I hope, Max thought. Until they found Liz, nothing else mattered, but he could hardly tell his foster parents that. They didn't know anything about his alien origins, let alone the dangers he and Isabel often faced because of those origins. Max saw the miserable look on his sister's face as he wrapped up the call home; he knew she hated lying to their mom and dad.

Isabel and the others kept their voices down until he hung up the phone. They were all seated around a circular table at a roadside pizza parlor on the outskirts of Carlsbad. An obvious tourist trap, Caverns of Cheese was decorated with a subterranean motif, complete with sparkly, aluminum foil stalactites, plus rubber bats hanging on strings from the ceiling. Sort of the Carlsbad Caverns version of the Crashdown Cafe, in other words.

Max was in no mood to appreciate the campy decor. "Well, that's taken care of," he announced glumly, "but that doesn't get us any closer to finding Liz." He blamed himself for Liz's abduction; it had been his plan, after all, that had gone so badly astray. "I can't believe everything fell apart like that."

"Yeah," Maria agreed. A whiff of rosemary oil mingled with the aroma of the pizza between them. "I don't get it. Why did Morton unplug the phone in his motel room?"

Sitting next to Maria, melted cheese dripping from the pizza slice in his hand, Michael offered a possible explanation. "When I talked to Morton on the phone, he got all freaked-out and paranoid about the line not being secure. Guess he was worried about wiretaps or something. He must have unplugged the phone to keep me from calling that number again."

That makes too much sense, Max thought. Not that it really mattered anymore; Liz was still missing and they had no idea where Morton had taken her, or if she was even alive. *No! She can't be dead*, he thought passionately. *I'd feel it if she wasn't still out there somewhere!*

Alex wandered back to the table, cell phone in hand, having briefly stepped outside to make an important call in a slightly more private environment. "Okay, I finally got hold of Valenti," he told his friends, lowering his voice so it wouldn't carry to any of the other tables. "There's an all-points bulletin out for the unnamed suspect who shot up the Denny's, but the local police haven't caught up with him yet. The worst part is that they found Morton's Chevy abandoned on a back road near the northern end of the park. They also found the body of Morton's partner, who turns out to be a Dr. Wilson Okada of Las Cruces University, lying in a ditch next to the road."

Maria gasped, shocked by this confirmation of Morton's murderous nature. Isabel looked noticeably less surprised, having already witnessed firsthand the gunman's brutal execution of his previous partner.

"The only silver lining is," Alex continued, "they haven't found Liz's body. In fact, the cops aren't even aware yet that any girl has been abducted; I'm not sure if that last part's a good thing or not." He sat down at the table next to Isabel and helped himself to a slice of pizza. "There's not much Valenti can do right now, but he's going to keep his ears open. He'll let us know if the local cops turn up anything new."

"Thanks," Max said sincerely, appreciating Alex's efforts even if the news was less than encouraging. *If the State Patrol can't find Morton or Liz, what chance do we have?*

As if on cue, a bell rang as the front door swung open and two uniformed police officers strolled into the pizza place. A hush fell over the table as the five teenagers looked at each other nervously. None of them was looking forward to being interrogated regarding the events at the Denny's and Motel 6. *How did they find us?* Max worried, trying to look relaxed and unconcerned by the cops' presence. *Our cars and license plates look completely different.*

So did Michael and Isabel, whose fake air force uniforms had been transmuted back into ordinary street clothes during the chase through the desert.

He forced himself to munch casually on a piece of pizza, like any other hungry teenage boy, all the while watching the police officers out of the corner of his eye. At the same time he took a rapid inventory of the parlor's available exits, just in case they needed to make a break for it. His free hand wrapped around the car keys in his pocket, making sure he could get to them right away.

Despite all his hasty preparations, however, the two policemen simply marched up to the counter and ordered a couple of slices to go, paying no attention whatsoever to the tense teenagers. *False alarm*, Max realized, trying not to let his massive relief show. He saw the same realization dawning in the eyes of his partners in crime, but everyone around the table remained a bit on edge until the uniformed duo left Caverns of Cheese with their hot slices.

"Whew!" Maria exclaimed, speaking for all of them. "I don't know about the rest of you, but I was definitely feeling like America's Most Wanted there."

"Tell me about it!" Alex agreed readily. "I was already reviewing my Miranda rights, with special emphasis on the right to remain silent."

Michael and Isabel were markedly less vocal about whatever trepidations they might have just experienced, as was Max. *Perhaps that's because,* he speculated, *we've lived like fugitives every day of our lives.*

His own sense of relief was short-lived, driven out by his persistent fear and guilt regarding Liz. "I should have killed Morton when I had the chance," he accused himself pitilessly. His mind kept replaying that moment in room #19, when he'd hesitated before striking out at Morton with his powers. "I should have blasted him to ashes."

"Don't say that, Max," Michael said, giving his best friend and leader a worried look from across the table. "That's not like you. That's not who you are."

Anger flared inside Max, tempting him to lash out at his friend. *If Michael hadn't planted all those doubts in my mind*, he thought bitterly, *maybe I wouldn't have hesitated when it mattered most!* He swallowed the surging resentment, though, refusing to blame Michael or anyone else for his own fatal error. "It's all my fault," he insisted. "If I had struck first, if there had been no second thoughts, Liz might be safe now!"

"Maybe so," Michael conceded, "but it's not that simple." He fixed his friend and leader with a probing look. "What's worse, Maxwell, thinking twice before killing someone, or doing it without thinking?"

Max didn't have a ready answer.

Isabel broke the silence around the table. "We still have one more lead," she reminded them, fishing around in her handbag until she retrieved a crumpled slip of paper. "Lieutenant Ramirez's phone number."

Max's eyes lit up. "What are you thinking, Iz?"

"Maybe if I call Ramirez, I can convince him to help us," she suggested. "We know there's no love lost between him and Morton. Maybe if he knows that an innocent girl's life is in danger, he'll do the right thing."

It's a long shot, she thought, but they were running out of options. *The trick will be not telling Ramirez any more than he absolutely needs to know.*

Max nodded, considering Isabel's proposal from every angle. He looked more hopeful than he had before, something that made Isabel herself feel more confident. "It could work," he decided. "Judging from what Michael and I saw in Slaughter Canyon, we know that he's an unwilling partner in this whole enterprise. Morton is blackmailing him." He handed the cell phone to his sister. "Let's hope that, no matter what Morton has on him, Ramirez draws the line at kidnapping."

She accepted the phone, then took a deep breath, working up her nerve. Her slender fingers hovered about the push-button dial.

"You go, girl!" Maria cheered her on. "If this works, I will never mock your Pod-given talent for flirtation again, I promise!"

"Like I really care," Isabel shot back tartly, the brief exchange of repartee providing a boost to her confidence. She dialed Ramirez's number and tossed her hair back before lifting the phone to her ear. "Watch and learn."

The lieutenant picked up on the second ring. "Hello?" he answered, and Isabel thought his voice sounded more strained than it had at the Caverns. *Bet he had a sleepless night,* she guessed, *especially after Max and Michael crashed his midnight rendezvous with Morton.* "Who is this?" he asked worriedly.

"Hi, David!" she said cheerily, not wanting to lower the boom right away. "This is Isabel." It took her a second to recall what alias she had used before. "Isabel DeLuca. From the Bottomless Pit, remember?"

Maria shot daggers at Isabel, but the name rang a bell with Ramirez. "Oh yeah, right." A bit of enthusiasm crept into his voice, but he still sounded worn-out and distracted. "Thanks for calling, doll, but, umm, now is not really good for me. Maybe some other time…"

Isabel spoke quickly, before he could even think of

hanging up. "That's what I'm calling about, David." Her fingers nervously shredded a paper napkin as she trapped the phone between her head and shoulder. "I'm afraid I wasn't entirely honest with you yesterday." She winced and chewed on her lip. "You see, I know all about your... arrangement...with Joe Morton."

Dead silence greeted her unexpected declaration. "David? Are you still there?" At first, she thought maybe he had dropped the phone and run away, but then she realized she could still hear breathing coming over the line. Fast, erratic breathing, like someone in a state of shock. "David? Talk to me."

"Who are you?" he whispered hoarsely, in a broken, wretched parody of the deep, masculine voice he had used with her in the caverns. He didn't even sound like the same person anymore. Instead of a cocky air force test pilot, confident in his appeal, Ramirez now sounded like a man whose nerves had been stretched to the breaking point, if not beyond. "For God's sake, who are you really?"

Isabel felt like the straw that broke a once-proud soldier's back. "That's not important now," she told him bluntly. She would have time enough to feel bad for Ramirez later. "What you need to know is that Morton has kidnapped a friend of mine, an innocent young woman, and we believe her life is in danger."

"A woman?" Ramirez couldn't believe his ears. "What are you talking about? I spoke with Morton five minutes ago, and he didn't say anything about a woman!"

Isabel's breath caught in her throat. Ramirez *was* in touch with Morton, and maybe even knew where the gunman was right now. "Listen to me, David," she said urgently. "You have to believe me. Morton abducted our friend at gunpoint only a few hours ago. If you know where he is, you have to tell us."

But the distraught lieutenant sounded more obsessed with his own swiftly unraveling future than with Liz's safety. "I don't understand," he pleaded. "Who are you? How do you know all this? Who told you?" His voice went from a whisper to a tortured wail. "Are you FBI? CIA? Majestic?" He grew more panicked by the moment, until she could practically see the blood draining from his face. "Oh, good Lord, you're with the Special Unit!"

Hardly, Isabel thought. "I'm not out to get you, David. That's not what this is about. We just want to save our friend."

"We?" Ramirez echoed. "Who is 'we'?" He started shouting into the phone, so loudly that Isabel had to pull the receiver farther away from her ear. "Leave me alone, why don't you? For God's sake, leave me alone!"

He hung up abruptly. "David?" Isabel asked, but he was already gone. She redialed hastily, only to listen to the phone ring repeatedly, going unanswered. *Don't do this, David,* she thought despairingly. *Talk to me.*

But the futile ringing went on and on. Isabel finally gave up and put the phone down. "It's no good," she informed the others, all of whom had been hanging on her side of the dialogue with Ramirez. "I think he knows where Morton is, but he won't pick up the phone anymore." She looked at Max apologetically. "I think I scared him off."

"You did your best," Max assured her. "He's trafficking in

top secret materials, remember. At this point, the slightest hint of exposure probably causes him to wig out." He regarded Isabel thoughtfully, and she recognized the pensive expression on her brother's face; he was thinking strategically, like a general. Or a king.

"There may be another way," he stated after a few minutes. "Isabel, I know this is asking a lot of you, but do you think maybe you can contact the lieutenant more directly, mind to mind?"

"I don't know, Max," she said, shaking her head dubiously. She wanted to help, but... "You know that I usually can't enter anyone's thoughts unless they're sleeping, and Ramirez didn't sound like he was planning to take a nap anytime soon. In fact, he sounded like he hasn't been sleeping much at all."

And who could blame him? she thought. She wouldn't want to have her life and liberty in the hands of a hot-tempered sociopath like Joe Morton. *Should I have told Ramirez about Okada's murder,* she wondered, *or would that have just panicked him more?*

"I understand," Max said, entreating her with his eyes. Even if she didn't entirely approve of their risky relationship, Isabel knew how much Liz Parker meant to him. "I'm not asking for any guarantees—I realize the odds are against this working—but please, Iz, for Liz's sake, *try.*"

Feeling the weight of her brother's hopes and fears settling heavily upon her unsteady shoulders, Isabel picked up the scrap of paper bearing the lieutenant's phone number. Generally, she preferred to have an actual photo to focus upon, but perhaps she could use this improvised calling card, personally inscribed by Ramirez to her, as a stepping-stone to his unconscious mind?

"No promises," she reminded everyone, as she held the scribbled phone number before her eyes. *Paging David Ramirez,* she thought.

Ready or not, here I come.

24

It took Lieutenant Ramirez much longer than expected to find the uncharted cave, so that Morton was impatient and irritable by the time, several calls for directions later, that the overwrought air force pilot arrived at the entrance to the cave, flashlight in hand. With her wrists bound, Liz couldn't check what time it was, but she guessed that it had be to around three in the afternoon. Her stomach grumbled unhappily, reminding her that she hadn't eaten since breakfast. *That's the least of my problems,* she thought, wondering how long she could keep her captor thinking that she was an alien. Would her noisy stomach pangs give her away, or would Morton just assume that extraterrestrial humanoids got hungry, too?

"What the hell took you so long?" Morton griped as Ramirez entered the cave, the beam of his flashlight darting over the rough, uneven stone floor. "I've been cooling my heels in this goddamn rockpile for hours!" the bad-tempered gunman complained.

"It's not my fault!" Ramirez insisted, looking much as Isabel and Max had described him, only a lot more agitated and disheveled. Sweat streaked his bronzed features and soaked through his blue, short-sleeved dress shirt. "This place isn't exactly on the map, you know. Besides, the roads around here are prowling with State Patrol cars. I got stopped and questioned—three times!—before I finally found a place where I could park my car and head into the hills."

His flashlight searched the crevices of the secluded hideaway, quickly falling upon Liz's captive figure, duct tape and all. A tic in his cheek twitched alarmingly as he stared wide-eyed at Morton's prisoner. "Jesus Christ!" he exclaimed, going pale beneath his coppery tan. "It's true. You *have* snatched some girl!" He spun around, exposing Morton to the harsh white beam. "You kidnapped a teenager!"

"No," Morton rebutted, without a trace of remorse. "I captured an alien." He advanced on Ramirez, suddenly sounding suspicious. "Who told you I took the girl? The police? The news?"

But Ramirez, shocked by Morton's insane explanation, wasn't listening to the gunman's questions. "An alien? Are you out of your frigging mind?" He swung the flashlight back toward Liz, confirming that she looked entirely human, then unleashed a flood of hysterical invective at Morton. "You maniac! You rabid psychotic! You've gone completely insane!"

Squatting on the cold stone floor, several feet away, Liz saw a potential opportunity arising from the escalating conflict between the two men. *This might be my chance to make a break for it*, she realized, *if Ramirez distracts Morton enough.* Her gaze turned again toward the gaping darkness at the back of the cave, and her nerve faltered. Did she really want to run blindly into that unknown abyss?

Ramirez shoved past Morton, the beam of his flashlight sweeping the cave. "Where is my money, you lunatic?" he demanded, the shadows under his ravenous eyes making him look like one of the living dead. "You promised me the rest of my money!" The shifting light revealed the open backpack, lying next to the locked attaché case, and the frenzied lieutenant descended upon the canvas pack like a ravenous vulture, only to find it frustratingly empty. "Where is it?" he shouted at Morton, throwing the worthless pack to the cave floor. His cheek twitched spasmodically, like a severed frog's leg attached to a galvanic current. "Where is my money, you blackmailing son of a bitch!"

The hefty killer stood his ground, one hand on the grip of the pistol stuck in his waistband. "Later," he barked. "Tell me more about those state troopers. How much do they know about the girl?"

Good question, Liz thought, more than a little curious about that herself. She cautiously flexed her stiff leg muscles, restoring their circulation. Her whole body tensed, poised to run the minute Morton's full attention was elsewhere.

"Don't 'later' me!" Ramirez yelled, snapping completely. "I've had enough of this!" He kicked the leather briefcase with his foot, propelling it across the cave so that the case landed only inches away from Liz's bound wrists. "I want my money and I want it now!"

Morton laughed contemptuously, shrugging his burly shoulders. "Sorry, sport. I haven't got it on me. Guess you're going to have to wait until you get me to Mexico."

"Damn you!" the maddened pilot swore, pushed too far.

With an inarticulate cry of rage, he charged at Morton, colliding with the stocky gunman head-on and knocking him back against a roughhewn limestone wall. "You monster! You've ruined my life!"

Watching intently, Liz knew she would never have a better chance to get away. She sprang to her feet, fighting to keep her balance even though her arms were still bound behind her back. On an impulse, she bent quickly and half-kneeling, fumbled for and grabbed the handle of the attaché case with both hands, lifting it off the floor as she dashed for the concealing darkness. The bottom of the case banged against the back of her legs as she ran, but Liz held onto the handle tightly, suddenly unwilling to let Morton, or anyone else, profit from the hijacked alien technology. *These secrets belong to Max and the others,* she thought with fierce determination, *and to nobody else!*

The cave floor was bumpy and irregular beneath her sneakers, but Liz managed not to stumble or fall as the stygian depths enveloped her. What sparse daylight had penetrated the cave from outside swiftly evaporated, but, to her surprise, Liz discovered that she could still see dimly in the dark, winding corridors of the cavern. *How?* she wondered, marveling at the faint silver radiance lighting her way, then realized that the unexpected glow was coming from the incandescent handprint on her stomach, exposed again now that her headlong flight had thrown open the flaps of her torn blouse. *Thank you, Max!* she thought, gasping at this unexpected stroke of luck. In a sense, his miraculous touch had once again come to her rescue!

A shot rang out behind her, making her jump. She heard a cry of pain, then something metallic (the flashlight?) clattering onto the limestone floor, followed by the sound of a body hitting the ground. Liz prayed that Morton had somehow ended up at the business end of his own pistol, or that the lieutenant had been carrying a firearm as well, but those hopes were dashed when a familiar, bellicose voice registered her disappearance. "Damn!" Morton cursed loudly, his malevolent roar reverberating through the cramped underground tunnels. "Come back here, you alien witch!" he roared. "Come back right now, or you're as good as dead!"

No way, Liz thought. She'd rather take her chances with whatever pitfalls lay ahead, even if it meant getting hopelessly lost hundreds of feet beneath the surface. *Just like Becky Thatcher* in The Adventures of Tom Sawyer, she thought, shuddering. Except that Joe Morton was more real, or better armed, than Injun Joe ever was.

Hearing loud, stampeding footsteps behind her, she plunged deeper into the lower reaches of the cavern, her eyes probing the darksome gloom even as she rushed down a sloping corridor, trusting in luck, fate, and the preternatural light of the silver handprint to keep her from running into a jagged rock formation—or tumbling into a bottomless chasm.

"You can't get away from me, you freak!" Morton shouted, sounding far too close behind her. "You're dead, you hear me? I shot you once and I'll shoot you again!"

That's what I'm afraid of, Liz thought.

25

Where are you, David Ramirez? Why can't I find you?

Her eyelids squeezed shut, Isabel did her best to tune out the sights, sounds, and smells of the busy pizza parlor. She rubbed the vital scrap of paper between her fingers until it felt as thin and fragile as tissue. Her heightened consciousness reached out, sifting through hundreds of churning minds, before zeroing in on the one distinct psyche that could tell her what Max so desperately needed to know. She nudged at the fringes of the lieutenant's identity, seeking admittance. *Here I am, David,* she called out silently. *Let me into your dreams.*

"Any luck yet?" Maria asked, breaking Isabel's concentration. The alien beauty's eyes snapped open, impaling the other woman with a royally ticked-off glare. The entire table shushed Maria in unison, causing the exasperated teen to tilt backward on her chair, throwing up her hands. "Sorry! My bad," she apologized, sort of. "Excuse me for wondering how she was doing."

Outside Caverns of Cheese, the afternoon sun remained

high in the sky, yet Isabel felt the day slipping away, taking with it any hope of liberating Liz from Joe Morton's murderous clutches. A handful of soggy pieces of crust were all that was left of two pepperoni and Tabasco pizzas, but her friends kept ordering additional snacks and desserts just to avoid being asked to leave their ad hoc base of operations. Isabel feared they were wasting their time.

"It's no good, Max," Isabel confessed, feeling like a failure. She hated to disappoint him, but it was the truth. "I can sense him, somewhere nearby, but wherever he is, he's awake, not dreaming." She tried to explain, to make Max and the others understand why, no matter how strenuously she labored, she couldn't come through for them. "It's like his waking mind forms a wall around his identity, his essence. I can't slip inside until that wall comes down." She looked at her stylish designer watch and saw that it was not even 3:30 yet; the only creatures sleeping right now were the bats at Carlsbad Caverns. "He might not go to bed for hours."

Alex put down the cell phone, which he'd taken custody of earlier. "I keeping trying his number," he volunteered, "but no luck. Either he's not home or he's not answering."

"Great," Michael said sarcastically. "For all we know, the damn ringing is keeping him awake." He shoved his plate away from him in frustration. "Isabel is right, Max. This is getting us nowhere. We need to get out there and start looking for Morton and Liz."

"What do you suggest, Michael?" Max asked skeptically. "That we drive up and down every back road between here and the Rio Grande? We don't even know what kind of car he's driving now, if he's on the road at all. For all we know, he could be holed up anywhere."

He turned toward Isabel, his face drawn and haggard. Isabel hadn't seen him look this bad since that time he thought that Liz had cheated on him with Kyle. "Please, Iz," he begged her. "Try one more time."

If it will make him feel better. "Okay," she agreed, giving the worn scrap of paper her attention again. Caverns of Cheese slowly receded from her awareness as she closed her eyes and went into a familiar trance. *One more time,* she thought, with little hope of success. *Just to ease Max's mind...*

The floor of the cave was moist and surprisingly cool. Lieutenant David Ramirez lay bleeding where he fell, unable to move at all. Morton's bullet had shattered his spine, he realized, after blowing a hole in his chest. He couldn't feel anything at all below his shoulders, which was probably a mercy of sorts. He felt cold and dizzy, light-headed even.

He was dying, he knew that, alone in a cave with no one to hear his last words or confession. *So this is how it all ends,* he thought bitterly, mourning his once-promising future. He wished he'd never heard of Roswell or aliens or secret UFO technology. *At least,* he thought, *this spares the air force the expense of a court-martial.*

His eyelids drooped, and he found it hard to stay awake. *Just as well,* he decided, his ebbing consciousness surrendering to the encroaching darkness. Oblivion called to him and the lieutenant decided not to fight it anymore. *Goodbye,* he thought, shutting his eyes forever. *Guess this qualifies as a dishonorable discharge.*

Then, just as he was letting go of life, he heard another voice calling his name.

David? Is that you?

The wall came down, disintegrating into nothingness, and Isabel slipped into Ramirez's unresisting mind. She realized at once that this was no ordinary dream; the colors were strange and distorted, gray and monochromatic in some places, while luridly bright and garish elsewhere. Shapes and angles were stretched and pulled out of proportion, as though glimpsed in a funhouse mirror. *What's happening here?* Isabel wondered, disoriented. *Where am I?*

It took her an instant or two to get her bearings, then she found herself standing in an unfamiliar cave, less grandiose than Carlsbad's magnificent caverns, and more like the hidden Pod Chamber outside of Roswell. The ruffled limestone walls of the cave were black-and-white, like an old-time movie, but fluorescent golden sunshine, brighter than daffodils, invaded the rocky chamber from an opening to her right, giving her just enough light to see by.

A feeble moan caught her ear, and she looked down to see Ramirez lying at her feet, a gaping wound in his chest. The injured pilot was black-and-white, too, but someone had colorized his blood, which glowed as psychedelically as the pigments in a black-lighted painting. Neon-red fluid pooled beneath the lieutenant's body and leaked from the corners of his mouth. Isabel stepped back in horror, yanking the toes of her boots away from the spreading pool of gore, and threw her hands over her mouth. She suddenly became aware of a rhythmic throbbing noise, pounding in the background like rolling thunder many miles away. The muffled thumping, which she instinctively knew had to be Ramirez's own failing heartbeat, grew slower and fainter by the second.

"Oh my God," she realized. The lieutenant wasn't dreaming, he was dying! Morton must have shot Ramirez, just like he killed Okada, and the biker in the alley. But where was Liz? Isabel looked about rapidly, but saw no sign of the kidnapped girl, only Alex's backpack, lying crumpled on the stone floor. Where had Morton taken Liz after shooting the lieutenant? Perhaps only Ramirez knew.

I have to hurry, she thought, and not just for Liz's sake. She had wondered sometimes about what would happen to her if she stumbled into someone's mind at the very moment of their death; now she seemed dangerously close to finding out.

And, even more terrifying, she knew she would have to go even deeper into the dying man's consciousness to learn everything he knew of this place, and of Liz's fate. *What if I stay too long?* she worried, dread eating away at her resolve. *What if he takes me with him wherever he's going?*

"David?" she whispered, then tried again more loudly. "David!" The dying pilot's eyelids flickered momentarily, but that was all. All around her, the fading pulse ticked away toward its inevitable cessation.

Unable to avoid kneeling in the sticky, sickening crimson pool, she took Ramirez's head in her hands and tried to rouse him from his terminal slumber. "Wake up, David!" she shouted into his face. "Talk to me, please!"

At first, there was no response and Isabel feared she was too late. Out of the corner of her eyes, she saw ebony shadows creeping in on them from every corner of the cave, threatening to extinguish Ramirez's last spark of life. She could barely hear his faltering heartbeat anymore.

His eyes opened, making contact with hers. "Isabel?"

She dived into his deep brown orbs, the portals to his soul, and instantly landed inside his head, looking out through those same eyes at the craggy ceiling of the cave. Darkness closed in perilously, obscuring his/her view, but Isabel found what she was looking for in the churning recesses of his memory. *Yes!* she thought ecstatically, swimming back toward the rapidly shrinking light. *Time to go.*

Part of her regretted leaving Ramirez to face the ultimate blackness alone, but then she remembered how, on the phone, the blackmailed lieutenant had worried only about his security, not Liz's. She decided not to lose too much sleep over Ramirez's tragic end, despite the intimate bond they had just shared.

"Good-bye, David," she whispered, using his own quivering lips, then woke herself up....

Max was there, right where she'd left him, watching her with eyes so naked in their agonized hope that she had to look away. The rest of her friends were there as well, seated around the empty pizza trays. Alex took her hand and offered her a sip of water. "How did it go?" he asked gently.

She appreciated the tender treatment, but declined the water, unwilling to let her tormented brother suffer in suspense an instant longer.

"I did it," she told them, the salvaged memories and impressions still fresh in her mind. "I know where they are."

26

"I'm coming for you, space-girl! You can't get away from me! Give me back that case or I'll dissect you myself!"

Morton's threats reverberated through the twisting labyrinth of underground chambers, the echoes making it impossible to guess just how near or far away he was. Hiding in a chapel-like grotto, carved out eons ago by seeping water and sulfurous gases, Liz kept her eye out for the telltale gleam of Morton's flashlight, which she assumed he had appropriated from Lieutenant Ramirez, who had no doubt joined the gunman's ever-growing list of victims. Periodically, over however long she had been fleeing through the convoluted caverns, she had glimpsed the leading edge of the beam falling upon a glistening limestone wall nearby, spurring her onward through yet more branching tributaries and tunnels.

The incandescent handprint upon her belly, which seemed to glow all the brighter the more frightened she became, was an extremely mixed blessing. On the one hand, it helped her navigate, albeit randomly, through this lightless subterranean realm, helping her avoid stumbling into solid walls or yawning chasms; on the other hand, it made her visible to her relentless pursuer, advertising her location like a neon sign on a moonless night.

For the moment, however, she seemed to have gained a slight lead on Morton, who must have taken a wrong turn somewhere amid the diverging corridors. Liz took advantage of this lull in the chase to do something about the sticky tape binding her wrists together. Locating a sturdy stalagmite with a notably jagged tip, she backed against the stony fang, using it as a saw to gnaw away at the overlapping strips of duct tape. Doing so meant dropping the purloined attaché case, but Liz decided she needed her hands free even more than she wanted to hang onto the coveted spacecraft debris.

"I know you're in here, Tess!" Morton called out, still laboring under the false impression that that was her name. Liz wasn't sure how she felt about facing death with that particular name on her would-be killer's lips. *Do I want to spend my final moments on Earth mistaken for a trampy blond homewrecker from another planet?*

The duct tape was maddeningly durable and hard to cut through, but she eventually succeeded in poking a hole in the tape between her wrists, then used that tiny gash as a starting point for tearing away at the gluey fibers holding the tape together. It was taking way too long, though, and Morton sounded like he was getting closer.

"Don't be stupid!" his booming voice railed at her. "It won't do you any good to get hopelessly lost down here. You're just going to starve to death in the dark!"

He had a point, Liz realized, but the alternative, putting herself back in Morton's bloodstained hands, was even less appealing. She'd cope with finding her way out if and when she finally got away from the murderous gunman. *Tom and Becky ultimately made it out of the caves,* she recalled, clinging to that storybook happy ending for comfort. *So can I.*

Only a few gooey strands held together the tape confining her arms. She tugged her wrists apart with every ounce of strength she could muster, while simultaneously sawing away at the last fraying filaments. All at once, her wrists sprang apart and Liz discovered she could see her own hands for the first time in hours. *At last!* she thought gratefully, savoring this one small victory over Morton's brutality. Eager fingers peeled away the rest of the tape, revealing wrists that were red and chafed, yet blissfully free.

Moving quickly, to get farther away from Morton, she rescued the briefcase from the floor and headed away from the sound of his approaching voice. Feeling like some exotic bioluminescent lifeform, evolved to exist far below the Earth's surface or at the bottom of the sea, she turned her silver light upon the escape route ahead of her.

Two separate pathways—one wide, one narrow—diverged before her. Liz hesitated, uncertain which natural aperture to take. Morton might have trouble squeezing his bulk through the skinny crevice, but what if that aisle kept on thinning until it ceased to exist? She shuddered at the thought of getting wedged into a dead end, unable to turn around and go back the way she came without running straight into Morton; all the killer would have to do is wait right where she was standing now for thirst or starvation to drive her back into his clutches. *Okay,* she decided, *the wide door it is.*

"There you are!" Before she could even act on her

choice, Morton suddenly rounded a curve, less than twenty yards behind her, his flashlight beam sweeping across both Liz and the juncture ahead. Liz looked back in surprise, squinting into the glare of the flash, and spotted Morton's intimidating bulk charging toward her, only seconds away. "Give me that case!" he yelled. "Give it back, you alien freak!"

Changing her plan at the last minute, Liz raced through the narrower opening. Swinging behind her at the end of her arm, the briefcase caught in the doorway, holding her back, and she had to stop and turn the case sideways before making it completely through the gate. The delay cost her precious seconds, so that Morton was almost upon her by the time she got the briefcase loose. His body slammed into the limestone walls of the skinny archway, but, just as Liz had prayed, he was too large to pass through the gap in his entirety. An arm and one shoulder squeezed into the shallow corridor, groping wildly for the escaping teenager. "Come back here! Come back or I'll shoot!"

He drew back from the slender opening, aiming both his flashlight and his gun at the murky passage into which Liz had fled. Hearing his threats, and knowing from experience that Morton had no qualms about gunning down those who crossed him, Liz quickened her pace, looking frantically for a turn in the corridor. Straight lines were her enemy right now; only a more crooked path would keep her out of Morton's line of fire.

No! Not again! she thought, unable to hold back painful recollections of the first and only time a bullet tore through her body. The jarring impact, the searing agony, rose like restless phantoms from the memories lodged in her flesh and bones. The handprint upon her stomach, where the mortal wound should have been, flared all the brighter for her terror. *Please, no! Not again!*

At the last minute, the confining wall fell away to her left, and Liz ducked into the much-needed detour, only an instant before the blast of a gunshot disturbed the sepulchral quiet of the caverns. Jagged chips and flakes exploded from the end of the improvised shooting gallery she had just abandoned, followed by the dancing beam of Morton's flashlight as he feverishly sought to see if Liz had been hit or not. A volcanic curse erupted from the enraged killer when he discovered that no humanoid body, alive or otherwise, lay in the path of the searching beam.

(Liz had to wonder just how Morton had expected to retrieve his precious attaché case from the far end of the skinny corridor, in the event that his angry shot had killed her instantly. Then she realized that the bad-tempered gunman was beyond reason at this point; as his behavior at the Crashdown had proven years ago, he was more than capable of shooting first and dealing with the consequences later.)

"Where the hell are you?" he roared in frustration. His hate-crazed voice echoed through the winding catacombs. "Don't think you're getting away from me for good, space girl. I'm not leaving this godforsaken hellhole until I've got that briefcase—and your alien hide!"

The side-tunnel she had so luckily discovered was no wider than the narrow passage she had just escaped, and it continued to constrict inch by inch, until Liz had to turn sideways just to squeeze her way forward. Increasingly afraid that she had trapped herself with no way out, except past Morton, she was forced to slide with excruciating slowness between the unyielding cavern walls, which, she recalled from her science courses, consisted mostly of the petrified remains of prehistoric mollusks and coral. Would her lifeless bones, she wondered, also become part of this vast prehistoric mortuary, buried for eons away from the light of day?

She felt horribly sorry for her parents, who might never find out what had befallen her. Would Max or Maria explain to them about Morton and his deadly schemes, or would that risk exposing Max's and the others' alien roots? She hoped that, somehow, her mom and dad could receive some sort of comfort or closure. Surely, Max would make sure of that, in her memory.

Max. She couldn't believe she might never see him again. There was so much that she still wanted to share with him, so much of their future yet to be written. *At least Romeo and Juliet died together,* she thought mournfully, *not separated by hundreds of feet of solid rock.*

It occurred to her that, in a sense, she had been living on borrowed time ever since that fateful shooting at the Crashdown. Perhaps death, once again in the form of Joe Morton and his ready pistol, had finally caught up with her.

Claustrophobia added to other fears plaguing her mind, but just when she was half-convinced that the dwindling corridor was destined to become her eternal tomb, the aisle opened up and, expelling an enormous sigh of relief, she stepped into what appeared to be a spacious underground grotto, perhaps the size of a high school classroom. Gnarled stalagmites sprouted from the stony floor while towering columns reared up toward a ceiling whose full altitude and dimensions were hidden by the all-encompassing blackness shrouding the roomy vault.

Liz listened anxiously for the sound of Morton's heavy footsteps, not at all certain how many separate routes or entrances might lead to this particular grotto. She didn't hear anyone approaching, but something else caught her ear: an unusual rustling coming from high above her, accompanied by occasional high-pitched squeaking and chittering.

Bats, she realized with a shiver. The grotto sounded as though it were home to a great many bats, all roosting overhead. The air smelled like a zoo, she swiftly noted, while the floor of the chamber was slick with accumulated bat guano, causing Liz to wrinkle her nose in disgust. Glancing at the lighted face of her watch, she saw that sunset was still three or four hours away; the bats would not be flying forth in search of their evening meal for quite some time.

Liz emitted a frustrated sigh. In theory, the bats' nightly departure might have pointed her toward a way out of the confusing maze of caverns. Was it possible she could stay put here until dusk, she speculated, or would Morton catch up with her before then?

Tired of carrying the awkward briefcase around with her everywhere, and remembering how it had almost slowed her down fatally back at the juncture between the two corridors, she looked around for something she could use to break open the lock. A slender stalagmite, about the size of a model rocket, attracted her eye, and she grabbed onto the tip of the tapering calcite formation with both hands, trying to break off the top. *Might make a decent weapon, too,* she thought, admiring its jagged point.

As before, actually doing something, taking positive action, helped to keep her post-traumatic fears at bay. Her desperate struggle to survive was proving excellent therapy, if nothing else. *Go figure,* she mused, wondering what Alex would make of that.

The twisting stalagmite was denser than the inverted icicle it resembled, but she eventually succeeded in snapping off the top six inches or so. She dropped to her knees next to the briefcase and pounded its shiny bronze clasp with the wide end of her improvised hammer. Every noisy blow made her wince and look about her nervously, afraid that the clamor had alerted Morton to her whereabouts, but, after about half a dozen savage strikes, the clasp broke apart and she yanked open the lid.

Inside, the salvaged Crash materials were just as she'd last seen them, back at room #19. Grateful for their amazing properties, she wadded up the mysterious silver foil into an easy-to-carry ball, which she placed in the pocket of her jeans, along with fragments of that strange tan plastic. Then she hid the looted attaché case in a crevice in the wall, so that it would not inform Morton that she had passed this way. Fortunately, the case's stylish black-leather appearance rendered it virtually invisible in the obsidian darkness of the cave.

That's better, she thought, hefting the stalagmite tip like a dagger. It wasn't much compared to Morton's semiautomatic, but it was something. At this point, *anything* that made her feel less like a defenseless victim was of incalculable value.

Now the question was, stay where she was or keep moving? Listening again for Morton's menacing voice or footsteps, while keeping a close look out for even a flicker of light from his flashlight, she thought she heard a slow, steady dripping coming from the far end of the grotto. She licked her dry, dehydrated lips, suddenly realizing just how thirsty and hungry she was. Stepping cautiously between the scattered stalagmites, taking care not to hurry beyond the radiance of the silver handprint, she made her way across the chamber until the eerie glow was reflected by drops of clear water, falling beat by beat, from some unseen stalactite high overhead.

The muddy floor, coated with wet bat dung, got more and more slippery as she neared the dribbling water. Cupping her hands, she caught the falling droplets and lifted them to her lips. The captured liquid had a funny taste, like mineral water, but was refreshing nevertheless. In time, she realized, thinking like the scientist she wanted to be, the calcium in the water would gradually build a new stalagmite or column, right where she was standing now. Liz hoped to be long gone before then.

Distracted by her successful quest for water, she was caught by surprise when a harsh white spotlight illuminated her from behind, throwing her distorted shadow onto the floor of the cavern. She spun around in a panic, almost slipping on the slimy rock beneath her feet, to see Joe Morton standing in an open archway not far from where she first entered the bat cave. His flashlight shone in her face, forcing her to shield her eyes with her hand. Morton himself was visible only as a looming black presence behind the blinding glare. "Don't move a muscle, freak!"

he growled, then chuckled cruelly. "Bet you thought I'd given up!"

Not really, Liz thought, searching futilely for some way out. She felt exposed and vulnerable, like an escaping convict caught by the watchful eye of a prison searchlight. Many feet above her, the bats, perhaps disturbed by Morton's bright light or bellowing voice, rustled and screeched unhappily.

Inspiration struck, and the imperiled teenager hurled the pointy stalagmite tip at the ceiling, while simultaneously throwing herself onto the slimy floor. Not surprisingly, Morton fired his pistol, the explosion sounding like the big bang itself in the vaulted underground chamber.

Facedown in the muck, Liz couldn't tell whether it was her calcite missile or the answering gunshot that most upset the bats, but the net result was the same: Hundreds of Mexican free-tail bats abandoned their roosts and began flapping madly for the quickest route out of the grotto—which just happened to be the wide-open archway where Morton was standing. The gunman screamed in fear and agony, his horrified cry almost lost amid a chorus of high-pitched squeaks and the frantic flapping of hundreds of leathery wings. The beam from his flashlight zigzagged wildly over the uncaring walls of the cavern as he flailed hopelessly at the unstoppable deluge of bats.

Liz scrambled to her feet and dashed in the opposite direction. The ground sloped steeply ahead of her and she ran downhill, following a trickle of water that she prayed led to another exit. The deafening sound of the bats' mass exodus had only just begun to lessen in volume when she gratefully spotted a gap in the wall ahead. She plunged into the shadowy void, even knowing that her downward trajectory was only taking her farther away from the surface, away from the sun.

Behind her, Morton howled in pain and fury. "I'll kill you, you witch! I'll shoot you full of lead!"

Won't be the first time, Liz thought.

27

Following the directions Isabel had lifted from Lieutenant Ramirez's mind only seconds before his death, Max and his comrades soon found Ramirez's car, a snazzy, metallic-purple Porsche, parked alongside an isolated dirt road in the foothills of the Guadalupe Mountains, less than five miles from where yellow CRIME SCENE tape fenced in the area surrounding Morton's abandoned blue Chevy. Driving just below the speed limit, so as not to invite the attention of the police, the Jeep and the Jetta had hurried past the site of Okada's murder, resisting any temptation to rubberneck.

Now Max hit the brakes next to Ramirez's Porsche, then jumped out of the driver's seat onto the rocky ground. "Is this it?" he asked Isabel fervidly. "Is this the place?"

His sister looked around, peering over the top of her mirrored sunglasses. "Yes," she confirmed promptly. Climbing down from the Jeep, she pointed toward a craggy ridge about a mile and a half away. "That's where he went. The cave is up there."

That was all he needed to hear. Without waiting for

Michael and the rest, currently parking the Jetta behind the Porsche, Max sprinted across the arid soil into the hills. The more he ran, dodging cacti, boulders, and ditches, the less need he felt for any directions at all. He could *sense* Liz's presence—and her danger. "Hang on, Liz!" he whispered, his pounding legs propelling him up a steep mountain trail, while the blazing sun beat down on him, causing the rugged, reddish-brown landscape to ripple before his eyes like a mirage. "I'm coming!"

"Max! Wait!" Isabel shouted behind him, her voice already sounding faint and distant. He heard the others chasing after him, with not only his worried sister yelling at him to let them catch up with him.

"Wait up, Max!" Michael called. "Don't do this alone!"

But Max couldn't stop. He couldn't even slow down. He had hesitated before, back in Morton's motel room, and Liz was now paying the price. *I can't fail her again,* he thought, stricken with remorse. The closer he got to the ridge, the more he could feel Liz's fear and despair, calling out to him via the special bond they shared. Time was running out, he understood, and Liz needed his help. He *had* to get there in time.

He knew that Michael was worried about him facing Morton alone, afraid that he might do something he would regret later, but Max no longer feared losing control. His overpowering, post-traumatic hatred of the homicidal gunman had been superseded by an even more compelling emotion: concern for Liz's safety. He had his priorities straight at last, and protecting Liz took precedence over any burning desire for revenge. If he had to kill Morton to save Liz, then that's what he would do, but with a cool head, his actions determined by the circumstances, not by stormy emotions beyond his control. *This is about Liz now,* he affirmed. *That's all that matters.*

His legs were aching by the time he crested the ridge, where he found the cave entrance just as Isabel had described it: an open mouth in the inhospitable hillside, partially concealed by an overhanging shelf of rock. He could see why it appealed to Morton as a hideaway. Thank goodness Isabel had "inside" sources of information!

He was about to enter the cave when a thunderous rumbling, surging up from deep within the Earth, warned him to leap to one side, only seconds before an explosion of bats erupted from the mouth of the cavern, flapping madly into the daylight. Confused and disoriented, hundreds of bats spiraled upward like a leathery tornado before winging into the hills in search of safer roosts elsewhere.

Max blinked in confusion. He had no idea what would cause the bats to abandon the cave in droves, hours before sunset, but he knew it had to do with Morton and Liz. *This can't be good,* he thought, wondering briefly whether Michael and the rest had seen the swirling cloud of bats as well. Perhaps one of them would know what it meant.

Ducking his head to avoid smacking it on the top of the gate, he rushed into the cave. Psychic energy crackled around his fingertips, ready to attack or to defend, but all he saw right away was Ramirez's lifeless body, lying at the center of a pool of congealed blood. Glazed brown eyes, now forever beyond fear of blackmail and extortion, stared blindly at the ceiling, while a disguised wire hanger and a torn silver shower cap, both completely worthless, rested on the cavern floor only inches away.

Max wasted little time contemplating the lieutenant's corpse, instead searching the dimly-lit cave for clues as to the whereabouts of Liz and her abductor. He had no flashlight, but he didn't need one; with a moment's concentration, a silvery halo radiated from his hand, lighting up the area around him. His eyes swiftly spotted footprints in the dust, leading farther into the cave. The smaller prints he recognized as Liz's, while a series of larger bootprints indicated that Morton had gone deeper into the cavern as well.

"Liz!" he called into the shadowy throat of the cave. "It's Max! Can you hear me?"

No one answered, leading him to wonder how far Liz and Morton had descended into the unexplored depths ahead. *She's down there somewhere,* he knew, convinced by both the footprints and his own undeniable sense that the girl he loved was nearby. He didn't know why the kidnapper and his victim had chosen to disappear into the lower regions of the cave, but he knew without hesitation that he had to follow them.

"Max! Where are you? Wait!" Michael's voice invaded the primitive confines of Morton's hideout. Max heard his best friend, who had obviously taken the lead among the others, scrabble up the gravelly ridge outside. "Hang on, Max! Wait for me! I'm right behind you!"

Sorry, Michael, Max thought. *No time. Liz needs me now.*

Like an alien Orpheus, braving the underworld in search of his Eurydice, he charged into the waiting darkness, using his gleaming hand as a torch to light the way.

"I'm coming, Liz! I'm coming!"

28

The deeper she descended, the colder it got. Liz knew from her goose bumps and trembling arms that she must be several hundred feet beneath the surface. She was lost as well, not at all certain that she could ever find her way back uptop, even if she *wasn't* being hunted by a crazed, gun-wielding killer.

She could hear Morton rampaging down the sloping passages behind her, perhaps following her oozing footprints through the bewildering network of tunnels. She had hoped that her trick with the bats would have discouraged him for good, but instead it only seemed to have made him even more insanely driven to kill her and regain his merchandise. "Run, you alien slut! Run while you can!" he bellowed, completely out of his mind. "You can't get away!"

The beam of his flashlight nipped at her heels, and Liz constantly had to shift directions to avoid giving him a clear line of fire. She darted left, right, then left again, taking any turn offered by this never-ending limestone labyrinth. *I really have become a mouse in a maze,* she realized, remembering what she had written in her journal many hours ago. According to her watch, it was almost five P.M., which meant that Morton had been chasing her through the uncharted caverns for at least an hour and forty-five minutes. *How much longer can I keep this up?* she thought, exhausted and scared. *Or do I have to keep on running through these endless catacombs forever?*

Max's palm print blazed upon her bare stomach, its phosphorescent radiance warning her right before she ran over the edge of a dangerous subterranean cliff. *Yikes,* Liz thought. *That was close.* No helpful guardrails protected travelers from the sudden drop-off, whose ultimate depth Liz couldn't even begin to guess. The yawning abyss stretched before her farther than her meager light could penetrate. Looking both left and right, Liz was dismayed to discover that the only way remaining to her appeared to be a narrow ledge running along the length of the chasm, at the base of a towering wall of petrified limestone draperies. The ledge was maybe a foot wide at best, making it extremely risky to venture out onto.

She looked back quickly over her shoulder, hoping she could still backtrack to a more promising escape route. In horror, she saw instead the darting beam of Morton's flashlight. He was only minutes behind her!

There was no time to look for another path, nowhere else to go. Swallowing hard, her back pressed tightly against the overlapping limestone drapes, Liz eased onto the ledge, trying with all her might not to look down. The darkness concealing the height of the chasm was a blessing, sparing her from vertigo, as, facing the abyss, she inched along the ledge, the tips of her sneakers actually extending an inch past the brink of the precipice. She felt like some silent-movie comedian climbing around outside the top windows of a twenty-story skyscraper, except that there was nothing at all humorous about her dire situation. *Don't look down,* she warned herself. Short, fearful breaths misted before her lips in the chilly subterranean atmosphere. *Even if you can't see anything, don't look down!*

Morton's cowboy boots pounded the floor of an adjacent tunnel. "I'm getting closer!" he threatened loudly. He sounded practically just around the corner. "I can smell your fear, you glowing freak!"

Liz looked down at her luminous belly, wondering if she dared cover her only available source of light. *I guess it's too much to hope for,* she thought bleakly, *that Morton will accidently fall over the edge of the cliff.* Alas, the batteries in his flashlight still seemed to have plenty of juice in them.

Creeping sideways along the narrow shelf, with Morton closing in and no place else to go, she experienced a brief surge of hope as the ledge eventually widened beneath her feet, so that she could actually face forward without toppling over the brink, thus allowing her to flee faster and less gingerly. Her relief was short-lived, however, when she abruptly ran into a dead end straight ahead.

"Oh my God," she whispered. Her precarious trek along the ledge had led her only to a couch-sized limestone balcony overlooking the bottomless crevasse. Walls of solid rock blocked her path on her left and to the front, while the deadly precipice dropped away on her right. She was trapped, with no way out except the way she came. *What do I do now?* she despaired. *I've run out of cave!*

"Liz!"

The unmapped caverns were a labyrinthine network of detours and false trails. In theory, it should have been impossible to track a missing person through all these convoluted tunnels, yet Max intuitively sensed that he was on the right course. He could *feel* Liz's presence in the dank catacombs, the very molecules of the air seemed to vibrate with the lingering reverberations of her recent passage. He knew that she had tread the exact same path he was taking now, and not very long ago.

He also knew that she was in terrible danger. The silver nimbus around his left hand, the same hand that had once brought Liz back from the verge of death, flared brighter than it ever had before, as if urging him onward to ever greater speed. Through some sort of subliminal psychic link, he felt her raw terror and hopeless desperation as though they were his own. *At least she's still alive,* he thought emphatically, hanging onto that conviction as he descended deeper and deeper into the underworld. *But for how long?*

A bullet hole defacing the wall of one limestone corridor proved that he was following in his quarry's footsteps, as well as confirming that Joe Morton was indeed armed and dangerous. Max gulped apprehensively, but did not slow his pursuit of the vicious killer and his captive. Squeezing through an unnervingly tight fissure in the Earth, he entered a sizable grotto that reeked like an animal's lair. His lambent hand illuminated an empty chamber whose floor was literally carpeted in excrement. *This must be where all those bats came from,* he realized. Glancing up, he saw that a handful of winged mammals, perhaps less excitable than their fellows, still hung upside-down from the ceiling. As before, he couldn't help wondering—and worrying—what had frightened all those other bats.

Morton's gunshots?

Hurrying across the grotto, he found disturbing evidence of recent violence. Fresh bloodstains mingled with the accumulated bat dung, leading across the sludgy floor to a darkly opaque exit at the bottom of a slippery slope. Did the crimson stains come from Liz, he wondered, or from Morton?

The sight of small, muddy footprints, proceeding rapidly away from the bat cave gave him renewed hope that Liz was still unharmed. Even better, the trail of bloodstains seemed to accompany Morton's larger bootprints more than they did Liz's much more petite tracks. Had Liz somehow managed to injure Morton? *Good for you,* Max thought.

The spilled blood, along with the dual sets of footprints, left no doubt as to which way to go. With his incandescent hand held aloft, he followed the clues that Morton and Liz had inadvertently left for him, which led farther downward, deep into the bowels of a planet he didn't even belong on.

He could no longer hear Michael and the rest behind him. Lacking his special connection to Liz, they must have been slowed or stymied by the cavern's many twists and turns. *Fine,* he decided. He would deal with Morton alone, one way or another.

"Liz!" he shouted again, throwing caution to the wind. He knew he was sacrificing the element of surprise, but that couldn't be helped; he *had* to let Liz know that she wasn't alone in this hellish underworld. "Hang on, Liz!" he cried, his feet racing over the trail of drying blood and muck. "Don't give up! I'm almost there!"

The light from his hand was almost blinding.

Cornered!

Unable to run any farther, backed against the wall, with solid rock on one side of her and a gaping chasm on the other, Liz held her breath as she heard Joe Morton's relentless footsteps drawing nearer. Now she cowered in total blackness, having done what she could to hide the shining fingers emblazoned on her flesh. In her heart, however, she knew that the darkness alone wouldn't be enough.

Indeed, only minutes later, a shaft of light pierced the absolute blackness, advancing to the very brink of the precipice—and beyond. "Whoa!" Morton exclaimed, taken aback by the sight of the yawning crevasse. "That step's a doozy!" He stomped up to the edge of the underground cliff, then swept the surrounding area with his flashlight.

It took him less than a moment to locate Liz, crouched upon the limestone balcony at the other side of the rocky ledge. The merciless spotlight showed him an exhausted young woman with nowhere to flee. Realizing that the moment of truth could no longer be avoided, she rose to her feet unsteadily, resolved to face her persecutor, the assailant who had haunted her traumatized psyche, once and for all. "That's right," she said as defiantly as she could, wishing she could manage as withering a remark or glance as Maria or Isabel surely could in her place. "You've found me. Now what?"

"What now? You want to know what now?" His voice,

already hoarse from filling the caverns with his barbaric shouting, was so clotted with murderous hatred that it barely sounded human. "Look what you did to me, you witch! Look!"

He turned the flash on himself, revealing a face shredded by dozens of bloody bites and scratches. His thinning hair was askew like a madman's, while loose flaps of reddened skin hung off his torn and ravaged scalp. Crimson stains splattered his collar and shirt, making him look like a homicidal psycho straight out of one of those gory slasher movies Kyle was always renting. "Thought you were pretty cute with that bat trick, didn't you," he snarled, "Take a good look, you outer-space freak! Look what you did to me!"

His bulging, bloodshot eyes glared at her with more pure malice than she had ever seen from a human being, or even a Skin, before. This wasn't about the "merchandise" anymore, she realized with a chill. It wasn't even about whether or not she was really an alien. This was about making her pay in blood for the bats and everything else.

"What about what you did to Lieutenant Ramirez?" she challenged him. "What about Okada, and that biker my friend saw you kill in that alley?" She hurled two years of suppressed trauma back at his mutilated face. "What about what you did to me that day in the Crashdown Cafe! You almost killed me, you slimy bastard!"

Morton spat contemptuously into the chasm. Blood or tobacco, Liz couldn't tell. "So?" he said callously. The recitation of his victims, even the one she could not possibly have known about, did nothing to dim the predatory bloodlust in his eyes. "Hell, you're not even a person, Tess."

"My name is Liz," she said. "Liz Parker. And a lot more people care about me than anyone ever will about you."

"Whatever," Morton muttered, unimpressed. He raised his semi-automatic and aimed it straight at Liz. "Time to finish what I started at that stupid diner."

The gun fired, the boom resounding in Liz's ears, and she felt the bullet strike her below the ribs, just like it had two years ago. This time, however, the lethal projectile bounced off the flexible silver foil that she had wrapped around her midsection, underneath her blouse. (In his pain and fury, Morton had never noticed that the glowing handprint was no longer visible.) Unable to pierce the miracle metal, the bullet ricocheted back at Morton, winging him in the right shoulder. "Arrgh!" he shouted, his handgun flying from his fingers into the chasm beside him, falling for several seconds before Liz heard it strike the bottom hundreds of feet below. "What—?" he grunted, clutching his wounded shoulder. "How did you—?"

"Thanks for the merchandise," she said, flashing open her blouse to give him a glimpse of the silver foil girdling her waist. The shocked look on his face was almost worth all that she had endured since bumping into Morton in another cavern the day before. "This stuff really is worth everything you paid for it."

"You—!" He staggered toward the ledge, his good arm reaching out for her, his bloody fingers clutching spastically, as though they couldn't wait to choke the life out of her. Liz backed against the cool limestone wall behind her, suddenly afraid that the injured gunman still possessed the strength and the ferocity to kill her with his bare hands. "That belongs to me!" he howled, saliva dripping from the corner of his mouth. Heedless of the fatal drop awaiting him if he slipped, Morton dragged himself onto the ledge and began inching inexorably toward Liz. "I'll take my merchandise from your cold, lifeless body if have to," he vowed, "or even if I don't!"

Liz saw her end approaching. It was ironic; in the end, a crimson handprint around her throat would trump the silver handprint that had saved her once before. *Good-bye, Max*, she thought. *I always loved you.*

"Liz!"

Max's voice rang out in the cavern as he came racing out a tunnel, holding up a glowing hand. His unexpected appearance startled Morton, who pivoted in surprise, losing his balance on the narrow ledge. "Who the hell are you?" he blurted, then toppled over the brink.

His falling scream terminated in a final, bone-crushing thud, many long seconds later. Then silence.

"Liz!" As quickly as he could, Max crossed the ledge and took her in his arms. She could feel his body shaking with emotion. "Oh my God, Liz, are you all right?"

"Yes," she said truthfully. She had stared her worst nightmare in the face, and come out of it alive and well and exorcised, finally, of a lingering demon. Beneath the lifesaving silver foil, her stomach tingled for an instant, and she knew intuitively what had occurred. Pulling away from Max's comforting embrace, just long enough to confirm what she had already guessed, she peeled away the silver wrap, revealing smooth, unblemished flesh underneath.

The glowing handprint was gone, this time for good.

EPILOGUE

"Just think," Alex said with a grin. "Joe Morton was at the center of an international conspiracy to hijack top secret alien technology—and he would've gotten away with it, too, if not for us meddling teenagers."

The entire booth groaned out loud, but even Isabel looked like she was having a good time. "Somebody give Shaggy here a Scooby-Snack to shut him up," she quipped, giving Alex a playful look to let him know she was just kidding.

Liz couldn't believe how carefree and relaxed everyone seemed, especially after their weekend from hell in Carlsbad. Maybe the eventful road trip really had been just what they'd all needed, after all. Certainly, Michael and Maria, and Alex and Isabel, had come through for each other during their out-of-town adventures, and seemed stronger as couples because of that. Liz enjoyed seeing her friends so happy together, even as she watched the front door of the Crashdown, waiting eagerly for Max to get back from the sheriff's office.

Five Rigelian Ripple sundaes, and two bottles of Tabasco sauce, were consumed before Max finally joined them. He slid into the booth next to Liz, then brought them up to speed on what he had learned about the official police investigation of the events at Carlsbad.

"According to Valenti," he began, "the FBI wants to keep this case low-profile; after all, they can hardly announce to the media that Morton's rampage in Carlsbad was all about classified UFO technology stolen from the air force. The official story is that Morton killed Ramirez and Okada, possibly as a result of a drug deal gone bad, then fell to his death while hiding out in an unexplored cave."

"What about the foil and the other fragments?" Michael asked. After recovering the attaché case from the bat cave, Liz and the others had safely stowed all of Morton's extraterrestrial "merchandise" in the hidden Pod Chamber, where they could be preserved along with other evidence of the teenage hybrids' alien heritage.

Max shrugged. "Officially, those materials never existed in the first place, so no one's making a public fuss about them being missing—although I imagine that the FBI and the Pentagon will be busy searching that cave for months." He smiled, clearly amused at the prospect of all those dogged Feds wasting their time.

"So that's it?" Maria asked. "No loose ends?"

"Yep," Liz stated confidently. For the first time in two years, she was no longer afraid of the man who shot her. At last, she could leave that trauma in the past where it belonged. "No more loose ends."

About the Author

GREG COX is the *New York Times* bestselling author of The Q Continuum trilogy, along with several other popular STAR TREK novels, including *Assignment: Eternity*, *The Black Shore*, *Dragon's Honor* (with Kij Johnson), and *Devil in the Sky* (with John Gregory Betancourt). In addition, he has written many novels based on Marvel Comics characters, as well as a nonfiction look at *Xena: Warrior Princess*. His short fiction can be found in such anthologies as *Star Trek: Enterprise Logs* and *Alien Pregnant by Elvis*.

Greg lives in New York, where he is a Consulting Editor for Tor Books.